Die at the Races

An Eva St. Claire Mystery
by
M.K. Stabley

D1530242

Keith
I hope you
enjoy them.
M.K. Stabley

This book is a work of fiction. Names, characters, and incidents are either the product of the author's imagination or are used fictitiously. Any resemblance to actual persons or events is entirely coincidental.

Dedication

This book is dedicated to my amazing husband, who is the inspiration for Eva's husband. For all the times I've asked you to read over a scene, to make sure it sounded okay and for all the support you've continued to give me throughout our marriage, and with my writing. You deserve the world. I'm so lucky and so blessed to have you as my forever. Love you, always and forever.

Table of Contents

Prologue

Kris stood still and silent. After a moment, Jake cleared his throat. "Did you hear what I said Kris?"

Blinking several times before looking over at his friend, Kris started to say something when he heard a gasp coming from the hallway outside his den.

He jogged the short distance to find his wife Eva, with her hand over her mouth and wide eyed .

"Eva, what's wrong?"

She looked back and forth between the two men standing in front of her, worried looks were evident on both faces.

"Is she okay Kris?"

"Well, I'm just going to go out on a limb here, but I think she may have overheard you talking about wanting us to work with you, with the FBI."

She just stood there, not saying a word, but shaking her head in acknowledgment.

Eva was quite petite, but very curvy, with blonde highlights and shoulder length hair. She was in her forties, as was Kris. He towered over her, standing at six feet. He was a big guy, with a partially shaved head and a full beard, with gray patches in it. He always told her that each gray patch has a name; one was the kids, one was from work, and the other was from Eva. Obviously he was joking, but Eva didn't find her designated patch a bit funny.

"Can we all go back into the den, and talk for a bit. I would like to explain what I'm looking for, and how you both may be able to help me. Yes, it would entail working with the FBI."

Jake was pleading with them to listen to his proposal. He wasn't used to dealing with civilians as possible colleagues. Jake ran his own show, most of the time. He didn't have a partner, because he didn't get along well with others. He had a team that would help every now and then. He's been an FBI field agent for twenty years. Jake was quite competent in his skills and his record for cases being solved was pretty impressive as well. He'd been Kris' college roommate for three years while at Penn State University.

Jake Long was a few inches taller than Kris, with a full head of black hair, cut into a neat quiff, where it was tapered on the sides and in the back, but the top was longer and swept up off to the side, not quite spiked, but it was a stylish hair cut for a man in his forties. His olive colored skin showed his Italian roots, he was sporting a two day old scruff on his chiseled face, and his broad shoulders filled out the fitted gray suit he was currently wearing. Staying in shape was a daily routine for him, even before joining the FBI. Jake had played defensive tackle for Penn State Nittany Lions, under the infamous Joe Paterno, in the early 90s.

Jake had yet to marry, not that his chosen profession allowed for it, but now that he was here in his friends house and seeing the way he lived, and how he reacted to his wife, it made Jake think of the possible prospect of the whole institution.

He was thankful they agreed to sit and talk to him. He felt guilty for wanting to use Eva's talents, but this could be a game changer.

Eva was already regretting agreeing to sit down and listen to whatever this guy had to say. Kris looked equally uncomfortable.

"Okay, so here's the situation. I know what you can do, Eva."

She internally cringed at the admission, but said nothing.

I have a case that is of high importance right now, in Louisville, Kentucky and it is centered around the Kentucky Derby.

Eva sat up straight, "what does this have to do with me?"

Kris glared at Jake, "You want to take her to Louisville, and have her do what she does, don't you?"

"Yes."

"I know nothing about horses or the Kentucky Derby. What am I supposed to do?"

"I need you to perform whatever it is you did here, to catch a killer.

"I can't just leave town, or my job, just like that."

"You'll be paid by the FBI. We use psychics and mediums all the time, you would be categorized under that, for all intents and purposes."

"It's not about being paid, I have our kids to take care of as well."

Jake was on the verge of saying anything he could to get Eva and Kris to go to Louisville.

"Listen, I know this is sudden, and I wouldn't ask if I wasn't desperate. Please, I need your help."

Jake was not one to beg, for anything, but if it worked, he'd do it. He needed to close this case before the Kentucky Derby race next Saturday.

Kris moved to the edge of his seat, his elbows on his thighs, and looked from Eva to Jake. "Maybe my parents could take the kids for a few days. If she does this, I'm going with her." Kris was adamant about that.

Jake looked to his friend, feeling hopeful. "Definitely, you can come with her. I had planned on both of you. So, do we have a deal?"

This was the last thing Eva wanted to be getting into. She wanted the magic part of her life back where it was in the past, but she couldn't bring herself to say no to Kris' friend, and FBI agent. If there was a possibility she would be able to find and get another killer off the streets, she had to try.

"Okay, fine. Deal." She held out her hand to Jake, to seal it with a handshake, to which he complied.

"Thank you. This means a lot to me. I honestly am not accustomed to asking for help, where my job is concerned. How soon would you both be able to head to Louisville? I can have your accommodations made as soon as you want."

"Pretty desperate to get her down there, huh?"

"Sorry man, I know this is short notice, but the sooner the better, like yesterday."

"Alright, let me call my parents and see if they mind keeping the kids a few more days, and we can head out this afternoon."

Jake smiled his thousand watt smile, "perfect. You have my cell. Call me when you have confirmation that you can leave today, and I'll set up everything else. One tiny detail, one you may not like... Eva will have to pose as my wife, while I have you staying somewhere else with the equipment."

Eva's ears perked up when she heard the last detail. "I'm sorry, what?"

Kris looked like he was going to strangle the guy. "No, you can't use her as your wife. How the heck would that work? Can't you think of another way?"

"I need her with me at the Lodge, where we're all going to be staying. This will need to look as unplanned and unsuspicious as possible. If there was another way, I would do it."

"I like how you left that detail out until after we agreed. If you do anything to her, I swear I will hunt you down."

Jake looked appalled. "I would never disrespect her or anything else, you have my word."

Kris walked Jake to the door, with Eva on their heels. "It was nice to meet you Jake, or should I say, husband?" She laughed, nervously, trying to make light of the situation.

Jake nodded, "Likewise Eva, and thank you. I'm sorry if I caught you off guard by showing up today. You have no idea how much I appreciate this."

"It's fine."

He shook Kris' hand and made his way to his car.

Kris shut the door, and turned to see Eva giving him the stink eye. "I know you're mad."

"Mad? No, not mad. Confused, yes. You, of all people, who want me to keep my past under wraps, and you are okay with me doing this?"

"I don't want you to do this, no, but I don't think you can say no at this point. I don't think Jake would reveal your talent, but I can't be sure."

"You think he'd make what I am public knowledge?"

"No, I don't think so, as long as you're working with him."

"Blackmail?"

"Not entirely, but you have something he wants and needs. And, I'm not too keen on the whole pretending to be married thing either."

"Oh for the love. That doesn't make me feel all warm and fuzzy inside here."

"I'm going to call my Mom and see if they can keep the kids a few more days. You start packing."

"What do I pack for something like this? I need my book and I'll wait until we get to Louisville to buy any supplies. I will take a duffle bag with some of the items I know I won't be able to find there, plus a backpack if I have to carry stuff to different locations. Jake will have to take us to the scene and I'll need more information from him on this murder. I didn't even think to ask him any details. Oh, and do you still have the goodies he sent you before, that we used last time? In case, you know, I need them."

"We'll figure it out. After I call my Mom, I'll call him and get more information. You need to call Chrissy and take off work for a few more days. Do you think she'll be okay with that?"

"I guess I'll find out, won't I? I'm not telling her why I need off though. The less she knows, the better."

"Good idea, she would probably want to come along with us."

Chapter 1 - The week before the Kentucky Derby

Louisville, Kentucky in late April is beautiful. The city was abuzz with the Kentucky Derby right around the corner. All the jockeys had been in town for the last couple months; to train and prepare for the biggest race of their life.

Penelope Rivers, owner and horse trainer at Estrella Equine Village Ranch, was taking in the quiet sunrise with a quick ride on her stunning sable colored thoroughbred, Sandy. She usually took this time in the morning as part of her meditation, before the jockeys arrived at the stables, for the day.

Her ranch was where all the jockeys boarded their horses and did their training runs, for at least two months out of the year. Those couple of months are her busiest of the year. If it weren't for her contract with Churchill Downs, she'd never make ends meet. Penelope had been widowed for six years, and is putting her daughter Chloe through Vet School at the University of Kentucky. She needs all the money she can get.

She doesn't have but one ranch hand to help her. Brett has been with her since not long after her husband passed away. Her daughter helps when she can too, but that is getting less and less as she gets older.

"Okay Sandy, take in the quiet now, it's going to get busy out here soon." The horse gave her a whinny and galloped along at a trail run pace. Not too fast, but not a slow walk either.

The sun was rising over the East, coming up over the bigger barn.

"Is that a beautiful sunrise, or what?" She said that more to herself, than to the horse.

"Looks like it is going to be a perfect day for training."

Penelope jerked her head behind her, as a young man with a french accent, and his gray thoroughbred were trotting up beside her.

She recognized the gentleman right away, as Florent Prat, one of the jockeys racing in this year's derby. He is one of three that came in from Toulouse, France. While jockeys are typically on the shorter side, Florent stood at 5'6 and looked to be in his thirties. His dark, thick wavy hair stood out in contrast to the light green eyes that glared at her now. Handsome, but a bit of a chauvinist when it comes to women and racing horses. That right there put him down a few notches on the good-looking male scale, in her book.

"You're out early, Mr. Prat. Trying to get in some extra training?" She couldn't help herself by goading him, just a bit.

"On the contrary, I needn't much more practice. Pegasus is in his prime. He'll be ready."

"A good positive attitude is the attitude to have. Takes the nerves away." She may have said that a little too sarcastically, but there was just something about him that annoyed her. Maybe it was a French thing. They are known to be somewhat pretentious.

"Ms. Rivers, I am rarely nervous. I know, I am good at what I do."

"I'll see you around Mr. Prat. I've got to go and prepare breakfast for everyone, before it gets too late."

And with that, Penelope sped up her horse's gait a little more. Leaving him behind before she said what she was really thinking.

Chapter 2 - Juliette

Juliette Sutherland opened her eyes to yet another sunny day in Louisville, Kentucky. It was only about a week until the biggest day of her life. She made it to the Kentucky Derby. Not many women can say they raced in one of the biggest, and most prestigious races in the world. But she will be able to after next Saturday. Juliette has been preparing for this race her whole life.

Growing up in Cotswold, England, on a horse farm, it was practically a birthright that she rode a horse from the time she was four. Her family was wealthy, and her parents made it a priority to start her horse training at an early age. Anyone who was anyone knew the proper way to ride a horse.

She started off with the basic training; learning to mount and dismount, grooming, the different gaits the horses would do, and she was a natural. Soon she was showing her parent's geldings and winning medals, but her real passion was pushing herself and her horse to the limit. She felt the rush the first time she took her first thoroughbred around a track at record speed. This was what she was meant to do.

Juliette had moved from England to the states a few years ago, and started her journey to the derby after she purchased her beautiful thoroughbred, Tennessee Whiskey. She chose the name because of the horse's coloring. It was as smooth and brown as the best Tennessee whiskey from the Smoky Mountains

That first year of training was typical, she and her horse getting used to each other, making tweaks here and there, with how she handled him, and he responded to her well. It only took six months for her to feel ready for their first race. She started midway in the racing season, but it was merely to get the experience and a feel for it. She did well, always placing in the top ten.

When the new season started back in September, she focused on winning more than anything else. The first race, Iroquois, at Churchill Downs was surreal for her. She knew the last race in May, would be right back here if they performed well. She managed 3rd place in that first race. Not exactly her best, she was always her worst critic, but she was able to continue on. They went from American Pharoah, to Breeders' Cup, Belmont Stakes, and ending at Pegasus, in Monmouth Park, and the other twelve races in between. They managed to place in the top three, every race.

Now she was right back where she started, the biggest race of all, The Kentucky Derby.

Juliette and Tennessee have been training here at Estrella Equine Village Ranch for a couple of months now. She really did like the ranch. She met a lot of the other jockeys, and spent some down time with them. This has been the most social she's been since arriving in the states. She left her boyfriend of four years, Kai Armstrong, back in England two years ago. It had been a difficult decision, but one she hadn't regretted. She didn't see any real future with him. It was for the best. She had goals to reach. Eye on the prize, as she put it.

Juliette pulled the covers off and climbed from her queen sized bed that she has been sleeping in for six weeks now, and padded over to the mirror in her bathroom. She looked at her mass of curly brown hair, that looked much like a rats nest, and grunted.

"Looks like a french braid kind of day."

Juliette is petite, as all jockeys are, maybe reaching 5'1" in height. She made up for her shortness with her long curly chestnut brown hair, hazel eyes and alabaster skin, that was always flawless. At 29 years of age, she didn't look any older than 21, at the most. The male jockeys never shied away from her; she had gotten the attention of a few. Some good, some not so good.

She had a few dates with one of the jockeys she'd be going up against soon, but she didn't feel any real strong feelings there. Phillipe Cardoza, a 32 year old racer from Sao Paulo, Brazil, had caught her attention early on, his long silky black hair, that he'd typically have pulled into a ponytail, but it was his penetrating dark chocolate eyes that pulled her in, at first. That and his squared chin, chiseled cheekbones, and his deep tanned skin, along with a body of muscles, even at only 5'7, he was quite the package, but alas, no spark. Not for lack of trying, of course. Juliette had a bigger spark with his beautiful black Thoroughbred, Brazilian Bomb.

Then there was Florent Prat, the Frenchman, from Toulouse, France. He made it abundantly clear that women shouldn't be racing horses, and definitely not in The Kentucky Derby. He surely wasn't a fan of Juliette's, and he made that known on a daily basis. He was the quintessential chauvinist pig. Juliette just ignored the grumpy Frenchy. The Brits and the French tolerate each other, but that's as far as it goes.

Getting ready for today's schedule, Juliette pulled out her notebook that listed the day's events. She grabbed her pen, and jotted one extra thing on her list... *Talk to Brett*

Chapter 3

Brett Singers was filling each of the horse stalls with bales of hay and fresh water when Penelope and her horse Sandy came trotting in.

"Morning!"

"Hey Brett, you're out early."

"It's going to be a warmer day, I wanted to get the horses more fresh water and make sure they have plenty of hay.

"Good thinking. Most of the jockeys should be arriving soon, or getting to the kitchen sooner. I wonder why some of them chose to stay at the Bourbon Inn and the Inn at St. James Court, instead of right here, where their horses are and they could get meals?"

"I wondered that too. I see you already had to entertain Prat this morning."

"He's like a rash, he just won't go away, the man is a pig. He still lives in 1950. His thinking is very caveman-like. Women shouldn't own businesses, they shouldn't race horses, blah, blah, blah. I wanted to deck him, but I need his money."

Brett snickered and shook his head.

"Yeah, he seems old fashioned.

Penelope dismounted from her horse, and looked back to see the man in question galloping toward the stables.

"Can you take care of getting Sandy back to her stall, while I run back to the lodge to prepare breakfast, and so I don't have to endure anymore Florent?"

"Yeah absolutely, get out of here."

Brett took the reins from her and started to guide Sandy to her stall.

"Morning Mr. Prat."

"Hello Brett. How are you this morning?"

"It's a beautiful day, I'm doing great, and yourself?"

"Wonderful, thank you. Was Penelope in a hurry for some reason? She seemed to rush off."

"She has to get breakfast ready for the guests before they all start their training for the day."

"Of course. I had mine at the Bourbon Inn. It was okay, but it's the same continental breakfast every morning for the last six weeks. You would think they would change it up. That is the correct use of wording, yes?"

Brett controlled his urge to smile.

"Yes, that is the correct use of words. Well, if you would have stayed here, Penelope changes the menu every few days; you would have had better choices. Why did you decide to stay at the Bourbon Inn, instead of here, where your horse is, if you don't mind me asking?'

"Ah, the PR lady at Churchill Downs, Sophia Barrere suggested it. Lovely woman, beautiful, actually. I rather think she fancies me, a little too much. I've noticed her in the bar at the Inn, on multiple occasions, and she strikes up a conversation with me, every time."

Brett was having a really hard time not rolling his eyes at Florent.

"Maybe you should ask her out to dinner sometime while you're still in town."

"I was thinking that. It has been a while, if you know what I mean."

His eyebrows shrugged. Brett nodded. "Gotcha."

"Well, if you'll excuse me Florent, I need to get Juliette's horse ready for her to take out after breakfast."

"Of course. I will leave you to your job. I still can't believe the odds on her winning this year's Derby. Have you seen them? They're giving her 8-1 odds, and me, 3-1. It's absurd, don't you think?"

"She is the odds on favorite. I don't think it's absurd, she's trained hard, and has proven to be a pretty good competitor. She may only have a year and a half of racing under her belt here, but she used to compete in England too. Mostly showing horses, but she got her first taste at racing ten years ago, and has trained for that, since. Are you afraid of a little competition Prat, from a female?"

He couldn't help egging him on, it was so easy.

"I'm not afraid, no, but you know quite a bit about Miss Sutherland, don't you? If I didn't know any better, I'd think you had a crush on her. Is there something going on between you two? I don't think she has made any of her past known to any of us."

"Of course not. I try to research each jockey the same, so I can better prepare their training, and handling of their horses."

He really hoped the french fry bought that answer. He did like Juliette, they got along really well. She was always nice, with a sweet demeanor, and her beauty just personified that. He knew he spent more time on her and Whiskey, than some of the other horses, but he tried not to be obvious about it.

"How thoughtful of you. Pegasus has certainly been spoiled here, that's for sure. He seems very happy. Handling him has been much easier."

I'm glad you think so. Now if you'll excuse me, I need to get back to work."

Brett took off before Florent could corner him anymore than he already had.

Chapter 4 - Chloe

Trying to stay undetected, while she sat staring at Brett leaving the barn, Chloe couldn't help but admire the man. She's had a crush on him since the first day her mom hired him.

Chloe Rivers, Penelope's 20 year old daughter, is a large animal vet student at The University of Kentucky. She has the same stunning auburn hair as her mother, her eyes are much greener, like fresh ivy after a rain. She is a bit taller and slimmer than her mom, but both have the same ivory skin.

Chloe always had her fair share of boys calling, but not one of them has interested her, the same way Brett does. Brett made it very clear to her though, that she was too young for him and he didn't feel the same about her, plus he would never date his boss's daughter. Chloe was still pretty bitter about those comments, and made it her life's mission to change his mind.

She sat up straighter, as she looked the man right in the eyes, he'd caught her in the act of ogling.

"Crap, how did I not notice him look over here? He's going to think I'm stalking him."

She immediately tried to recover herself by waving in his direction, hoping he'd just assume it was just a friendly stare.

"He doesn't look to be buying it."

His brow furrowed in irritation, but nodded a greeting.

"What is up with him? I'm not exactly a dog to look at. If anything, I'm too pretty for him. Maybe that's it, he thinks I'm too good for him."

Chloe decided to get out of her car and go talk to him. She needed to be close to him. He was gorgeous, muscled, and his hair was crazy shaggy, but in a beach bum, surfer dude way.

Brett noticed her exit her car, and internally cursed as he noticed her coming his way. "Why me, why today? First the french fry, now the princess."

Walking toward the barn where he was prepping the stalls for the jockeys, she did so, slowly with purpose. She wanted him to see she wasn't some little kid.

"Hi Brett, how are you this morning?"

Looking a little put out, Brett aimed for nice. "I'm fine Chloe, and you?"

"I'm good, thanks for asking. My finals are coming up soon. So I've been concentrating on studying, but after that I'll be here everyday to help out at the Ranch. It'll be fun to work together, again. Maybe we can even go out sometime, you know, like colleagues."

This time he couldn't hide his disdain too well.

"Um, I don't think that would be a good idea Chloe. I don't mind working with you, but I don't do outside activities with people I work with."

Chloe was stunned speechless.

"Well, that's just ridiculous," she accused.

"Sorry, it's just my own rule."

"So, if I didn't work the ranch, we could go out sometime?"

Brett knew he'd just landed in a trap. He definitely wasn't getting out of this conversation, not easily anyway, and not without hurting the girl. The truth is always best, he thought.

"Listen Chloe, I think you're a really nice person, but we won't be anything but friends and co-workers. I just don't feel the same way about you, as you appear to feel about me, not that I am not flattered, but I hope you understand."

"Yeah sure, no problem."

She was clearly upset, but wasn't about to make a scene.

"Good, thank you. I've got some stalls to prep here before everyone arrives. I hope you have a great day, and good luck on those finals."

His attention was suddenly diverted to the main ranch house, and Chloe turned to see what caught his attention so quickly. That's when she saw her; Juliette Sutherland was walking toward the stables.

Seriously… That's who he has eyes for, she thought.

Chloe pulled herself together before the woman in question made her way to them.

Brett gave her one of his perfect smiles, that would've melted the crabbiest of people, and she responded in kind. Chloe thought she was going to be sick.

"Brett, good morning," she beamed.

"It is a good morning Juliette. How are you?"

"Ready to get in some riding, with Whiskey."

Juliette looked to Chloe and smiled, a genuinely friendly smile, and greeted her in her posh british accent. "Chloe, right? How are you?"

Chloe was about to throw up, but she pasted a smug smile on her face, and exchanged quick pleasantries with the woman in front of her.

"Yes, it's Chloe. I'm fine. I was just talking to Brett here, letting him know that once my finals are done, I'll be back to working here at the ranch, everyday for the summer."

"That's fantastic, best of luck to you on your exams. If you'll excuse me, I'm going to go check on Whiskey. It was lovely to see you both."

Brett piped up, "he's quite a beautiful horse. I fed and brushed him a little this morning. He is a friendly guy."

"Well thank you for taking such good care of him for me. You didn't have to do that."

"I love horses, it was my pleasure, and it is sort of my job." He laughed.

Chloe couldn't take it anymore, she made her way past the two, before she said something she'd regret.

"Excuse me, I need to get going."

"See ya Chloe." Brett said without even looking her way.

"Yeah."

She was back at her car slamming the door of her 1968 black convertible Mustang that her grandfather had given her for graduation. She sat there for a minute just watching the pair, getting more and more irritated.

Chloe had enough. She peeled out in front of the house where she was parked, pulling looks from multiple people on their way to the stables, including her mother. Chloe noticed the look of anger on her mother's face through her rear view mirror. She didn't care; she was ticked. No man has ever turned her down, and this stable hand had done it without even flinching.

She headed over to Churchill Downs to speak with her grandfather.

Terrence Rivers, estranged father-in-law of Penelope, and the only connection to Chloe's father that she had. He was on the Board of Directors at Churchill Downs, a billionaire, with the looks of John Forsythe. He was also one ruthless bastard. Terrence made his billions on the backs of others' work and is an avid gambler, but he loved his only son's daughter, his granddaughter Chloe, more than anything. She was going to play on that love.

Chapter 5 - Brett and Juliette

Brett was watching Juliette tend to her horse like he was her child. She loved and nurtured the horse as she probably would a child. He had to admire her for that. He also admired her, for her. He wanted to get to know her more, maybe even take her out to dinner.

Juliette was certainly aware of Brett watching her, as she caressed her dear Thoroughbred. For some reason she was nervous around him, suddenly unable to speak in full sentences. There was a spark there for sure. But she had no time for a personal life, not with the most important race of her life coming up. Though the thought of dinner or a drink out wouldn't be unheard of. Her sudden acknowledgement to that made her stop and turn in the direction of her admirer and smile. He gave her one of his blazing pearly white smiles right back. She felt her heart skip a beat, and she quickly turned away.

Brett couldn't take it anymore, he was going to go over and talk to her. He saw the blush in her cheeks when he smiled at her; she felt the spark too.

"Juliette, can I ask you something," he said, now standing a foot from her.

She jumped at his question, unaware that he had made it that close to her, without her hearing him.

"Sorry, I didn't mean to startle you." He smiled.

"No, it's fine. You are pretty stealthy, aren't you?" She laughed, nervously.

"Honestly, I wasn't trying to be." He felt bad for scaring the woman, but it just confirmed what he had been thinking. He had gotten to her. A smile formed on his handsome rugged face as he looked at her, wanting to ask her a multitude of questions, wanting to know more about her. He saw how easily she blushed and got flustered around him.

"So, are you excited about being the only woman in this year's Derby?" He thought he'd start out slow, and build up to the real question burning on his mind.

She smiled, and was thankful at this line of questioning.

"I'm excited, yes, but very nervous. This is the race I've been wanting to be in, since I was a little girl. And, the fact that the polls are giving me an 8-1 chance of winning this year's Derby, puts even more pressure on me to do well."

He knew the odds, she was a favorite to win this year. He could only imagine the pressure she felt.

"I'm sure you will do great. Are any of your family and friends from Cotswold coming to watch in person? A boyfriend, maybe?"

That was obviously a personal question. He knew it might have been too soon to ask, but it was out there now. Brett waited for her to answer. It looked like he'd taken her off guard, but she recovered herself quickly.

"My parents will be unable to come, unfortunately. As for a boyfriend, I don't have one. With my schedule it's hard to have much of a personal life."

He felt her disappointment at the last comment, but he was going to take it for what it was. She was single, and that was all he needed to know.

"Do you ever go out to dinner?"

Brett almost thumped his head with his palm with that question. Way to just blurt it out there buddy, he thought.

The corners of her mouth tipped up into a slight smile, and the pink in her cheeks deepened in color, as she shyly started brushing her horse.

"On occasion, I go out to dinner, why?"

Now it was his turn to be stymied.

"Um, I was just wondering. I mean, I'm sure you go out with the other jockeys and stuff."

"I've made friends with a few, but they are just friends. Florent Prat doesn't like to hang around me much, as I am sure everyone can tell. Phillipe Cardoza is a very nice man; we have gone out a couple of times, but nothing came of it. We train together on occasion."

"That Prat guy is a chauvinist ass. He's afraid to lose to a woman. Might hurt his ego and all that. It would serve him right if you won, maybe take him down a few notches."

Juliette couldn't help but laugh. "You nailed him to a T."

"I have talked to Cardoza on multiple occasions. He seems nice, hard to understand sometimes, but I'm getting used to his accent."

"Yes, his accent is very strong." she said, with a smile.

Brett couldn't help smile back. She had a beautiful smile, and he loved her british accent.

"Juliette, would you want to have dinner with me tonight? We could go to Sarino's."

"I'd love to."

She didn't even hesitate, which shocked both him and her.

"Great! I'll meet you at the front of the main house. Say 7 o'clock tonight?"

"Sounds lovely, I'll be there."

"Okay, it's a date then. Before you change your mind, I have to take off and muck a few stalls."

He took off but could hear a faint giggle from behind. Brett smiled the whole way to the other side of the stables.

Chapter 6

The day seemed to be dragging for Juliette. She still couldn't believe she said yes to a dinner date with Brett. The smile pasted on her beautiful face said she was happy with her sudden decision though. She shook her head. Her head definitely wasn't in the game, on the track today. She didn't even hear the horse and jockey coming up behind her.

"Juliette! Juliette!"

Phillipe Cardoza was trying hard to get Juliette's attention, but she was quite distracted. He didn't want to scare her, so he continued to gallop towards her faster. Once he was within five feet, he yelled her name, again.

"Juliette!"

She jerked her head back, startled.

"Sorry, I didn't mean to scare you." The look of chagrin on his bronzed face showed his embarrassment.

"Phillipe, don't apologize, I wasn't paying attention. How are you and Brazilian Bomb doing this sunny morning? She thought he really was a pretty horse."

"Ah, we are doing wonderful, and you and Whiskey? You seemed to be off in the distance somewhere. Winners Circle, maybe?" He was chuckling at his own sense of humor.

"Whiskey and I are doing great, I just have a lot on my mind. Winners Circle is one of them."

"Anything I can help with? You seem a little nervous. Why don't we grab dinner later and talk."

"That's sweet of you, but I'm fine."

"Okay, so just dinner then?"

"I already have plans for dinner, but thank you."

She didn't want to have this conversation with Phillipe right now. When they first arrived in Louisville, Juliette and Phillipe got pretty close. They went on a few dates. There was nothing there; no spark for Juliette, but Phillipe still harbored some feelings for her. She wasn't sure why she didn't feel anything for him. He was beyond handsome.

Phillipe is from Sao Paulo, Brazil. He's a little taller than her, has bronze skin, long hair that was black as pitch, that he usually wore in a ponytail, plus a chiseled face that is reminiscent of Greek Gods. He is quite good looking, beautiful even, but it wasn't enough for Juliette.

"Ah, you have a date?"

She noticed the sardonic tone of his voice; she didn't like it. Juliette didn't think it was any of his business, but she replied anyway.

"Actually I do, with Brett."

She didn't care who knew. Once they were at Sarino's, people would see them together anyway.

He laughed. "The stable hand? Interesting…"

Juliette jutted her chin out, at his disdain for Brett.

"He's not just a stable hand. He manages the whole ranch Phillipe and you know it. And why is it so interesting that I am having dinner with him?"

He tried hard to recover his attitude, but fell short.

"I didn't mean anything by it, really. You are an International Jockey, a multiple race winner. I just didn't think a guy like him would be your type. He's so ordinary, isn't he?"

Her temper was about to get the best of her and she could feel it.

"My type?! What do you know about what type of guy interests me, other than it isn't you? And he is not ordinary. He is very kind, smart, good with the horses, and very knowledgeable about their needs, if you haven't noticed."

"Well, I guess you put me in my place, didn't you? I only asked you out because you were new to the circuit. I was being friendly."

Phillipe Cardoza knew he was good with the ladies. They loved his accent and his hair. Once they found out he was a jockey, they swarmed like flies. He wasn't going to let her see that he was disjointed about her not returning his feelings.

"Well, I guess we're done here. Juliette, it was a pleasure seeing you. I guess I'll see you after I cross the finish line, huh?"

Why that smug, arrogant slimeball. He is almost as bad as Florent Prat.

She smiled, her pearly white smile and gave him her most sincere goodbye.

"I believe, I will see you looking on as Whiskey and I will be presented with the Garland of Roses." With that, she and her horse took off around the track.

Phillipe looked on, stock-still and cemented in his position. Anger radiated off him in droves. No woman has ever been so ill tempered with him.

"She'll get what's coming to her, I'm sure. I don't care if she does have 8-1 odds in her favor."

The anger he suppressed, he channeled through to his training for the rest of the day. His thoughts were muddled with visions of him beating her and taking home the Derby trophy. She'd regret being so rude to him.

He also had an idea to run into the couple later tonight, at Sarino's. He would have to give Miss Sophia Barrere a call and ask her to accompany him. She couldn't say no, she was Churchill Downs Public Relations lady and he'd spied her staring at him many times.

Chapter 7

Brett was just finishing up for the evening and getting ready to head to his home located on the ranch when Phillipe came trotting in on his black Thoroughbred, Brazilian Bomb. The horse was stunning; the rider not so much, he thought. Brett got the impression the man was a little in love with himself more than anything or anyone else.

"Excuse me, Mr. Singers, are you leaving already? I could really use your help."

Phillipe knew he was getting ready to leave and exactly where he was going. Being the good stable hand he knew he was, he wouldn't leave without helping him. Brett took pride in his job, Phillipe could tell.

"Yes, I was getting ready to leave.. I have plans tonight. What did you need help with?"

This guy rubbed Brett the wrong way on so many levels. Maybe it was his primadonna attitude, or just the way he treated the hands that worked at the ranch, like they were peons. There was something about this guy, Brett didn't like..

Phillipe was thinking of the one task that would take the longest, whether it needed tending to or not.

"I think one of his shoes is loose. Could you look at it? If it needs replacing, you could handle that, right?"

Brett looked at the man, who was now smiling down at him from atop his horse. If that wasn't an evil smile, he didn't know what was, he thought to himself. He was definitely getting a strange vibe from him. He had never given him this feeling before. Maybe he was just getting nervous about the Derby. Jockeys tend to get a little needy the closer they get to the race. But he didn't want to be late meeting Juliette, either.

"Sure, I'll check him out. Which shoe are you worried about?"

"Um… the back right hoof." Phillipe had loosened it himself.

"Fine. Why don't you get down? I can take him back to his stall and check it out."

Philipe did as he was told, slowly, dragging out as much time as possible.

"I do appreciate this. Would you be able to replace his shoe today if need be?"

Brett was beyond agitated with Phillipe now. He needed to go back to his house, clean himself up, and be back to the main house by 7:00 to meet Julliette. He checked his watch and saw that it was already 5:30.

"We will see what we're dealing with first, then I can determine what will need to be done."

He took the horse by the reins and guided him into his assigned stall. Brett tethered the reins to a hook in the corner and pulled a stool into the stall, so he could check the horse's shoe.

Phillipe's Thoroughbred is a beautiful horse with a black silky mane, broad muscles, and strong. Brett noticed him the first day he trained.

Sitting on the stool next to the horse, he pulled up the back right foot.

"Okay boy, let me check this shoe, see if it's loose. Hopefully it won't need replacing."

As Brett examined Brazilian's shoe, he noticed nothing was really wrong, but it was a bit loose. There was a scratch mark on the side, not from rocks or debris, but from some kind of tool.

Phillipe stood leaning against the stall door, his feet crossed at the ankles, as well as his arms crossed over his chest, watching Brett with his prized horse. He was hoping it wasn't obvious that he had tried loosening the horses shoe. He figured if he started making idol conversation, Brett wouldn't notice particulars.

"So, I hear you and Juliette are going out. How nice for you."

Brett looked over his shoulder at the man, his words were laced with jealousy, that, he had no doubt.

"We're going to dinner, yes. From what I can see here the shoe is merely loose, and won't need replacing. I'll tighten it and he will be good to go. However, I'm not sure what you used to loosen it, but I wouldn't do it again."

Irritation showed on his face, and in the tone of his voice, putting Phillipe into a defensive stance.

"Are you saying I did this to my horse on purpose?"

"That's exactly what I'm saying. Would you like me to show you the tool mark? Listen, I don't know what your deal is, but if you did this to make me late for my date with Juliette, it's not going to work. I will tighten your horse's shoe and log it in our books, so if there is ever a discrepancy, we have proof. We make computer copies of all of this as well, so if you plan to destroy my paper copy, I'll have a back up."

"Excuse me, I am hardly jealous of you. I can have any woman I want. In fact, I have a date tonight with Sophia Barrere. She does PR for the Derby and Churchill Downs."

"Congratulations."

Brett made a couple of adjustments to the shoe, which took him only a couple of minutes, and the horse was good to go. He made his notes in his log book, had Phillipe sign off on it and scanned it into his phone to download to their records later.

"Phillipe, Brazilian is all good, so if you'll excuse me, I need to go get ready for my date. You and Miss Barrere have a wonderful evening."

Annoyed by the stable hand's remarks, Phillipe nodded and replied curtly, "thank you."

Brett was through the stable building in seconds and high tailed it back to his place to get a quick shower and put on some decent clothes.

Chapter 8

Juliette had showered, blown her hair dry, and was searching through all of the clothes she brought with her. She changed outfits three times. She was never this nervous going out to dinner with anyone before, why now, she thought.

She was still mad at Phillipe for how he had acted when she told him about going to dinner with Brett. It truly was none of his business. She wasn't going to let his attitude ruin her evening.

Juliette decided on a pair of khaki chinos, a white oxford shirt, and her loafers. She felt like she looked understated, but neat. Her long brown hair hung down in wavy curls, to the middle of her back and her makeup was subtle. Juliette didn't need a lot to look decent. She was thankful for her good genes, because she didn't have a lot of time to fuss around with primping. .

She got to the bottom of the stairs and almost to the front door, when she saw a white Mercedes CLS Coupe pull around the front of the round driveway. She peeked through the window to see who it was. The man that exited the car made her lower jaw drop in surprise. The man was dressed in khaki chinos, a white linen button down shirt, with the sleeves rolled up, brown moccasins. If he hadn't still had the blonde shaggy hair, scruffy beard, and those amazing blue eyes, she would never have thought it would be Brett.

She pulled the door open as he was taking the steps two at a time. He stopped short and gasped.

"Wow, we look like twins," he said, laughing.

She looked down at her ensemble and had to keep herself from cringing, but a small laugh escaped.

"Maybe I should change my clothes real quick."

"No! You look great. I don't mind, if you don't."

"If you're sure?"

"Absolutely. Let's go."

They walked down the steps in silence. He showed her to the passenger side and opened her door with a flourish.

"Your door madam."

Juliette laughed. "Why thank you, sir."

"My pleasure."

She watched as he rounded the front of the car and then took notice of the interior of the car. It wasn't a low end Mercedes, she was sure of that.

"I gotta say, this isn't exactly the type of car I was expecting you to drive," she said, as he sat down.

He looked down at her, "I'm full of surprises."

And with that, Juliette found herself speechless.

Most of the drive to Sarino's was made in awkward silence. Brett wasn't usually this nervous. He just didn't know what to say.

Juliette felt his unease and decided to break the silence.

"So, how was the rest of your day? Mine seemed to drag on, and Phillipe Cardoza didn't help matters much."

He looked at her, surprised. "Phillipe got up into your business too, huh?"

"What do you mean, too?"

"He caught me at the end of the day. He asked me to check his horse's shoe. He wanted me to see if it was loose or coming off. He also asked me if I would stay to replace it right then and there. Thankfully it had just been loose, but on purpose. I noticed that pretty quickly. He wasn't too happy after I said something to him about the on purpose part."

"Whoa, what do you mean, on purpose?"

"I think he took a screwdriver to the shoe on purpose, to delay me tonight."

"Really? Interesting. He asked me to go to dinner tonight, but when I told him I had plans with you, he wasn't too happy. I can't believe he would stoop so low, as to do something to his horse, to wreck our plans."

"Well it didn't work, here we are and we are going to have a wonderful dinner."

Juliette took a second to look in his direction and smiled. She still didn't like what Brett told her.

"I'm not going to let him ruin my evening. I never go out, so this is a treat."

"It seemed to me that you and Phillipe had a thing going at one time, from what I remember."

"We had gone to dinner a few times, but I told him I didn't see it going anywhere. I told him I hoped we could remain friends. Did he say something else to you about it?" The irritation in her voice was impossible to miss.

"He didn't say you were necessarily dating, but he seemed put out by the fact that I was taking you out tonight. He rubbed me the wrong way after the stunt he pulled today, with the horseshoe. Watch out for him, okay. He's a fierce competitor and he is probably feeling a little inferior with the odds of you winning the Derby being so high."

"He's such a tosser. Can we talk about something else? No Derby talk tonight, okay?"

"I can do that, but first, what's a tosser?"

"Oh, it's British slang for a Jerk."

"Good to know," he laughed.

When they pulled into Sarino's, the parking lot was pretty busy, but Brett knew to call ahead, to get his name on the list just in case.

Juliette didn't miss the crowded parking lot. "Wow, what's going on here tonight? We may not get a table."

"Never fear, I called before we left and had our name put on the list. They said it would only be a 20 minute wait."

Brett angled himself out of the car, walked around the front to the passenger side and gently opened the door for Juilette to get out.

"Your mother must have been something else. Your manners are impeccable. Thank you. I'm not used to this kind of spoiling."

He held out a hand to her and she took it. They walked to the front door, with hands still entwined.

They headed to the hostess station to let them know that they were there. She gave them a pager and told them it would only be a 10-15 minute wait.

"Do you want to grab a drink at the bar while we wait?"

"Sure, a glass of Merlot sounds great."

"It's such a nice evening, how about we go to the outdoor bar?"

"Perfect"

They found a couple of bar stools open and grabbed them. After giving the bartender their order, Juliette took a minute to look around the outdoor area. It was a warm evening, especially for the end of April. They still had the large gas heat lights on the patio area, to keep it warm.

She was eyeing the different food selections on the menu, so she wouldn't waste too much time when they got seated, when Brett let out a grunt in disgust.

She looked in the direction of his sudden sour mood. That's when she saw the man exiting a BMW and opening the passenger door for his female companion. It was Phillipe, but who was he with? The woman didn't look familiar. She was stunning. The woman wore Louboutin heels, she was as tall, if not a smidge taller than Phillipe, and her hair was long and blonde. Her suit said Bloomingdale's, but her makeup screamed Walgreens, once they got closer. Juliette thought to herself, *why so much make-up? She didn't need it. Actually, she would look lovely without it. Maybe a little blush, a paler lipstick...*

"Juliette, we could go somewhere else, if you prefer," Brett said, breaking her out of her judgement and back to the here and now.

"No! It's fine, maybe they won't see us."

No sooner had she said that, she heard the infamous shrill of her name being called, in the all too familiar Brazilian accent.

"Juliette, what a surprise. I didn't know you would be here tonight."

She had to control her every impulse not to roll her eyes at him. He knew very well they would be here tonight.

"I'm pretty sure I told you, not even five hours ago that we were coming here tonight."

Her annoyance level was peaking off the charts. Brett put his hand on the small of her back to calm her. She looked up at him and smiled in appreciation.

The woman at Phillipe's side now looked vaguely familiar to her, but she couldn't place her. She finally held her hand out to the woman, to introduce herself, since Phillipe wasn't going to do it.

"Hi, I'm Juliette Sutherland."

The woman in question shook her hand enthusiastically, smiling.

"Oh, I know who you are. I'm Sophia Barrere, I do all the Public Relations for the Kentucky Derby and all that is Churchill Downs. You are a PR person's dream. It's a real pleasure to meet you."

Phillipe scowled at the woman next to him. "What am I, chopped liver?"

She quickly dissolved the situation. "No, not at all. It's just that Juliette is the first female that has only a year of racing under her belt, qualified for the Derby, and has 8-1 odds of winning this year. That's never happened in the history of the Derby before. You have to see that this is huge for the sport."

Juliette couldn't hide her astonishment at the amount of information this woman knew about her.

"Wow, you've done your homework. I'm not doing this for fame or publicity though. I do it because I love riding. I grew up with horses. It's what I've always done."

Phillipe was getting restless and irritated that all the attention was now centered on Juliette and not on him.

"Can we go now and get a table, I'm starving. I need a drink, as well."

Phillipe grabbed Sophia by the elbow and started pulling her along. She turned back toward Juliette and Brett. "Again, it was a pleasure meeting you."

"You too."

Juliette and Brett looked on as Phillipe ushered her through the door, knowing they were going to have to wait, just as they were.

"Well, that was awkward," she said, laughing.

"Phillipe wasn't too happy about the attention shift, that was for sure."

"I don't really like all the attention I get. I wish they'd just let me ride."

"You had to know this coming; that you would garner some attention, right?"

"Of course, but I'm still not used to it."

"I know. Sorry. We can leave, if you want."

She looked up at him, sincerity shined in the ocean blue eyes that were staring at her. She knew what she was getting into, especially with such a publicized race like the Kentucky Derby and she should just get used to it. She wasn't ready to end her first date with Brett so soon, either.

"No, I need to get used to the attention, right? And frankly, I'm not ready to end the night yet, if that's okay with you?"

The full on electric bright white perfect smile he gave her, eased her tension immediately.

"I'm glad, I wasn't quite ready to end the night yet either. Shall we enjoy our drinks, until they call us for our table?"

"We shall."

They clinked their wine glasses together, smiled at one another, and sat back to enjoy their wine.

Chapter 9

Inside Sarino's, sitting with a view of the outside bar area, Chloe Rivers looked on at the couple with disgust in her eyes.

"Seriously, he'll go out with her, but not me?"

She had said it mostly to herself, but it grabbed the attention of her companion and grandfather, Terrence Rivers. Chloe's mother, Penelope has been estranged from the man since her husband's (his son's) death, but he still keeps in contact with his granddaughter, because of his love for his son.

Terrence is a greedy, gambling man, who bears a striking resemblance to actor John Forsythe. He is six feet tall, with gray eyes, a full head of thick white hair, and wears Armani suits.

"Who or what are you talking about dear?"

Chloe looked at her grandfather with embarrassment on her face. She hadn't realized that she'd complained out loud.

"Oh, sorry grandfather. It's just Brett, who works with the horses at the ranch. He's here with Juliette Sutherland. She's the one female jockey everyone is raving about. I've been trying to get him to go out with me, but he told me that he has a policy of not dating anyone he works with, or his boss's daughter. Have you ever heard of such a thing? I mean, doesn't he technically work with Juliette?"

Terrence wasn't used to his granddaughter discussing men with him and he wasn't exactly comfortable with it, but he didn't like her feeling rejected either. He looked out the window to where Chloe was watching, taking in the young couple. They looked to be enjoying themselves. He wasn't sure how to handle this situation. He himself had a lot of money riding on this race. Juliette's 8-1 odds were going to make him a pretty penny. A lot was invested in this girl winning. She didn't need to be sidetracked by a man.

"I can always talk to Miss Sutherland and remind her she shouldn't get distracted from her training, right before the biggest race of her life."

"Grandfather, I don't need you to take care of me all the time. I'm twenty years old, I'll get over it. I don't think she's even that pretty. What does he see in her? What do any of these guys see in her? Phillipe was tripping all over her, too."

"She's just competition for Phillipe and the other jockeys. They may be trying to throw her off her game."

"I guess you're right."

Chloe couldn't keep the loathsome look off of her face.

She noticed them getting up to leave, walking toward the door to the inner restaurant. She hoped she and her Grandfather were hidden enough in the corner they were sitting in, so she could quietly and secretly watch them.

Chapter 10

The hostess seated them in the middle of the dining room of the restaurant. Juliette was feeling a little on display. She noticed people staring and got an uncomfortable feeling. Brett noticed and took the hostess off to the side to speak to her.

"Is there another table that isn't quite so front and center? I think my date is a little nervous about people staring at her. You see, she will be the only female racing in the Derby and everyone seems to recognize her."

The hostess looked over at Juliette, as Brett was explaining the situation and recognition came into her face.

"That is her, I hadn't been paying any attention. Are you sure you want to be moved out of the way, this could give her some good publicity."

Seeing the terror on her face, he immediately decided.

"I'm sure. If there is any way you can move us to another table, I would greatly appreciate it, as would she."

"Okay, sure. How about that table over on the West wall. It has a pretty nice view and not many people are over there, plus it's away from the parking lot windows and outdoor bar."

Brett thought that location looked perfect and the hostess sat them there.

Juliette gave her an appreciative look and thanked her profusely. "This table is so much better, thank you," she said.

"No problem. I got the feeling you were getting stage fright when you saw people staring."

She let out a small chuckle, but it didn't quite reach her eyes.

The rest of the evening went on without much more fanfare and they were both thankful for the respite. They were able to talk uninterrupted and find out more about each other. They'd asked what likes, dislikes and lots of questions about where they'd each grown up.

To her, he was a breath of fresh air, she didn't know she needed. She had learned that he grew up on a horse ranch in Santa Barbara, California. His parents had bred and raised horses, and still do. She had actually heard of his parents and their business, Pacific Coast Horse Ranch.

She learned that Brett was an only child, he's never been married, and loves not only riding and caring for horses, but was an avid surfer. She could have guessed that last one, on her own, just by the way he looked. He was also a pretty savvy businessman. He had bought 49% of Estrella Equine Village, after Penelope's husband had passed away, to help her and her daughter. According to him, her father- in-law, Terrence Rivers wanted nothing to do with the ranch, even though it would have helped his late son's family. He had offered to buy it, but wasn't going to keep it a horse training ranch and Penelope wasn't going to let that happen.

Juliette had read up on Mr. Rivers a little bit, after making it to the Derby, so she would have a little background on the event.

She was enjoying herself more than she thought she would. The food was amazing and the company was even better.

"I want to thank you for tonight. I really needed to get out, even though there were a few issues, which I know I have to get over. I'm having a lot of fun."

Brett smiled at her. He was having the best time too. Juliette was a joy to talk to and he had found out that she and her family are from Cotswold, England and even though he figured they were pretty wealthy, she never said anything about it. She wasn't one to flaunt it either.

He couldn't believe that she used to show horses and had been doing so since she was ten years old. He was pretty flabbergasted that she had only been on the racing circuit for a year. He knew she was new to racing, but still couldn't get over just how new. When he had watched her on the track, she didn't have the new jockey look. Her horse Whiskey was very in tune with her and vice versa.

Brett was pleased to hear that she didn't currently have a boyfriend, too. She had an ex- boyfriend that was still back in Cotswold, but he had been out of the picture for a while now. She had mentioned that earlier, but during dinner, he got the full story.

"I'm happy you're enjoying yourself. I wasn't so sure there at the beginning. It could have gone south quickly, if Phillipe had anything to say about it."

"I'd rather we forget about that, if you don't mind?"

"Agreed."

"Are you ready to head back to the ranch?"

"Ready whenever you are."

He proceeded to get up from his chair and walked over to hers, holding out his hand for her. She looked up at him, smiled, and slipped her hand into his.

They walked from the restaurant to his Mercedes, where he again opened her door, let her get situated, and closed it.

He smiled to himself as he walked around the front to his side and angled himself in behind the wheel.

The drive back to Estrella Equine Village was quiet, both were thinking about what the other might be thinking. Neither one broke the silence until he pulled into the circle drive and put the car in park.

"Don't move, I'll let you out," he said.

Before she could get a word out, he was out of the car and walking to her side. He opened the door once more for her and held his hand out for her to take. Brett gently pulled her to a standing position, with her looking up into his eyes.

He wanted to lean down to kiss her, but wasn't sure if she would be ready for that, yet. He took her hand in his, shut her door and walked her up the steps. He paused on the top step, turned them around, and pulled her down with him to sit.

"Mind if we just hang out a little longer, it is such a nice evening out here?"

She was more than happy to hang out with him as long as he wanted.

"I'd be happy too."

He loved to hear her speak. He still couldn't get over the british accent. She sounded so sophisticated, even when she was being sarcastic.

They hadn't been back at the ranch for more than three minutes, when a BMW 5 series pulled into the circle drive. Brett didn't recognize the car as anyone he knew. They waited until the mystery visitor exited the car.

A young man in his thirties, with walnut brown hair and eyes, full beard, extremely handsome, wearing a black suit, with a red tie, walked towards the steps. A full on perfect set of teeth smiled at Juliette.

Juliette's eyes went wide with recognition and she almost swallowed her tongue. Shock, anger, trepidation, annoyance, all played at the facial expressions that were forming on her beautiful face. She said nothing. Brett looked back and forth to both people, waiting.

"Juliette, you're looking lovely. I have so missed you. Aren't you going to greet me properly?"

Juliette sat there, speechless. She glared at the man standing in front of her.

Brett stood up, grabbing her hand and pulling her with him. He held out a hand to shake the mystery man's hand.

"I'm Brett Singers. You apparently know Juliette. Who may I ask are you?"

The man shook his hand and looked to Juliette, who was still silent and holding Brett's hand in a death grip.

"Sorry chap, my name is Kai Armstrong, I'm Juliette's boyfriend from England."

The sudden boyfriend admission brought Juliette out of her shock induced stupor. She glared at Kai.

"Ex-boyfriend Kai, not boyfriend." Juliette put a strong inflection on the Ex part of her comment.

Kai just shrugged off her comment.

"That was not my doing," he said.

"What are you doing here Kai?"

"Maybe I should let you two talk in private," Brett jumped in.

"That would be kind of you chap."

"No, you're not leaving Brett, Kai is."

She gave a pointed look toward Kai. " I don't know why you're here and frankly I don't give two figs, but I suggest you leave."

Kai jutted his chin out, "I came here to see you race in the biggest race of your life. It's what people do for those they love."

Juliette gave him an indignant look.

"Pfft...well, you can go back to England Kai, I don't want or need you here. And news flash, I am not in love with you. We broke up over two years ago, and until now you hadn't so much as emailed me since."

"Oh bloody hell, Jules. We all made mistakes, yours was leaving Cotswold to come here and mine was not giving you a bloody shout out."

"You can be such a wanker Kai. I don't regret leaving England to pursue racing or breaking up with you. Now, for the last time, take your arse back to where you came from. I'm on a date."

"I'm sure your friend won't mind if I take a few minutes of your time, right old chap?" Kai smirked in Brett's direction.

Brett was sensing Juliette's discomfort with the situation and wasn't going to leave her yet. He was enjoying listening to the conversation the two were having though. He found their slang words more entertaining than those used here in the states.

"Actually, I do mind. Maybe you should have contacted her before you showed up unannounced. From what I'm sensing, she'd like you to leave. Call her tomorrow and set something up, but right now, she's still my date."

Kai and Juliette both looked at Brett, one with the look of annoyance, the other with glee.

"Is that what you want Jules," Kai asked.

"Yes Kai, please be on your way. If there was something you needed to talk to me about, you should have called first. I have a feeling I already know why you came all this way. You were hoping I would let you train me and I would be your in, in the racing world here in the states. But I don't need a trainer, I have one."

"That's not why I came here. I mean, yes, I could totally help you, but that's not the only reason."

Juliette knew he had ulterior motives for being here and it was probably money related. She wasn't about to let him profit off of her success.

"Kai, you never change, it's all about the money and the show. I know you, and I am not interested. And stop calling me Jules, I always despised that and you know it."

She stepped over to Brett and took him by the hand. They walked through the front door of the main house, leaving a speechless Kai behind.

Chapter 11

Shutting the door and locking it, Juliette breathed a heavy sigh of relief.

"I'm so sorry Brett, I had no idea he was coming into town. I hadn't heard from Kai for two years. Of course the one time I decide I am ready to go on a real date, he shows up."

She put her head in her hands and shook her head, frustrated.

Brett took her by the hand and walked her into the sitting room. It was a large room, with a full wall of windows facing the stables, exposed wooden beams in the twenty foot ceilings gave the room an open feel. There was a large comfy brown leather sofa and matching loveseat, as well as two upholstered wing back chairs facing the stone fireplace, it was the focal point of the room. It made the feel of the room cozy and welcoming. He motioned her to sit on the larger sofa and he positioned himself a foot away, not wanting to seem too forward.

"Sit, we'll just talk for a bit. I apologize for saying my peace to Kai, I hope you aren't mad."

"Are you kidding, I was thrilled that you spoke up. You could tell I was uncomfortable with him being here and you said something. I appreciate that so much. He's pig headed and ignores me when I tell him to leave. One of the many reasons I broke up with him. That, and his incessant need to be front and center and make a lot of money. I'm not in this for the money or fame, I just love to ride my horse."

Brett felt an ache in his heart. He was falling for Juliette Sutherland, and hard.

"I'm sorry our date was ruined and I would like to make it up to you, if you'll let me."

"You don't have to do that. Besides, I don't think it was ruined. I had a great time, all things considered. But I wouldn't be opposed to another date."

She smiled at him, butterflies tickling her belly. She felt like a teenager, all shy and awkward. She never felt like this with Kai, in the couple years they dated. She was really taking a liking to Mr. Brett Singers.

Juliette didn't know what to say. For the first time, in a long time, she had no clue what to say. She looked down at her and Brett's hands, still entwined and felt wistful. A peace she didn't know was missing in her everyday life, fell upon her.

Brett saw the look on Juliette's face and couldn't resist placing his hand on her cheek. She looked into his big ocean blue eyes and was swimming. He was going to kiss her and her stomach started doing flip-flops. Why was she so nervous? She wanted him to kiss her.

He leaned in slowly and placed the chastest of kisses on her lips, it was like a butterfly had fluttered it's wings upon them. Her eyes closed briefly, enjoying the sensation. When she opened them, Brett was smiling his beautiful, perfect smile at her.

"Well, I should really be going. And you need your rest. I'll think of something for us to do tomorrow, if you're up for it."

Feeling a little breathless, Juilette shook her head in agreement. "Sounds good."

Brett stood and headed for the front door, he turned and smiled, "Sweet dreams, Juliette."

Chapter 12

Juliette was so keyed up after Brett went home, she decided to go for a walk and breathe in some cool evening air. Hoping to take her mind off the kiss that just happened, she made her way to the stables, to check on her horse. Horses were always her saving grace. They kept her calm and balanced, in an otherwise wonky world.

Tennessee Whiskey was standing in the far back corner of his stall, against the wall. She thought that was a little odd, considering it was pretty late and he was usually sleeping by now, but she made her way into the stall to brush him, but there wasn't much in the way of light out there and she tripped over something hard and slipped across the ground right inside the stall gate. Once she balanced herself, she took her cell phone out and turned the flashlight on, shining it on the ground where she'd just come through. It took her hot second to see what she had run into.

"Oh bollocks! Oh for bloody hell, Phillipe!?"

He was lying there inside Whiskey's stall, surrounded by a pool of blood, streaming from his head. Juliette inched her way over to the horse, to check him out, to see if there were any injuries to him.

Kneeling over Phillipe, to check his pulse, she heard a slight shift in the stables and went rigid with fear. After a minute, she heard nothing but silence and resumed trying to find any kind of pulse on Philippe, but there was nothing.

"What do I do?" She muttered to herself.

Her cellphone was still in her hand, but she was shaking like a leaf. She knew she needed to get help. Her brain wasn't working on all cylinders yet and another noise came from the other end of the stables, where the doors were. She froze where she was, leaning over Phillipe's body.

Juliette heard the sound of boots coming closer and closer, until she could see the tips under the stall gate. Whoever it was, was right there, in front of her horse stall. She held her breath, hoping they would keep walking.

She looked up and saw the wide green eyes of Penelope Rivers.

"Oh my God! Is that Phillipe? Juliette, what did you do?"

Hearing Penelope ask her the pointed question, brought her out of frozen silence.

"Me? I didn't do this. I just came out here to see Whiskey and found him like this."

Penelope opened the stall gate and got on her knees checking for a pulse, just as Juliette had done.

"He's dead Penelope, I already checked."

"Well, I have to call 911. What happened out here? Did you get into a fight?"

On the defensive now, Juliette brought herself to a standing position, looking affronted by the accusation.

"I found him this way. I almost tripped over him. Bloody hell Penelope, I don't know who did this. You have to believe me." She sounded hysterical, but she couldn't help it. Juliette had never seen a dead body before.

"Alright Juliette, calm down. I believe you. But we have to call the police. Is your horse okay, he's not hurt at all, is he?"

"No, he's fine. Who would do something like this?"

Penelope looked around, trying not to touch anything, or disturb any more than they already had. "I don't know, but we have to get out of the stall, before I call the police. We may have destroyed evidence, and if we did, we'll be in big trouble."

She called 911 and explained the gruesome scene to the operator, who informed her that they both needed to stay where they were, until the officers got there and spoke to them.

"Great, we have to stay here until the police come. The operator said they'll want to talk to both of us. Hope you didn't have any plans to sleep tonight."

Juliette felt nauseated. She squatted down, wrapping her arms around her knees, hugging them close to her body. She was trying to wrap her thoughts around the whole idea that there was a dead guy in her horse's stall, when she jumped up. "Why was Phillipe in Whiskey's stall?"

"Good question. That's not going to look good for you."

Juliette was getting annoyed with Penelope and her pointing fingers at her. She didn't do anything wrong. But she was right, it wasn't going to look good for her, in the police's eyes. Her thoughts went to her horse again. "I wonder if he was trying to hurt Whiskey and someone saw him and stopped him. Is there any way we can get a Vet out here to check Whiskey out, just to make sure?"

Juliette was pacing now and could now hear the faint sounds of sirens in the distance.

"I'll call doc Montgomery in the morning and have her check him out."

"Thanks."

"Here they come. This is the last thing I need at my ranch."

Penelope was thinking of all the bad press this would bring to the Estrella Equine Village. They will have a field day with this, she thought. And so will Terrance.

Just as expected, two police cars, an ambulance and the coroner's van were all pulling into the back part of the stables, dust flying behind the cars, making it hard to see.

Two officers from each car exited, along with paramedics and the coroner. They made their way through the stables to where the two women waited.

One of the first officers that reached them, removed his hat, and nodded to both women.

"Ms. Rivers." Then he turned to Juliette. "Ma'am."

"Hey Jackson, this is Juliette. She's one of the jockeys set to race Saturday. She found the dead guy."

Penelope made introductions, as the other officers made their way closer to the crime scene, looking inside the stall. A couple made disgusted noises, while the others, it seemed like any other day at the office to them.

"Ah, so you're the female jockey that's getting all the buzz around here. I'm Sergeant Jackson Tripp. "

"Yes, I guess that would be me. I'm Juliette Sutherland."

"Jackson, can we get on with this, I don't want this to draw too much attention, if you know what I mean."

Penelope was fidgeting and trying to get the officers and coroner to make the call and pronounce Phillipe dead already, so she could get back to a normal routine.

Juliette remained quiet and waited for the inevitable to come.

"Ms. Rivers, I understand that this may cause a mess for your ranch, but I am going to need to ask both of you some questions. It's apparent that you both know the deceased. What is his name, by the way?"

"Sorry Jackson, it's been a rough season. Of course I'll answer any questions you have. His name is Phillipe, but I can't remember his last name. I'm sure I have it in the files."

"It's Phillipe Cardoza," Juliette whispered.

"And you know Mr. Cardoza how?"

"We were both jockeys. He was supposed to compete in the Derby, too."

"Were you friendly with him, or was it strictly competitive?"

"Um, we had gone to dinner a few times. I'm not one to get jealous of other jockeys, if that's what you mean. I certainly would never hurt anyone."

There was yelling coming from the outer area of the stables, that made everyone look up from what they were doing.

"Juliette! Juliette!" Brett was yelling as he was running to the stables, after seeing the amount of emergency vehicles outside the ranch.

Sergeant Tripp pointed to one of his men to go see what the commotion was.

"Now Ms. Sutherland, would you consider your dinners with Mr. Cardoza to be dates? Were you romantically involved with him?"

"Please call me Juliette, and no, we were not romantically involved."

The voices were getting louder at the stable entrance. Juliette knew it was Brett's voice and he was getting mad.

"Will you please tell your men to let that gentleman in? I need to see him."

"Who is it," Tripp asked her, intrigued by her sudden need to talk to whoever was out there.

"He's the stable manager or stable hand, whatever you want to call him. He's probably worried about the horses."

"Stay right here, please."

Juliette was freaking out and when her anxiety takes over, she shuts down, completely. She needed to see Brett, so he could see she was okay. She knew from the tone of his voice, he was more worried about her, then the horses, but she wasn't about to admit that to Sergeant Tripp.

Brett came running to her side, looking her over, making sure she was unharmed. Taking her by the elbow, he leaned in and asked her, "are you okay? They won't tell me what's going on?"

"It's Phillipe, his body is in Whiskey's stall. I nearly tripped over him when I went to check on Whiskey."

Brett was silent for a second, while processing what she'd just told him.

"Wait, Phillipe is dead?"

She was having trouble holding the tears that were threatening to descend, back. He looked at her and pulled her to him, in an all encompassing embrace.

"You're okay Juliette."

He was doing his best to reassure her, when Sargeant Tripp cleared his throat to get their attention.

Brett put a little distance between him and Juilette, but didn't let go of her hand. He could feel her squeezing it for all her worth. She was hanging on by a thread and he wasn't about to let go of her.

"Can I have your name again, sir?"

"Brett Singers, I'm the stable manager here."

"Mr. Singers, do you know Mr. Cardoza very well?"

"I only met him a month ago, when the jockeys that are going to be in the Derby set up shop here, to train. We've talked a few times, but nothing other than that. I was checking his horse out earlier today. He thought it had a shoe issue, but I resolved that."

"You're obviously close to Ms. Sutherland here, though, aren't you? How would you categorize your relationship with her?"

Brett wasn't sure how to answer that, they had gone on their first date, just tonight.

"I guess I'd say we are dating. We had our first date tonight, but I don't see the relevance here."

"It goes toward motive, Mr. Singers. We will be questioning everyone on the property, but your protective nature towards Ms. Sutherland makes me think there is more to this story. Care to explain?"

Juliette jerked her head up and felt the anger bubbling under her skin at the audacity of this man.

"Oh bloody hell, neither of us had anything to do with this. We had just gotten home from dinner, not even half an hour ago. I came out to check on my horse and almost tripped over his arse. You're wasting your time talking to us, we did nothing wrong."

Everyone within earshot, turned their attention to Juliette's outburst. She suddenly realized that everyone was staring at her. Brett put an arm around her shoulder, pulling her close.

"I think she's made her point, are we free to go now," Brett asked.

Sergeant Jackson looked flummoxed, and scowled at both of them.

"Do you both reside on the grounds here?"

"Yes," they both said in unison.

"Well, I live here full time. My house is at the far end of the property, but Juliette is only here until the Derby is over."

"God help me, this better be over before that," Penelope piped up.

The coroner walked out of the stall, walking toward the group.

"The victim wasn't killed out here, Jackson, he was dumped here."

"Seriously? Now I have to find out where the man was killed? This just keeps getting better and better."

"Yeah, once the PR people get a hold of this, it'll be bad. They'll be on your butt, to get this solved before the Derby next week. If it hurts them financially, the crap will hit the fan. I suggest you bring in higher ups on this one."

"Higher ups? You mean the FBI? You don't think I can solve this?" He looked at the coroner, indignant.

"I'm just saying, if I were you, I'd want all the help I could get."

"Uh huh."

Jackson ran a hand through his thick blond hair, frustration emanating from him.

"Crap. Okay, here is what's going to happen. You two are not to leave town; Ms. Rivers, you gather all your guests, first thing in the morning, to a central meeting area on the ranch. I will be here at 9am sharp, with extra help. As for now, this stable will be off limits, while we get the Crime Scene Investigators combing the place for any evidence they can find. Everyone got that?"

They all shook their heads in acknowledgement.

"Are we allowed to return to the main house, to go to bed," Juliette asked.

"As soon as I see the CSI team that I had sent to your room, return."

"What? You had someone in my room without telling me?"

The smirk on Jackson's face was smug, but he wanted it to look that way. "This is a public ranch, you don't own any part of it, we are allowed to search, as we see fit. As soon as I spoke to you, I had them go to the lodge and start looking around. With Ms. Rivers okay, that is."

Brett put a secure arm around her waist, holding her to her spot, before she lunged toward the Sergeant. He could feel the anger vibrating off of her.

Just as she was about to say something she might regret, a group of people wearing coveralls came into the stables and nodded to the man, letting him know they were finished.

"Alright, you are able to return to your room, Ms. Sutherland. Mr. Singers, you're more than welcome to walk her back, as your house is next. And before you say anything, you too, do not own that property, so we are going in to search your place, as well."

"Brett, they're searching the main house as well, so it's not just you two he's singling out," Penelope said, hoping to tamp down any anger.

"You knew they were already searching and you said nothing?" Brett was more upset with Penelope for not informing them, then he was of them actually searching.

"And for future reference, I do own my house, and the land it is on here. But I have nothing to hide, so search on."

Brett grabbed Juliette's hand and led her out of the stable, fuming.

Chapter 13

Shaking his head and walking faster than Juliette's short legs could move, Brett suddenly stopped mid stride, dropping her hand and raked his fingers through his hair.

"I can't believe this, can you? She said nothing the whole time we were standing there. She knew our private property was being searched and said nothing."

"Maybe she wasn't allowed. I don't know. I'm not any more happy about it, than you are, trust me. But I don't have anything to hide, I had nothing to do with Phillipe's death, I hope they know that."

Brett slowly calmed down enough to think rationally. He knew she couldn't have killed Phillipe, she was so small and petite. She couldn't hurt a fly.

He held out his hand to her and she took it, wrapping her tiny fingers around his.

"Let's get you back to the main house, so you can get some sleep. You must be exhausted. This isn't exactly the way I envisioned our first date, by any means, but it definitely wasn't boring, that's for sure." He managed a slight laugh.

She turned her head to look up at him. It was dark, except for the moon and stars lighting their way. He really did have a beautiful smile, it was perfect.

She let a small chuckle escape. "It most certainly wasn't boring. Next time, can we make it a boring date? I like sitting in front of the TV and watching some ridiculous comedy and eating popcorn?"

"Sounds good to me. So, there is going to be a second date?"

"I thought we'd already established that," she laughed.

He felt the tension roll off his shoulders, taking in her beautiful smile and her innocent sense of humor.

"Looks like every light in the main house is on. They must have searched every room. I wonder how many people are waiting to ask questions? Are you sure you want to go back in, just yet?"

She looked up at the main house and stopped dead in her tracks. She hated attention and avoided it at all costs.

"Is there somewhere else we can go? I don't want to go up there."

"Sure, my place is pretty secluded on the other end of the property. We can go there, if you want, or we can go for a walk around the grounds. It's up to you."

She contemplated going to his place, but she didn't need any extra rumors going around.

"A walk would be nice."

"A walk it is then."

Brett once again reached for her hand and started walking in the opposite direction. He was hoping no one in the main house had seen them and decided to head in the same direction they were.

They walked for a few minutes in comfortable silence, until Juliette broke that silence.

"Brett, who do you think could have killed Phillipe? Do you think it was done on purpose? Was it just him they were after, or were they targeting jockeys in general?"

"I honestly don't know. Grant it, the guy had a bad attitude, but not so bad that he deserved to be killed. I am more worried about your safety right now, than anything else."

He gave her hand a gentle squeeze and smiled down at her. She gave him a hint of a smile, but it still didn't quite reach her eyes.

The moon and stars had been shining all night and they seemed to be illuminating their path. Juliette noticed in the distance, lights coming from a large structure.

"What is that place out there, that has lights coming from it?"

"The building on the left is another smaller stable, where I keep my horse Shasta, and the bigger structure is my house."

Surprised, Juliette halted their walk. "You have a horse here, too? I didn't realize there were any other stables on the grounds."

"When I started working for Penelope, I had asked her after I'd been here for a year, if she would mind if I built my own house and stable on the other side of the grounds, since it was all open acreage. Of course, I told her I would pay for the land, as well as having the buildings built and she agreed to let me do that. I figured she would want the extra money, since her husband had just passed away and I wanted my own living area, away from where I worked everyday."

"I don't blame you for wanting your own space."

As they got closer to Bretts house and stable, she started to make out the look of the property. The house was an A-frame log home, with a wrap-around porch that spanned both sides of the house. It was bigger than she expected it to be, for a single guy. The stable was made from cedar and painted a deep burgundy, from what she could tell in the dim lighting. It had black wrought iron trimmings and a sliding barn door.

"Can I see your horse, while we're here?"

"Sure."

He slid the barn door to the left and led her into the stables. The overhead lights worked on motion sensors. The deeper into the stable they walked, the more lights came on. It had four large stalls, made mostly of wood, with metal bars and arched tops. Each stall had large steel hooks on the outside, that held the tack for each horse, along with a grooming area at the one end, where the horse would be brushed and new shoes would be put on. Each stall housed an area where hay was kept and water could be distributed.

Juliette was impressed and a little jealous. "You have a great set up here. Your Shasta is well taken care of and maybe a little spoiled," she said, laughing.

"Thanks. She is in the stall at the far end. She is more like a kid than an animal to me, so I guess you could say, she is quite spoiled."

They continued walking toward the other end, when a nose peaked out of the stall and let her presence be known.

"Brett, she's beautiful."

Shasta was a pretty chestnut color, with a touch of white around her nose. She had a broad chest with rounder hindquarters. She looked solid.

The horse came closer to the two of them and nuzzled Brett's neck in a cute hello. Juliette couldn't help but smile. She ran her hand down the soft, yet hard side of her face and Shasta loved the attention. The horse turned her head in her direction, taking an instant liking to Juliette.

"She likes you. She doesn't let just anyone pet her like that."

"She knows a horse person when she sees one."

The barn door flew open and Chloe came running in, stopping dead in her tracks. She looked at the two standing close to each other, staring back at her.

Chloe, what are you doing here," Brett asked, annoyed.

"I was looking for you. I heard what happened to Phillipe and I wanted to check on you. Apparently you're just fine. What is she doing here?"

"We were taking a walk, to get some fresh air after being questioned." His hand stayed at the small of Juliette's back, keeping her close.

Chloe didn't like what she was seeing and she could feel her anger fueling, especially seeing him touch Juliette, like he was being protective of her. Chloe's anger flared more than usual lately. Maybe it was her upcoming finals. She felt off.

"Doesn't she have her own room in the main house," she said, referring to Juliette.

Juliette could see the jealousy and hatred Chloe had for her and she wasn't used to feeling irritated by such things. She had just had the worst night of her life and wasn't about to accommodate this young girl with snippy comments.

"I do have a room at the main house, yes, but there was a lot going on with the police and all the other jockeys being questioned. I felt like taking a walk and Brett was nice enough to accompany me. Is that alright with you?"

Brett let out a little snicker of laughter, but quickly righted himself enough to hold his own.

"Chloe, it really isn't any of your business what we are doing. You're on my land and this is my house. If we want to take a walk around the grounds, we can. Maybe you should get back to the main house to be with your mom, she could use some support now."

If looks could kill, they'd both be six feet under. Chloe turned on her heel in a huff and sauntered out of the barn.

"I'm really sorry about that. I'm not sure what her problem is lately."

"I think I know what it is. She's jealous that I'm here with you. I think she wants you all to herself," Juliette explained.

"Yeah, she has been coming on to me, more so lately. I told her nicely, that I wasn't interested. I was hoping she would get the hint."

"Can you blame her?"

Brett smiled, took her hand and gave it a gentle kiss.

Juliette had to keep her mind clear and in the game, or in the race, if you will. She didn't have a lot of time for romance right now, not with the Derby a few days away.

"I really should be getting back to my room, it's getting late and I need to train in the morning."

"Of course. I'll walk you back."

"Thanks."

Chapter 14

By the time they reached the main house, everybody had retreated back to their rooms to catch some sleep. Juliette wasn't ready to say goodnight to Brett, but she didn't have a choice and she knew it.

They walked through the main door, to find more people milling around and they all just turned and stared at the pair that had just joined them. They recognized Officer Tripp, Penelope and of course Chloe and Florent, but there was another older gentleman that Juliette hadn't recognized, but he looked familiar. After a second glance, she saw that it was Mr. Rivers. As they walked their way through the hall to the living area where everyone was huddled, she noticed Kai was back and sitting on the leather sofa, looking like he owned the place.

"Kai, what are you doing back here?"

He sauntered over to them. He tried to kiss her on the cheek but she pulled away before he could touch her. Still holding on to Brett's hand, she held her ground and waited for an answer.

Kai gave her a dirty look.

Juliette was wondering what his problem was, he never acted this arrogant, it was out of character for him.

"I heard what happened out here and I wanted to check to make sure you were okay. Obviously you're fine, so I'll be taking off, for now."

The Sargeant overheard what Kai said and stopped him before he could get out the front door.

"Excuse me sir, did she say you were here earlier? I need you to stay and answer some questions."

Juliette was laughing internally, but said nothing.

"The name is Kai, Kai Armstrong, and I was here for five minutes to talk to Juliette and then I left. Tell them I was here for just a bit, will you?" He turned to Juliette for some help.

Rolling her eyes heavenward, she sighed, "as far as I know, he left after our brief discussion."

Sargeant Tripp didn't look all that convinced. "Where did you go after you left the ranch?"

"I drove back to my room at the Bourbon Inn."

"Can anyone verify that you were there tonight?"

Chloe stepped forward, "I can. I saw him there. I was having a drink in the bar, when I saw him come in."

Everyone looked to her, questioning.

Juliette and Brett stood dumbfounded. They looked from Chloe to Kai, to see Kai's reaction. He didn't even flinch, no facial twitches at all. Maybe they do know each other, but she was thinking that was a long shot.

"Do you know Mr. Armstrong, Ms. Rivers," Tripp questioned.

Taken a bit off guard, Chloe stuttered, "not personally, no, but a good looking guy like him is hard to forget." She gave Brett a smug smile, as she recovered herself quickly.

"Fine, but Mr. Armstrong, you are not to leave town until this investigation is over, do you understand?"

He gave Juliette one quick smirk and turned his attention to the officer, "of course, I'll stay as long as needed."

Juliette wanted to run to the sanctuary of her room and never come out. She wasn't sure how her day had gone from good, to downright miserable, in less than 8 hours.

After another half hour of questions, Sargeant Tripp let the jockeys and guests leave to go to their rooms, or back to their homes. He made a point to tell everyone that this was far from over. They were informed that the FBI would be showing up tomorrow.

Most of the crowd had dispersed and went their own ways, but Brett and Juliette were sitting on the front steps outside. They saw Kai and Chloe head out together, which left them both shaking their heads.

"Do you think Chloe is telling the truth? Do you think that she actually saw Kai," Juliette asked.

"I was just wondering the same thing. I noticed her stutter, but she recovered rather quickly. She is something else, that's for sure. I knew there was a reason I didn't want to get involved with her, other than she isn't my type."

Juliette laughed, "she is definitely one of a kind."

Brett stood and took her by the hand, to help her stand with him.

"I should probably let you get some sleep, it's been a long day."

Juliette looked up into his blue eyes and shook herself out of the trance he seemed to always put her in. Every time she looked into those eyes, she was a goner.

"Yes, I should get some sleep, or try to. I have a busy training day ahead of me tomorrow. You need to sleep as well, since you're out there before any of us, tending to our horses."

He just smiled and looked down at the ground. All of the sudden shyness clouded his face. He picked her hand up and gave it a gentle kiss, dropped it back to her side and made his way down the steps.

Juliette was left staring after him, her mouth wide open and breathless.

"Bloody hell, how does he do that?"

She turned and made her way back inside, when she heard a heated discussion coming from the kitchen.

"Why are you here Terrance? I haven't seen you since Terry's funeral."

"I was having dinner with Chloe tonight. I dropped her off at her apartment, but she must have gone out again after, because she called me from the Bourbon Inn to tell me what happened. Looks like you have made a mess of the place, just as I thought you would. You should have let me buy this place from you when you had the chance. Now it isn't going to be worth a dime, after the media finds out about the murder."

"How dare you come in here and insult me and how I run this place. There isn't anything wrong with it. For your information, I am making a profit, thank you very much. No thanks to you."

"Well, after what just happened, I'll be surprised if you last six more months. No jockey will want to step foot on this ranch, Penelope. I'll refer them elsewhere after this."

"Is that a threat?"

"Not in so many words; more of a warning."

"I think you need to leave, now. Don't let the door hit you in the butt on your way out."

Juliette had to duck behind the half wall near the stairs, before Penelope caught her eavesdropping.

The older gentleman stormed out the front door, slamming it and shaking the walls in his wake.

Juliette eased out from behind the wall and quietly made her way to her room. She unlocked her door, turned on the light and locked herself in for the night. She lay awake for another hour, contemplating everything that happened over the course of the day. She tried to make some sense of it, but sleep finally won out in the end.

Chapter 15

Brett was up early, to get a headstart on getting the horses fed and ready for the day's training. They had moved Juliette's horse to another stall, at the end of the large barn, because her previous stall was now covered with crime scene tape and it still shook him to see that.

Tennessee Whiskey, or Whiskey for short, didn't seem to mind the change, thankfully. He was eating hay, drinking water and behaving the way he always did. The Vet had shown up first thing to do a quick once over on the horse and told him he was perfect.

Brett was brushing his mane when Juliette sauntered in, looking around and finally spotting them at the far end.

"Good morning. When did they move Whiskey?"

"Good Morning to you. Sorry, they had me move him and his things last night before I headed back to my place. They had already looked him over and all of his accessories. They were looking for clues or evidence, and when it didn't turn anything up, they asked me to move him to another stall. They needed him out so they had more room to look for any clues he may have been standing on. I would've let you know then, but I didn't want to wake you. The doc was here, too. She said he looked perfect. Did you sleep okay?"

"I was awake for a while. I walked into a heated discussion between Penelope and the older gentleman that had shown up. Anyway, they were not happy to be talking to each other, from what I overheard."

"Ah, Terrence Rivers, Penelope's father-in-law and board member at Churchill Downs. All around, not a very nice man. He hasn't been out to the ranch since his son passed away. I was a little surprised to see him last night, honestly."

"Interesting."

The sounds of talking coming from outside the stable stopped their conversation. A few of the jockeys were making their way into the barn, to get their training underway.

Florent made his way over to Juliette, a smug look on his face.

"Juliette, Brett...Big excitement here last night, huh? Afraid of a little competition Juliette? Did you feel the need to take Philippe out?"

Juliette's mouth went slack, "I would never."

"Hey Florent, where were you last night, before you showed up here," Brett interjected.

"I wasn't here at the time of the murder, if that's what you're implying. I didn't show up until later, after the news spread."

"That's not an answer."

"If you must know, I was having a drink with Sophia Barrere, PR lady from Churchill Downs."

"Really? Because we saw her at dinner with Phillipe last night."

The look on Florent's face was priceless. He obviously had no idea he had been second fiddle to Philipe.

"Well, I'm sure she is talking to all of us jockeys before the Derby," he said, and took his leave in huff.

Brett turned to Juliette to see her snickering.

"What's so funny?

"That was a good show. You flummoxed him good. I was about to throttle him."

He couldn't help but let out a bark of laughter.

"Throttle him, huh? I'll be sure to never get on your bad side."

They both laughed out loud, walking Whiskey out of the barn.

"Well, it's training time for me. See you on the flip side."

"I'll be here."

Chapter 16

Juliette was just finishing a run with Whiskey when she noticed a slew of black sedans driving down the long drive toward the ranch, whisking up dust devils on their way in.

She made her way to the barn, dismounted her horse, and walked him into the area where his new stall was located.

There were a few other jockeys finishing up for the day, as well and they all waved as she walked by.

Chloe strolled in, wearing her signature designer clothes, Prada shoes, her make up was flawless and she had an attitude to match.

Juliette rolled her eyes while she was facing her horse, so she wouldn't notice. The others put their heads down, concentrating on unbridling their horses, so she would ignore them. Juliette was the one she was aiming for.

"Crap on a cracker," Juliette whispered to her horse.

"Ah Juliette, just the person I wanted to see."

"Chloe, what do I owe the pleasure of your presence today?"

"Oh, I wanted to talk to you about your friend Kai."

"What about him?"

"Are you two really dating, or is he available? I mean, he says you're his girlfriend of a few years now, but I see you out with Brett, so which is it? Are you cheating on Kai, or are you and Brett just friends?"

"Kai misspoke, we haven't dated in over two years, so he is not my boyfriend. As for Brett, we just had our first date last night. Satisfied?"

"You don't have to get rude about it, I was just curious."

Juliette decided to turn the tables on Chloe. "Now I have a question for you? Did you really see Kai last night at the Bourbon Inn, because I could have sworn I saw you with your grandfather at Sarino's, when Brett and I were there for dinner."

Chloe stood back a couple feet, glaring at Juliette. "Are you stalking me, Juliette?"

"Hardly. I have more important things to do. You know, the Kentucky Derby? But you still haven't answered my question."

"You're not the police, I don't have to answer to you."

She turned on her heel and walked away. Juliette yelled behind her, "I guess that's my answer."

Brett walked in from outside the barn and headed for Juliette, who was still staring in the direction Chloe had just exited.

"What was Chloe doing in here?"

"She was being Chloe. She had the gall to ask me if Kai and I were still a couple, because apparently Kai is still in denial and she wanted to know our status, as well. She's a twat, I'm sorry."

Brett laughed, "don't be sorry, I don't know what a twat even is."

That had Juliette laughing. "It's a british slang word for the American version of a female dog."

Brett shook his head, as he understood. "What did you tell her?"

"The truth. Kai and I haven't been together for over two years and he's in obvious denial, then I told her you and I had our first date last night, not that it was any of her business. But, when I asked her if she really did see Kai last night, she wouldn't answer, especially after I'd told her that I had seen her at Sarino's, when we were there. She hightailed it out of there after that. I must have hit a sour spot."

Brett stood there, shaking his head. "You don't pull any punches, do you?"

"Why should I, she interrogated me, why don't I get a turn?"

"Hey, I think it's great. She needs to be taken down a notch or two. She's a little spoiled. Her Grandfather's fault, I believe. But she is the only one he's ever really nice too. He's pretty ruthless otherwise, I hear."

"I believe it, after the argument I heard between him and Penelope. Not to get off topic, but did you see where all those black sedans went that were coming down the drive?"

"I saw them go toward the main house. I'm sure it will only be a matter of time before they make their way to us here, in the barn."

"Are they the local police?"

"I don't think so, they looked like men in black suits. My guess is FBI."

"Oh."

Chapter 17

Jake and his guys pulled into the Estrella Equine Village Stables. They got out of their unmarked sedans, and headed to the front door.

"Okay, I'll be taking point here fellas."

He went to the front door of the main house, where he was immediately met with Penelope opening the door, staring up at him with a questioning look.

"Hello, can I help you?"

Jake gave a hint of a smile at the young looking mother and ranch owner.

"Ma'am, I'm Jake Long with the FBI's Midwest Division. I'm here regarding the murder of Phillipe Cardoza. May I have a word with you?"

She backed up slightly, letting him enter, then shutting the door behind them.

"What do you want to know? I'm not sure how much help I'll be, but ask away."

Penelope pointed Jake toward the sitting area in the living room. He took a seat in one of the brown leather club chairs, and sat perched on the edge. Looking stiff and uncomfortable, Penelope followed his lead and sat on the large leather sofa in the middle of the room.

"Mrs. Rivers, first let me say how sorry I am that this happened on your ranch, I'm sure you are still in shock."

"Penelope, please. And shock is an understatement. I want to find out who did this just as much as you do. This whole catastrophe could legitimately ruin my business."

"I understand, and that is why I'm here, to get to the bottom of this and ultimately find the murderer. Can you tell me what your relationship with Mr. Cardoza was?"

"Relationship? We didn't have a relationship, unless you mean a professional one. He had his horse boarded here and he did his daily training, but he was not a guest here."

"Okay, so he had his horse here; did you have any interaction with him at all? What was his demeanor like when you encountered him? Did he mention having any trouble with any of the other jockeys?"

"Wow, no holds bar, huh? I would see him out on the track training, if I was out by the stalls. He was generally pleasant, a little stuck on himself, if you know what I mean, but as with most jockeys, they aren't exactly tall in stature, so they tend to have a Napoleon complex, if you catch my drift. I wasn't aware of him having any issues with anyone here. My ranch manager may have a better sense of any issues, since he works directly with each Jockey and their horse. His name is Brett Singers. He is probably out by the stalls, or out by the track as we speak. It's only a few days until the Derby, the jockeys are pulling out their last minute training routines."

"I apologize for shooting the questions out so fast, but the more I ask, the more I know and the faster you get your life back to normal.

Will you be here for the remainder of the day? I may have more questions after visiting the stalls."

Penelope stood to lead the agent out, and he took that as his cue to leave. At the door, she turned to him, "I will be here doing my daily chores, if you need something."

She shut the door after him, and he stood there on the front porch quiet for a second, not sure what to think of Ms. Penelope Rivers.

He didn't have much time to contemplate the conversation he just had, when one of his men came up the stairs pulling him out of his head.

"Jake, the ranch manager is out by the track with the lady whose stall the victim was found in."

"Thanks Jason, I was just heading that way. Can you get me some information on Penelope Rivers? I want to know everything you can find on her and this ranch, ASAP."

"I'm on it. I just set up a small area by our cars in the driveway, with computers and everything we need."

"Great, thanks. Also, let me know when, and if you see Eva arrive, will you?" Jake winked, and the young agent nodded.

Jake took off for the track.

Chapter 18

Brett and Juliette both saw the gentleman leaving the main house, heading their way. They looked at each other knowing he was coming to speak to them.

"Here we go," Brett said.

"Is he coming to question us?"

"That would be my guess. He just left Penelope, so he's probably making his rounds. I'd rather just get it over with."

"I guess." Juliette had a sick feeling in her stomach. She couldn't get the uneasy feeling that Kai wasn't telling the whole truth last night. She didn't think he had it in him to kill, or at least she hoped he didn't.

Brett squeezed her hand, trying to convey some comfort that she wasn't alone, that he was there with her. She turned to look up at him, and he had the most beautiful smile, it lit up the whole room. It was in stark contrast with his beach bum tanned skin. Juliette felt herself smile on instinct, back at him.

Jake saw the couple he was heading for, and noticed they were holding hands. He wondered if maybe this wasn't the ranch manager, and that it was the jockeys husband or boyfriend instead.

As he approached, Jake spoke up, "Hello, I'm looking for Brett Singers."

Brett held out his hand to Jake, "that would be me."

Jake shook his hand, taken back for a second. "Nice to meet you." He then turned to Juliette, "and you are?"

Jake noticed the hesitant look on Juliette's face.

"I'm Juliette Sutherland." She took his hand, and gave it a quick shake, while pulling her other hand away from Brett's. She hadn't missed the agent looking confused at their situation.

"Juliette Sutherland? The jockey from England? You're projected to win this year's Derby, I read."

Looking embarrassed, she shook her head, "yes, I'm the jockey from England. The newbie. As for the winning projection, I can't really answer that. I don't want to jinx anything."

"Well, can you both take a minute to answer some of my questions about the murder of Phillipe Cardoza, then?"

Brett spoke up eagerly, "sure, what do you want to know?"

"First off, what was either of your relationships with Mr. Cardoza?"

Brett started off, hoping to ease Juliette's tension. "Well, I cared for his horse every day, since he arrived here. Not much else besides that."

"And what about you, Ms. Sutherland? Any competitive issues between the two of you?"

"Um, I'm not an overly competitive person by nature, Agent. When I first got here, Phillipe was very cordial, and helpful. We went to dinner a couple of times, but nothing became of it, not that he didn't try, but I wasn't into dating at the time."

Jake eyed the two, "but that changed after meeting Mr. Singers here, didn't it?"

Juliette's eyes widened.

"You were holding hands when I approached, so you weren't exactly hiding it," Jake stated.

"Oh bloody hell, I guess we weren't. We just had our first date last night. It's not like we've shagged or anything."

Both men stifled a laugh, as they weren't used to her choice of words.

She noticed, and felt the heat in her cheeks, as the embarrassment crept in.

"Sorry, you know what I meant."

Brett pulled her into his side, kissing the top of her head, "it's okay, I think he gets it."

"Anyway, you said that you and Mr. Cardoza had gone to dinner a few times. Was he mad that you didn't want to make the relationship more?"

"I don't know, I didn't think so."

The sound of gravel being run over at a high rate of speed had them all looking toward the ranch entrance. A black Mercedes was hauling butt toward the main house.

"Any of you know who that might be?"

Once the driver exited the posh car, both Brett and Juliette said, "Sophia Barrere, the Derby publicity person."

"Is it normal for her to be out here at one of the training facilities?"

"Not really, she would normally be speaking to the jockeys at Churchill Downs. I'm guessing she's here to try and put a lid on any bad publicity from Phllipe's murder."

They all squinted as they noticed the woman exiting the passenger side of the Mercedes.

"Well, she is walking this way with a purpose, that's for sure. Who is that with her?"

Sophia Barrere made her presence known everywhere she went. The high end designer clothes, shoes, and her signature blonde bombshell waves. Today was no different. The English gentleman with her, didn't hurt either. He had come to her office that morning, to introduce himself, and to give her the news of Phillipe's murder.

Juliette and Brett both sighed in exasperation, "that would be Kai Armstrong, Juliette's ex-boyfriend. He is in town from England." Brett didn't even try to hide the annoyance in his voice.

The two converged on the three, rather quickly. Sophia being the first to talk. She stuck her hand out to Jake, "Sophia Barrere, PR for the Kentucky Derby, who are you?"

Jake wasn't used to this kind of interruption, he did the interrupting. "Jake Long, FBI."

"Well, I am so glad you're here. We need to get this murder thing under wraps and quickly, before it hurts the race, economically that is. This is the biggest event of the year, you know."

Looking gobsmacked, Jake shook his head, "this is a murder investigation, not a PR stunt, Ms. Barrere. Did you know the deceased very well?"

"Of course, I apologize. I didn't know Mr. Cardoza all that well, but we did have dinner last night."

"Interesting."

"What do you mean, interesting," Sophia stuttered her words.

"Well, you just said that you didn't know Mr. Cardoza well, but in the same sentence interjected that you had dinner with him last night. Would you like to explain that a little further?"

Her cheeks turned pink from her blunder; she hesitated with her answer. "We knew each other, of course, he was one of the jockeys. It's my job to know all of them, but we weren't on a date or anything like that."

"I see. Can you tell me everything you did on your *dinner outing,*" he asked her, in air quotes. He was being a sarcastic ass and he knew it.

"There isn't much to tell, he picked me up at my office, we went to Sarino's, which is where we ran into these two," she said, pointing to Brett and Juliette. "Phillipe wasn't too thrilled with me when I started talking to Juliette, and the fact that she has 8-1 odds at winning this year's Derby. Did you know she could be the first woman to win the Derby?"

He looked at Juliette, giving her an appreciative nod, then steered back to his questioning of Sophia.

"Why would he be upset, it's just odds on paper. Was he that concerned with his ability to win?"

"I don't know, I never asked him. The rest of the night he talked about himself a lot, and I kind of tuned out, to be honest. After dinner, he took me back to the office and I got in my car and went home."

"Can anyone vouch for your whereabouts between 9:30pm - 11:30pm last night?"

"Why? Am I a suspect?"

"Ms. Barrere, everyone is a suspect right now. Now, do you have an alibi?"

Speechless for a minute, she contemplated her answer. She knew no one saw her, but her dog, and she wasn't a viable witness.

"Ms. Barrere?"

She looked up at Agent Long waiting for her to answer.

"I went home, but I live alone, so the only witness I have is my dog Bella."

Raising his eyebrows, he asked, "did you have any contact with anyone last night via phone between those times, that can vouch for you?"

She perked up, "yes, I do. I was on the phone with Florent Prat for almost an hour. He'd called me a little after 9:30. He should be here today. He may be out on the track training right now, but you can ask him."

"Florent Prat is another jockey?"

Brett spoke up, "yes, he is set to race this weekend as well. He should be out on the track, I can get him, if you'd like. If we're done here, that is?"

"I'd appreciate it, thank you."

Seeing the man with Sophia tense, Jake walked up to him, his hand out and introduced himself, "Agent Long, and you are?"

With his distinct British accent, Kai took his hand, "Kai Armstrong."

"Kai, can you tell me where you were between the hours of 9:30-11:30 last night?"

Blinking a little too fast at the question, Kai regained his composure and answered, "I was here talking to Juliette and Brett around 9, then went back to the Bourbon Inn, where I'm staying."

"Did anyone see you at the Bourbon Inn?"

Smugly, Kai remembered Chloe speaking up for him last night and vouched for him with the cops. "As a matter of fact, yes. A young lady that was here last night had said she'd seen me in the bar at the Bourbon Inn. I can't seem to recall her name though."

He knew her name, knew her well, but didn't want anyone else to know that.

Juliette recalled her name, and she wasn't a fan of the girl either.

She wanted to flog Kai right there, but instead she told Jake that it was Chloe who spoke up, and gave Kai his alibi.

"Who is Chloe, and where would I find her today?"

Jake was making a list of the people that he had already spoken to, and the new ones he would have to speak to.

"Chloe is Penelope Rivers' daughter. She was here earlier, but I believe she had class today. She goes to the University of Kentucky," Juliette said.

Jake continued writing while Juliette was talking. "Does she live here on the ranch or somewhere else?"

"I don't think she lives here, but I'm not sure if she lives on or off campus, sorry. Penelope can probably tell you that information. Can I go now, I really need to get Whiskey out on the track for training."

Jake nodded, "yeah, we're done here, for now."

Chapter 19

Kris and Eva were getting closer to Louisville, Kentucky when Jake called.

"Hey Jake, what's up? Tell me you solved this case all on your own and we can go home."

"Sorry St. Claire, not that easy. I have a list of possible suspects here and if your wife doesn't get here soon, I'm going to be working this case for a month or more. I was just checking in to see where you were? Your room is already set up at the Bourbon Inn and Eva is set to stay at the ranch. I sent you the address to both, did you get them?"

"I did, but I still don't like that we are in separate places."

"I need you to be able to set up the recorders and all of the electronics at the Inn, where no one will suspect you of anything. If you were to be here with her, they could catch you with the equipment, when they come in to clean. I need to keep my outside help quiet. At least at the Inn, you can tell them you don't need your room cleaned."

"I still don't like it. Who's going to be there with her, to protect her if she needs it?"

"I will. Remember, doting husband that I am?"

"I think I'd rather her be on her own."

Jake let out a bark of laughter, "dude, I'm not going to hit on your wife. Besides, I know she carries."

This made Kris laugh out loud, making Eva look up at him with a questioning look.

"What's so funny?"

"Jake."

Eva rolled her eyes and went back to her tablet, researching everything on the Kentucky Derby, as well as the typical horses that race in the Derby, along with the traditions and events that take place this week.

She had talked to her boss Chrissy for a bit before they left, knowing that she would know more about horses, and the whole history behind the race. Chrissy was pretty knowledgeable for the most part, but her understanding of the history was lacking, so she decided to do that much herself.

Chrissy ended up prying the information out of Eva, as to why she needed to know so much about the Kentucky Derby all of a sudden and when she told her why, Chrissy went into Yenta mode, wanting the 411 on where she was going to be, the address, the phone number, what the case was, who was murdered, and how. It was kind of disturbing to Eva, that Chrissy wanted the bloody details. All she could tell her was to read a certain article on The Courier Journal website.

Eva wasn't exactly privy to sharing that information with anyone, according to Jake. Even though Chrissy definitely tried to make her case about being the perfect partner, with her horse knowledge and all. Jake had shot that down, as soon as it hit the air. She was also sworn to secrecy to never mention where Eva was going to be this week, to anyone. Jake said he'd know if she told anyone, which made her conclude that he had bugged the salon, her house and maybe even her phone.

Kris hung up with Jake, just as Eva finished reading another article on the traditions of the Derby.

"So, what did he want?"

"He was checking in to see where we were on the road. I think he's a little anxious to put you to work and it still makes me nervous. I'm still not sure how he's going to explain your presence at the ranch."

"I was wondering the same thing. Maybe he would tell them that his wife was a big Derby fan, or something. Did you know that no female has ever won the Kentucky Derby, to date? There is a new female Jockey this year that has 8-1 odds at winning. Apparently those are great odds, I looked it up."

"You're just learning all sorts of new things, aren't you? Should I take you to Vegas and see what you can do there? Maybe you could win us some big money?"

She laughed, "I don't think that would be a good idea. I just did some research. I can perform helpful spells, I'm not psychic. I can't predict what the next card in Blackjack will be."

"Too bad, that could have come in handy."

"How much longer until we're there?"

"You're starting to sound like the kids. *Are we there yet? How much longer until we're there?*"

"Ha ha. I'm getting a little nervous, that's all."

He grabbed her hand, bringing it to his lips, kissing it lightly. "I know you're nervous. I'm sorry, I was trying to lighten the mood."

"I know. Thanks."

"We should be there in about thirty minutes."

Chapter 20

Brett was watching the jockeys out on the track, working their horses hard. It was only a few days away from the race and he hoped they weren't pushing the horses too hard. It could have an adverse effect on the horse.

He took note of Sophia at the opposite end of the track eyeing Florent, and trying to get his attention. Brett needed to get to him before she did, to make sure he would tell the truth to Agent Long, not that he thought she was lying, but to be on the safe side.

Brett jumped over the fence and waved at Florent to come over to him. He noticed the look on Sophia's face and she wasn't happy. Lucky for Brett, Florent didn't seem to notice her.

In his uppity French accent, Florent asked, "Hello Mr. Singers, did you need me for something? I'm in the middle of a training session with Pegasus here."

"Florent, there is an FBI agent waiting to speak to you about Phillipe's murder and he sent me to get you. Can you walk over with me, now? It won't take long, I'm sure."

"Why would he need to speak with me, I've done nothing wrong?"

"He's speaking to everyone, not just you."

"Fine."

Florent flung his leg over the horse's back and dismounted with a huff, handing the reins over to a ranch hand. "Lead the way, Mr. Singers."

Brett walked alongside Florent in silence for a minute, before speaking up. "How's training going? Do you feel good about the race?"

"Training is good and of course I feel good about the race, why wouldn't I? Just because you're in love with the front runner, doesn't mean she is going to win, I don't care what her odds are. Now that Phillipe has been taken out of the equation, those odds may change."

Brett stopped mid stride, grabbing Florent by the arm to stop him. "What does that mean?"

"We all saw you two last night at Sarino's, it's all over the internet. Someone took a picture and everything. It said something along the lines of "Farmhand and the Derby Princess.""

"I don't care about that, our picture can be all over the world news for all I care. I'm not ashamed of going out with Juliette. I'm talking about Phillipe being out of the equation. What did you mean by that? What did you do Florent?"

"Me! I did nothing. I am just saying that the odds may change now. He was close behind Miss Sutherland, we all may move to different odd standings now, even her."

Florent yanked his arm out of Brett's hand and continued walking toward the barn. The rest of the walk was silent.

Jake watched on as he saw the two men walking his way and wondered what the hostile confrontation was all about.

Brett introduced Florent to Jake, and started to leave, to look for Juliette when Jake stopped him short. "Hold up Mr. Singers. I'd like to ask you what that short confrontation was about when you and Mr. Prat stopped short of walking over here?"

"It was nothing, really. He mentioned that there were pictures of Juliette and I on the internet from last night and it caught me by surprise."

"I see. And this is a problem for you?"

"No, not at all. It was the mentioning of her odds of winning the Derby changing, now that Phillipe is dead, and her and I dating. They think she may not be as focused on the race. I made it clear to Florent that she and I dating shouldn't affect anything. Can I go now, I would really like to find her before she gets taken off guard by this."

"Okay, go ahead."

Brett hightailed it out of the barn, in search of Juliette.

Jake took a long look at Florent Prat, who seemed to be getting antsy by the second.

"Mr. Prat, this should only take a couple of minutes, do you mind telling me where you were last night, between 9:30pm and 11:30pm?"

"Why?"

"Because that is the time frame for which Mr. Cardoza's murder would have taken place, that's why. Now where were you?"

Florent made a show of looking concerned, but in truth he couldn't careless and didn't want to be bothered by this whole interrogation. "I was back at my room at the Bourbon Inn, reading."

"Did anyone see you?"

"I have a single room with no roommate, so no."

"Did you happen to speak with anyone during that time, or were you strictly reading only?"

"No, I didn't speak to anyone last night."

Sophia had just entered the barn as Florent's last words came rushing out, making her pale. She gasped and the men turned toward her, staring.

"Ah Miss Barrere, just in time. I'm sure you heard Mr. Prat's statement. Of course I'll be checking everything out for myself, but would you like to change your response to the earlier question, as to what you were doing last night?"

Her mouth dropped open, dry and unable to speak. She gave herself a mental shake and admitted, "okay fine, I was with Phillipe last night after we had dinner, but I swear I didn't kill him. I left him at 9:20 and he was very much alive."

"Why did you feel the need to lie to me? It doesn't make things look very good for you, if you start off by lying, Miss Barrere."

"I panicked. I'm not supposed to fraternize with the jockeys. I could lose my job."

"Would you rather be in jail instead?"

"No!"

"I believe you and Mr. Prat will be coming with me."

Both Sophia and Florent looked appalled, and taken back. They both looked at Jake like he was joking.

"You can't be serious," Florent said, exasperated. "I need to get back out on the track to practice."

"And I need to get back to Churchill Downs. Press conferences are going to be starting soon. If I'm not there, Mr. Rivers will be furious."

"Mr. Rivers? I thought Mrs. Rivers' husband was deceased."

"He is. I'm talking about the elder Mr. Rivers. He is a big wig at Churchill Downs."

"I see. Would he be there now, by chance? Does he have much contact with the jockeys?"

"I'm sure he's there, why?"

"I may need to speak to him. Why don't the three of us take a ride to Churchill Downs, together."

Florent made a sound of disgust. "I don't have time for this. I did nothing wrong."

"Then you should have no problem coming with us. The sooner we get there, the sooner you get back here to practice. Now, if you'd board your horse, we'll get going."

"Fine."

Jake rolled his eyes heavenward, thinking he needed a different job.

Chapter 21

Kris and Eva were pulling into the Bourbon Inn parking lot and called Jake to see what they were supposed to do as far as checking in.

"Hey Jake, we're at the Bourbon Inn. When I check in, is the reservation under my name or yours?"

"Hold on, let me go somewhere I can talk."

"Okay, no problem."

Kris could hear Jake excuse himself from whoever he was with.

"Okay man, sorry. I am about to head over to Churchill Downs with a couple of high maintenance people, to question someone else."

"Sounds like you'd rather have a root canal."

"Oh yeah, for sure. It would be less painful. Anyway, your reservation is under your name. We didn't have time to get you any other identifications. However, when Eva comes this way to the ranch, she'll be known as Eva Long. Since she is posing as my wife while she's here, no one will suspect her of doing anything else."

"Dude, that one is still a little hard for me to swallow."

"I know, but you know otherwise. It means nothing. You know I'll keep her safe."

"Yeah, yeah…"

Jake let out a bark of laughter. "You really are having a hard time with this aren't you? Don't you trust your wife?"

"Her I trust; you I'm still debating," he laughed.

"Trust me, please. I won't let anything bad happen to her."

"Alright, alright. Eva is giving me looks here and I'm going to have to explain this all to her. I'll go check in and send her on her way to the ranch."

"Sounds like a plan. Thanks again for doing this man, I appreciate it."

"Don't mention it."

And with that, they ended the call and Kris had some explaining to do.

"So, what is it you don't trust Jake with," Eva asked, smiling.

"You."

"Me? Why me?"

"Okay, I know it's stupid, but I know what he looks like and you've seen him, he's a good-looking guy Eva and you're going to have to pretend to be married to him. When you check in at the ranch, you're checking in under Eva Long. It's just rubbing me the wrong way, I know it shouldn't, but it does."

Eva reached out for his hand and clasped it in hers. She looked at her husband adoringly and couldn't help but chuckle.

"Kris, yes Jake is good-looking, but he's not who I would ever want as a husband. Nobody but you is right for me. He's not my type anyway. In my eyes, you're more than good-looking; you're loving, caring, sweet, and you make me laugh. I gotta tell ya, that right there is a killer combination in my book. No one could ever compete with you, remember that. I love you, always and forever."

"Ditto, Mrs. St. Claire."

She leaned over and kissed him briefly before pushing him out of her car. She hit the trunk button so he could collect his suitcases.

Eva rolled the window down, "I'll text you once I get to the ranch."

"Okay. Be careful Eva. I love you...always and forever."

Chapter 22

Jake, Sophia and Florent entered the main building at Churchill Downs, followed by a couple of Jake's agents.

"Where is Mr. Rivers' office," he asked, looking at Sophia.

"The offices are on the second floor."

"Well then, please lead the way."

They all headed to a bank of elevators while Jake took in his surroundings. There were life size replicas of racehorses with jockeys' on them, along with the roses hanging off them and an actual starting gate. These people take horse racing seriously, he thought.

As they headed out of the elevator on the second floor, there were lounges, banquet rooms, and windows everywhere. You could see the race track, no matter where you looked.

Sophia stopped in front of a closed door and knocked gently. She waited to hear the person on the other side acknowledge before she opened the door.

"Yes?"

"Mr. Rivers', may we come in?"

Terrence Rivers looked up from his spot at his desk at the people that were with her. He was sizing them up, as he always did with new acquaintances, before acknowledging their presence. It was his way of exerting his power. He had already determined the men wearing the black suits were feds, but wasn't sure what branch. The other gentleman with Sophia he recognized as one of the jockeys, but wasn't sure of his name.

Terrence motioned for all of them to come in. He stood and rounded his desk, to greet them.

"Sophia, who are your friends?"

Jake stepped forward, "Mr. Rivers', I'm Agent Jake Long with the FBI. I'm here investigating the death of Phillipe Cardoza. These gentlemen are my colleagues."

Terrence stepped back around his desk, and sank into his chair.

"Of course, it was terrible. How can I help?"

"We'd like to ask you a few questions. Did you know Mr. Cardoza personally?"

"I knew of him, of course. He was going to be racing this Saturday in the Derby. I believe I spoke to him on a few occasions, but I make a point to get to know all of the jockeys before the Derby."

"Where were you last night between 9:30pm and 11:30pm sir?"

"I had dinner with my granddaughter last night, and after that I dropped her off at her apartment. I went home after that, but when Chloe had called me later to tell me what happened, I headed out to the ranch. Am I a suspect, Agent Long?"

"Everyone is being questioned sir. Can you tell me the timeline of your dinner with your granddaughter?"

"Chloe and I went to Sarino's. We even saw Sophia and Phillipe. I guess it was around 7:00, but we left there around 8:30pm. I took her home after that. I did go to the ranch, like I said, after I heard what happened."

"Chloe? This is the second time I am hearing her name today. I guess I need to speak to her as well. Where can I find your granddaughter, Mr. Rivers?"

"She attends The University of Kentucky, so I'm pretty sure she is in class right now, but she has her own apartment off campus. The apartment complex is called Riverford Crossing, it's off John Davis Drive. Let me check my contacts in my phone for her actual address."

"I'd appreciate that, thank you."

Mr. Rivers was fumbling over his phone searching for what seemed like a little too long, to find his own granddaughter's address. Jake knew he was stalling, which was never a good sign.

"Oh, here we go. Her address is 8001 John Davis Drive, Apartment 3B."

"Thank you sir. I will advise you, like I have everyone else I've talked to, please do not leave the state until you hear from me."

Florent raised his hand in question. "May I go back to the ranch now, I need to finish training for today? I have already lost precious time."

"Like I said to Mr. Rivers', don't leave the state. I'll catch up with you if I have any more questions."

Florent let out an exasperated sigh. "Fine. I'll call a cab. I'm not even sure why I had to be here for this"

Jake and his colleagues headed back to the elevators, to regroup. He wanted to be outside before he said anything else out loud.

At the car, he turned to them, "Mr. Rivers texted someone, while he was searching for his granddaughter's address. My bet is, it was Chloe and he was giving her a heads up that we would be coming. We need to get over to that apartment. It is at least a half hour drive from here."

Chapter 23

Eva pulled into the circular driveway of the Estrella Equine Village Ranch. She looked around, hoping to see Jake on the grounds somewhere so she didn't have to check in by herself. Unfortunately she didn't see anyone around. She had noticed quite a few people over by the arena and stables, but those were farther out on the land.

"Well crap on a cracker."

She decided she better text Jake to let him know she was there. She hoped he would tell her he was on his way and she could wait for him to get there.

"*Jake, it's Eva. I just got to Estrella Equine Ranch. Are you close by?*"

"And now I wait…"

Not even thirty seconds had passed and her phone dinged, with a new text message.

"*Great! Go ahead and check in with the owner, Penelope Rivers. The guys and I are on our way to her daughter's place to question her. I should be back there in the next hour or so. Tell her your name is Eva Long. She is expecting you. See you later.*"

"I don't want to tell her my name is Eva Long. It's Eva St. Claire. Ugh, why did I agree to this again," she mused. "You can do this Eva. Let's just get in there and get this over with."

Eva knew she was stalling. She sat in her car for another ten minutes trying to psych herself up to go inside, when she saw a woman open the front door of the main house and look her way. She looked pleasant enough, casually dressed in jeans and plaid flannel shirt, along with some roughed up cowboy boots. Eva figured this must be Penelope.

She had no choice but to get out of her car now.

"Hello," Penelope called out.

"Hi there. Are you Penelope?"

"Yes I am. You must be Eva, Jake's wife."

Eva almost blew her cover, she was taken off guard when she said Jake's wife.

"Umm, yes I am. He said to check in with you and he would meet me back here in about an hour."

"Sure, I can get your things up to the room we have reserved for him."

Eva's stomach did a nose dive. His room? We were sharing a room? Of course they were, she thought, they were supposed to be married. She thought to herself, "it better have two beds."

"Grab your stuff and follow me," Penelope said.

Eva grabbed her two bags from the trunk, and headed up the stairs toward the main entrance. "Right behind you."

She followed Penelope up two flights of stairs to a long hallway. The inside was deceptively bigger than it looked from the outside. Penelope stopped at the last door and handed Eva a key.

"This is our biggest room. We normally only have one person in each room most of the time, so a lot of the rooms are smaller, but this one should suffice the two of you for a few days. If you need anything, please let me know."

"Thank you. I appreciate you giving us the larger room, he takes up a lot of space with his height and build. Well, you saw him." She tried to bring a teasing aire to her comment.

"He is rather tall, isn't he? Looks more like a football player to me, than a federal agent."

"He did play football in college. He played for Penn State years ago." Eva was glad to have had that pertinent information. A wife would definitely know those things.

"Well Mrs. Long, I'll let you get settled. I am going to get started on dinner, for those staying here who choose to participate. I serve a buffet at 6pm, if you and Agent Long are interested."

"Thank you. And please, call me Eva."

"Okay, Eva. Maybe I'll see you at dinner."

Before Eva could respond, Penelope was already retreating.

Eva put the key into the lock and opened the door to her living arrangements for the next few days.

She was pleasantly surprised at the size of their room. It didn't have two beds, but it did have a comfy looking brown leather couch on the one wall, which she figured she could sleep on, no problem. It had a king sized bed, a pine log coffee table and end table to match. There was also a small galley kitchen with a refrigerator, stove top and microwave. The bathroom was quite roomy, with a large glass enclosed shower, two sinks, with stone counters and hardwood flooring.

Eva felt a little more relaxed with the spacious room. They wouldn't have to be too close together, she thought.

She started to unpack her one bag when her phone dinged, alerting her to another text message.

"Eva, did you get to the ranch? Is Jake there? Let me know you got there okay, please. Love you."

"Crap! I forgot to text Kris when I first arrived."

Before she texted him back, she snapped a couple pictures of the room, so he could see how big it was.

"Sorry! Yes, I got here fine. Jake is off questioning someone else, so I checked in. Everything is okay here. It's a very nice place. I was quite relieved that there is this big leather couch in the room that I can sleep on. It's more of a small efficiency apartment, than a lodge room. As you can see from the pictures, it's pretty open. How are your accommodations? Love you!"

Kris replied quickly, as she thought he would.

"Ugh! I forgot you two would be in the same room. You have your gun on you, right?"

Eva let out a bark of laughter, and texted back, *"LOL, yes I have my gun. Why do you think I'll need it? Jake isn't like that, is he?"*

"No, but you never know. You are adorable, you know."

"I think you're a little partial, and he wouldn't get anywhere with me anyway, remember he's not my type."

"Ha ha... Alright, I better let you get settled. You two keep me up to date. I know he'll let me know when I need to start recording you for things. You have your earrings and Jake has the tracking device that he can inject into your arm. Be careful, please. And,don't do anything stupid. <3"

"Thanks for the vote of confidence. I'm nervous as it is, don't add to it. I have the earrings and I'll be texting you all the time. Talk to you later. <3"

Eva put her phone on the coffee table and began putting clothes in the drawers that were empty. She took her bathroom stuff into the bathroom, where she found a nice sized cupboard to put them in.

She picked up her other bag and opened it, it held all of the supplies she thought she might need to perform the necessary spells. She had a half dozen white pillar candles, sea salt, iodized salt, baking soda, honey, a jar of pig's blood, a white silk scarf, a notebook, her family's book of spells, and her .380. The .380 was not part of the magic process, but needed nonetheless for back up protection. She stowed the bag in the back of the closet, until she needed it.

"Now, I wait..."

Chapter 24

Chloe Rivers received her grandfather's text about the FBI being on their way, but she didn't care. She was Terrence Rivers' granddaughter, that meant something. She was sure her grandfather had already told them that she was with him last night anyway. She had given Kai Armstrong an alibi. She did have a brief, but strange interaction with him and she didn't even know him very well yet.

People owed her and she would collect on it, if she had to.

The buzzer on her intercom system went off and she responded, "Hello?"

"Miss Rivers', this is Jake Long with the FBI, may I come up with a few of my colleagues?"

"What is this regarding?" She already knew, but she thought she may as well play it up as good as she could.

"This is in regards to the murder of Phillipe Cardoza. We would like to ask you a few questions. We can do it here or down at the police station, your choice."

"Okay fine, come on up."

She buzzed them in and waited for them to get to her floor. A minute later, the knock at the door came. It was a harsh wrap on her steel door. She actually flinched at the sound.

Chloe opened her door to find four men that took up most of the hallway, with their sheer height and girth. She wasn't sure if they were really FBI agents or pro football players.

Jake was the first to speak. "Chloe Rivers?"

"That's me. And you are?"

"FBI agent Jake Long, ma'am. May we come in and ask you a few questions?"

Chloe smiled at Jake, thinking he was a pretty good-looking guy, but too bad he was a Fed.

She motioned for them to enter her apartment. "Sure, but I don't really have a choice, do I?" She smiled at Jake, giving him her flirty grin, hoping he'd take it easy on her and get the whole questioning thing over with as soon as possible.

Jake flashed his pearly whites and knew exactly what her game was. This wasn't his first rodeo. "Well, we could drive you to the station and do this there. Like I said, the choice is yours."

Chloe's smile immediately fell. He was onto her.

"No, let's just get this over with. What do you want to know?"

"First off, where were you last night between 9:30pm and 11:30pm?"

"I'd gone to dinner with my grandfather, at Sarino's around 7, and he dropped me off at my apartment around 8:30, then I went to the Bourbon Inn for a drink with friends. I was there until 9:30 or so, and then I stopped at the ranch after I found out about Phillipe."

"Do these friends of yours have names that can corroborate your whereabouts?"

Chloe started fidgeting in her seat and Jake could tell she was lying. She would keep lying, but he wanted to see how far she was willing to take it.

"I would really rather not involve them in this, if that's okay? I'm sure the bartender at the Bourbon Inn saw me and can vouch for me."

"Are you afraid your friends might not give you the alibi you're looking for?"

Jake wasn't pulling any punches and he didn't trust this girl for all the tea in China.

Chloe's eyes widened and her mouth dropped open.

"I did nothing wrong. Now, if you'll excuse me, I need to get ready for the press party at Churchill Downs that starts in a few hours."

She walked to the front door, opened it and waited for them all to walk out single file, Jake being the last one out. He turned to her, "I look forward to seeing you at the party tonight Chloe."

She slammed the door, ran to her cell phone, and called Brant at the Bourbon Inn. He was one of the bartenders that she was friendly with. She knew he would say anything for her.

She dialed his number and waited for him to pick up. "Come on Brant, pick up."

He finally picked up on the fifth ring, "Hello."

"Brant, it's Chloe. I have a favor to ask you."

"Chloe, hi. Anything for you dollface."

Chloe rolled her eyes. She had a feeling Brant had a thing for her, but she felt nothing for him. After all, he was just a bartender.

"If some FBI agents come by and ask if I was there last night, tell them I was there until 9:30pm, okay? And, I was there with some friends."

"Uh Chloe, are you in trouble? I don't like lying, especially to FBI agents."

"No, it's fine. They're questioning everyone about Phillipe's murder."

"But you were here with him last night."

"I know, but I don't want them to know that. I don't have time to get dragged into this, with the Derby coming up. I didn't do it, Brant."

"Okay, I'll tell them I saw you with a group of friends last night."

"Thanks, I owe you one."

She immediately regretted saying that, as she knew damn well he would collect on it.

"I'll hold you to that Chloe," he said, laughing.

"I'm sure you will. I have to go get ready for the press party. I'll talk to you later Brant, and thank you."

"Sure thing. Later Chloe."

After hanging up with Brant, Chloe headed for her oversized walk-in closet, staring at her wardrobe, searching for the perfect outfit to wear to the party. This was the official start of the Derby week festivities. The Press Party was just the beginning. A lot of influential elite's would be in attendance and it never hurts to hobnob with them.

Chapter 25

Jake had just pulled into the Estrella Equine Ranch, when he got a call from the local field office. As soon as he'd left Chloe's apartment, he'd called the office to see if they could get him into the press party tonight. He had asked them to pull some strings to get him and his "wife" tickets to the Derby Press Party tonight at Churchill Downs.

He was hoping Eva would be up for a little party tonight.

Jake entered the main house and was heading for his room, when Penelope stopped him.

"Agent Long, your wife has arrived and I've already given her a key to your room, I hope that was okay."

"Of course, thank you."

"I also got a call from my daughter. You went to her apartment to question her?"

"Yes, we did. We are questioning everyone surrounding the Derby and she was here last night. All I can say, is we have questioned her and we are following up with her answers."

"I see."

He could see the motherly worry in her eyes, but her daughter was an adult and if she has anything to do with this case, she will face the consequences, just like anyone else. Not that he didn't understand her worry.

"Umm, I was wondering... My wife and I were invited to the Press Party tonight, is it a formal party or casual? I'm just wondering if I need to take her shopping for a new dress?"

He wasn't used to playing the role of husband, let alone a doting one at that.

"Oh, well, I will be attending as well, and yes it is a little on the dressier side. She doesn't need a ball gown or anything like that, but if she has a little black dress, she should be fine."

"A little black dress?" Jake wasn't sure what that meant.

Penelope couldn't help but chuckle. "She'll know what it means."

"Oh, okay. Thank you."

Jake headed up to the second floor, to where his pseudo wife was. He was getting a nervous feeling in the pit of his stomach and he didn't know why. It was disconcerting.

He stood at the door for a second before putting the key in. He fumbled with the key a little before putting it in the lock, so she would hear him, and not be surprised. He had forgotten to text her that he was back.

Upon opening the door, he found Eva sitting on the leather couch, curled up reading a book. She looked so normal to him. But she wasn't normal. She had a rare background, that he himself still couldn't believe he was using. He didn't know the whole story of how she became what she was, but he was hoping to uncover a little bit of that, while they were together.

She looked up, smiling at him.

"Hey Jake! How's it going?"

He thought... This is so normal. This is what she does when Kris comes home from work everyday.

"Eva, I'm good, how are you? How was the drive down? Did Kris get checked in to his hotel? I hope this room is okay. If not, I can ask for a different one."

Good Lord, he was talking 90 miles an hour.

Eva let out a breathy little laugh. She could see Jake was just as uncomfortable with this situation as she was. And she appreciated that.

"I'm good. Just catching up on a book I'd started reading on the way down. It was an easy drive. Kris is all checked in at the Bourbon Inn. He has texted me a few times. He said you have the tracking device with you and I brought the earrings. And, the room is fine. I can easily sleep on this couch, it is rather comfy."

"The couch! No, you can take the bed and I'll take the couch. I'm not bending on this."

Eva's eyes got big. She wasn't sure if he was being bossy or overly polite.

"The couch is fine Jake, really."

Jake knew he had exerted a little too much force with the way he said it, and he felt like a giant bully. He softened his tone, and spoke in a lower voice.

"Please Eva, I insist."

She looked up at this big man, carrying a 9mm Smith and Wesson, and smiled. He really was just a big teddy bear, but had no idea how to deal with women. "Jake, this couch wouldn't fit you."

He looked at it closer and she was right, he was over six feet tall and he'd be hanging at least a foot over the edge.

"I feel bad having you sleep on the couch. My manners are better than that."

""It's actually very comfortable."

"Okay, you win. But, if it gets uncomfortable, tell me and I'll trade you."

She smiled, "deal."

He felt his shoulders relax for the first time all day. Now, he had to tell her they were going out in public, as husband and wife tonight, to a froo froo party. Jake wasn't a froo froo party kind of guy.

"So Eva, I know we are here undercover as husband and wife, for all intents and purposes and I was only going to be using your gift, if I have no other options, but…"

Eva sat up straighter, thinking, *Oh crap, what was she going to have to do?*

"But what?" She looked at him, a little weary.

"There's a Derby Press Party tonight, and I have tickets for it. We kind of need to go."

"A party? You and me, as husband and wife?"

Jake could feel her anxiety going through the roof. He understood it. Jake wasn't thrilled with the idea of pretending to be married either.

"I'm sorry. I wouldn't ask if it wasn't important."

"I know. I'm just trying to picture us playing the happy married couple," she said, laughing.

Jake laughed, too. "I get it, I'm not exactly husband material."

"No, it's not that. It's just, I'm not that good of an actress."

"It'll be fine. I'm not a great actor either, but we'll do what we have to do, to get the job done I guess."

"I guess. So, what do I wear for something like this anyway? I may need to hit the mall."

"Oh, I asked Penelope whether this was a formal shindig or casual, and she said it is more of a "little black dress" kind of event. She said you would know what that meant."

"I do know what that means and unfortunately, I'm going to have to hit the mall, now. I have nothing to wear that meets that criteria."

"No problem, let's go. We have a few hours before it starts. This shopping spree will be on me."

"You may regret saying that. I am a woman, after all."

"I deserve it. I got us into this party, I'll help you look the part."

Eva laughed as she got up from the couch, to fetch her purse.

She looked back at him, "You have no idea what you're in for Jake."

He smiled, even though he was secretly banging his head on the wall next to him.

"Let me just text Kris, so he knows what's going on."

"I'm sure I'll be getting a list of don'ts a mile long, soon after."

"You really do know him well, don't you?"

"Like a book."

Eva finished texting Kris and not even five minutes later, Jake was getting ding after ding with texts from Kris. He was right about a lot of it, but mostly, he wanted Jake to keep his wife safe, above all else.

Chapter 26

Jake had no idea how this shopping trip was going to go down. He prepared for the worst. She surprised him after only two stores and trying on only five dresses in black, Eva had found the perfect little black dress. He wasn't so sure about the shoes she'd picked out, they had at least three or four inch heels. Jake wasn't sure how she could walk in them without falling on her butt, but that was on her.

After putting on each dress, she would come out and look into the giant mirror at the entrance to the fitting rooms, turn, and either groan or smile. It was interesting to him, how the process worked. She even asked him a couple of times if a particular dress looked okay. He had no idea how to answer that without getting himself in trouble. She was petite, but pretty curvy. She looked good in almost all of them.

He decided she needed something to wear with the black dress, to finish off the outfit. He found the jewelry department of the store she'd found the dress and shoes at. He told her to pick a necklace, earrings, and a bracelet out that she would wear with the said little black dress. At first she refused his offer to buy her the new dress and shoes. Now she was almost adamant about buying her own jewelry, but in the end she accepted his kind gesture.

Jake always traveled with a few different types of suits. They were all similar styles, but in different colors, gray, black and navy. He figured his black suit would fit tonight's required attire bill. Eva had suggested he buy a new black silk tie to go with it, since his tie choices were limited to gray and red. She said the black silk of the tie would dress up the suit. Now he was hoping she wouldn't tell him to shave. He liked his rugged scruffy face.

They returned to the ranch with an hour and half to spare, before the party. He let Eva get ready first, since he figured she might need the extra time. He knew he only needed thirty minutes at most and he would be ready.

He could see the discomfort on her face, as she took everything in the bathroom with her, to get ready. He didn't blame her. Jake was still pretty much a stranger to her. They did have some time to talk, and get to know each other while out on their shopping trip, which was good. He was hoping that had eased her qualms about him a little.

She exited the bathroom, forty minutes later, dressed in the "little black dress", four inch heels, the shiny silver jewelry, and her hair and make-up completely done to perfection. She stood there waiting for him to say something. His mouth went dry, and he was speechless.

She cleared her throat to get Jakes attention.

"Earth to Jake."

He shook his head, clearing the fog that poured over him. It was such a huge change from when she entered the bathroom to now. He didn't want to sound like a pig, but he thought she looked pretty amazing, but how could he put that into words that wouldn't offend her.

"Oh sorry. I must have been daydreaming. You look very nice."

"Nice? That's it? You lost your ability to speak, over very nice?"

She let out a bark of laughter that made him raise his eyebrows. He hadn't heard her truly laugh, and he thought he really liked the sound. It suited her, and made her look younger.

"Actually, you look more than nice, amazing actually. Kris is going to be so ticked at me."

Eva shook her head. She understood him a little better now.

"Okay, thank you. You better get yourself ready. I'm sorry I took so long. I hope I gave you enough time."

"You only took forty minutes. I was expecting at least an hour. You gave me plenty of time."

He took his suit and all he needed into the bathroom with him, just as she had.

Eva took a selfie of herself all dressed up, in the full length mirror and sent it off to Kris. Ten seconds later her phone went off. It was Kris.

"*That should be illegal. You look stunning and I'm a bit jealous. Don't have too much fun. I'm bingeing shows on Hulu in my room and eating room service. I think I got the crap end of this deal.*"

She chuckled and sent him another quick text, "*I'm sorry. I definitely won't have any fun, but thanks for the compliment on the dress. Love you, always and forever.*"

Kris replied with his signature, "*Ditto.*"

Eva decided to sit and read a little more of her book, while Jake was getting ready. She was feeling a little more nervous as she sat there. She couldn't concentrate on what she was even reading. Her foot started to do that little shake thing it did when she was uptight.

Jake opened the bathroom door and stepped into the sitting room wearing a tailored black suit, white dress shirt, the black silk tie she picked out and black wingtip shoes. She felt her mouth drop open a little, but immediately shut it, before he saw. He'd left his face unshaven, but on him it looked good.

"Well, don't you clean up well."

"Um, thanks. I'm not much of a swanky party type of guy. This is a little awkward for me, so I will apologize now for anything stupid I may say or do."

"It'll be fine. You have a job to do and I have a role to play. We'll figure it out."

He was dreading telling her they might have to act like your typical married couple. Holding hands and touches, to keep up the pretense.

"We need to go over a few things before we leave. One being the fact that we are supposed to be married. I may have to hold your hand, or have my arm around you at some point. I don't want to take you off guard when I do, and you jump away from me. It would blow everything. I wouldn't do anything inappropriate, of course, but I just wanted to discuss this with you before we left."

She truly appreciated him being focused on her being comfortable and knowing all the possibilities of what's to come.

"I understand. I knew we would have to act married, at some point. It's fine."

He smiled at her, relieved that they were on the same page.

Eva held her hand out to him as she made her way for the room door. Jake looked down at her, she was smiling up at him. "Mind as well start now, husband."

He took her hand in his and they headed out. Her hand was so small in his large one. He hoped he wasn't holding it too tight, or hurting her. Jake figured she'd say something or move her hand.

They were immediately greeted by Juliette on the stairs, as she was heading in the same direction they were. No doubt going to the same party they were, too.

At the bottom of the stairs, Brett stood, staring at Juliette descending the stairs ahead of them. He had that smitten look on his face, Jake could tell he was a goner. Eva squeezed Jake's hand a little to acknowledge she saw the same thing. She was beaming from ear to ear.

"Ah, young love," Eva whispered under her breath, barely audible to even Jake.

Brett looked behind Juliette to see Jake and Eva following.

"Agent Long, who is this lovely creature with you?"

Jake almost blew it right off the bat, but Eva was right on it. She held out her free hand to Brett and introduced herself.

"I'm Jake's wife, Eva. What is your name?"

Brett looked surprised at the mention of Agent Long having his wife here with him, while on an investigation. Jake could see the toggles churning in Bretts head, but he quickly covered his butt.

"My wife loves horses and as soon as she found out I was coming here, she begged me to let her come down. She drove down once I was all settled in here. We're actually on our way to the Derby Press Party, which I'm guessing you two are off to, as well."

Brett shook Eva's hand and looked to have bought Jake's lame story.

"Yes, that's where we are heading as well. I guess we'll see you both there. Any new information on Phillipe's murder?"

"We have questioned a number of people and the ME will have the autopsy complete tomorrow morning. We should know the actual cause of death and go from there."

"Good to know. I hope this gets solved before the Derby on Saturday."

"That is the goal. Well, we will see you both at the party."

Jake held onto Eva's hand and walked to the front door, holding it open for her, like a true gentleman would do, or doting husband, he thought.

"Would you like to take my car? It's the gray BMW over there."

"Embarrassed by my standard issued FBI sedan, Mrs. Long," he said, teasing.

She snickered. "Not at all. I just thought you might like to drive something fun, for a change."

He walked her to the passenger side and Eva unlocked the car with the touch of her hand. Jake opened her door and gestured to her, "your chariot, madam," he said, with a flourish.

"Why thank you kind sir."

They rode in comfortable silence for most of the drive. Eva had so many questions stirring in her head, she decided to start the interrogation.

"Jake, can I ask you a few questions? I want to know more about you. You know, in case people at the party ask me."

He looked over at her, in the darkened interior of the car, with a slight smile. He knew this was coming. She was pretty inquisitive, he gathered.

"Sure. What would you like to know? My favorite color, favorite food, animal, where I grew up?"

"Those are good starter questions."

"Okay. Blue, pizza, golden retriever, and Pittsburgh."

"Wow! Right to the point."

"I didn't think I'd have to elaborate much on those."

"True enough. How about, why did you want to be an FBI agent?"

"Right to the big one, huh?"

"I have been wondering about that one since we met."

. "Okay. Well, when I was in high school, my cousin Hannah was abducted from the bus stop near her home, in broad daylight. It was a nightmare for my aunt and uncle, not knowing what happened to her, who had done this, and what she was enduring. There were cops, FBI, neighbors, and us family members combing the woods by their house, for hours. I had never been so scared and so mad in my life. We couldn't find any trace of her. Now, the bus stop was near a convenient store, and I knew they had surveillance cameras all around it, for shoplifters and people who tried to leave without paying for their gas. I mentioned it to one of the agents that was assigned to the case. He immediately took off for the store and asked the owner for permission to view the footage from the day before. He saw the whole scene unfold before him. It was like watching a bad movie. Hannah had gotten off the bus, and once the bus was out of site, a black van pulled up along next to her. A man with black curly hair, about my height, heavy set, and not even bothering to cover his face, grabbed her from behind. She was kicking and screaming. He just threw her into the side door of the van, where another guy was waiting to hold her down, so they could get away."

Eva's mouth dropped, she was speechless, listening to Jake recount the event. He continued his story.

"Once the agent put the faces into the facial recognition software, which was a fairly new thing back then, he also added the part of the license plate they were able to decipher off the van, as well, and they were able to come up with a 90% match in their database. Both men had prior arrests for pedophilia, and were both on parole. Their parole officer's had both men's addresses, and they immediately sent in SWAT to both places. Hannah was found at the heavy set guys address, in the basement, tied up to a bed. He was hiding in a secret room that Hannah was able to tell them existed, because she had seen him open it at one po

The agent I had told about the cameras had remarked to me, that if it hadn't been for me, and my knowledge of the cameras at the store, it could have been a much different outcome. Hannah had gone through a lot in those two days, but she had the support she needed at home to get through it. That day, I knew what I wanted to do after college. I wanted to help those who couldn't help themselves. I haven't regretted my decision. I do, however, envy Kris. He has a life I sometimes wish I had. Beautiful wife, kids, house... a normal life."

Eva was stunned. She didn't know how to respond.

"Well, the world is definitely a safer place, because of what you do."

"Thanks. I like to think so. Anything else you want to know? I'm not sure there's much else to tell."

"Your cousin is okay, now?"

"She is, yes. It was a long road, but she's a strong woman."

"That's great. It had to have been a scary couple of days for her. I can't even imagine. I only had a half hour or so of horror, and it was enough to last me a lifetime."

"I know. I heard the whole thing."

"Right. You did hear everything."

"Eva, can I ask you a question? You can tell me no, and I'll drop it."

"No, go ahead and ask away. You answered mine. It's only fair that I answer yours."

"How do you do what you do, exactly? The whole spell thing or magic?"

Eva knew that's what he was going to ask. She had been waiting for him to finally question her past.

"It's a little complicated, but you can trace my family all the back to the Salem witch trials, if you can believe that. My Great-Great-Great Grandmother, Elizabeth Howe was one of the witches put to trial, in 1682. She died at the stake, I'm told. I hold a family book of spells that has been passed down from generation to generation, but I vowed it was stopping with me, and I had planned to keep that vow. I don't know if it is something I was born with, or if it is truly just the simple spells that make things happen, but I always thought of it as more of a curse. I hadn't used my magic in twenty plus years, and now here I am, doing what I said I would never do after my mother passed."

"I'm sorry. I didn't know. If it's any consolation, I appreciate your gift. If you can help me find out what happened to Phillipe Cardoza, you've done a good service. You're not the first person with a special gift that we've utilized. We have psychics and mediums on payroll now and then. We don't advertise that we use them, but they have provided a lot of good information and help in previous cases "

"I understand that, and if it was for anything else, I would have said no, without hesitation."

"Understood."

They both went silent for a beat, as they were pulling into Churchill Downs parking lot. Jake pulled up to the front of the Paddock gate, where they had valet parking. The attendant opened Eva's door and offered her a hand, while the other attendant took the key from Jake.

Jake rounded the front of the BMW and held his hand out for Eva to take and she accepted it without hesitation.

"You ready to do this, Mrs. Long," he asked, with a teasing voice.

"I'm as ready as I'll ever be, Mr. Long."

Chapter 27

They followed the rest of the guests into the Paddock Gate entrance. They watched as groups were entering the elevator to the second floor, where the party was being held at the Rooftop Garden, according to the tickets he was given.

They waited for the elevator to come back down, because he didn't think Eva would be too keen on using the stairs in the four inch heels she was wearing.

As they entered the now empty elevator, Jake noticed Chloe, Penelope, Brett, Juliette and another gentleman, who was holding Chloe's hand, entering the building. He couldn't tell who the man with Chloe was, until they got closer and he noticed that it was Kai Armstrong, Juliette's supposed ex. He thought that was interesting.

Before they could get close enough to catch the elevator with them, Eva had punched the 2nd floor and the door shut.

"Don't like to share elevators with other people," he asked, amused.

"It's not that. I got a strange vibe from that group of people that were coming toward us. I don't think it was the two we'd met earlier, but I'm not sure which one was giving off the vibe and I panicked. Sorry."

"What kind of vibe?"

Jake was now really intrigued by what Eva just said.

"I'm not sure how to describe it, it was just a feeling in the pit of my stomach. I'm sorry, that's the only way to describe it."

"It's fine, don't worry about it. It's always good to go with gut instincts. When we get into the groove of mingling at this party, I would like to see if you can narrow it down, by hanging around some of the people from that group."

"You think one of them murdered Phillipe?"

"Maybe, but I'm not leaving any stone unturned."

The elevator doors opened and there was a gaggle of activity outside the entrance to the Rooftop Garden, as people were making their way through the doors. There was a table at the entrance where people were getting checked in by presenting their tickets to two women dressed in what looked like Churchill Downs uniforms.

Eva and Jake made their way to the table, where Jake showed them his phone where his boss had sent their tickets.

"Names sir?"

"Jake and Eva Long."

The girl searched her list of attendees and made the necessary checkmark next to one of the lines, which must have contained their names. She smiled and pointed toward the entrance.

"Mr. and Mrs. Long, the buffet is to your right and the bar is at the end on the left, you can't miss it. Also, you are seated at table 15, along with a couple of the jockeys. Lucky you."

Jake wasn't sure if she meant that sarcastically, or was serious. He smiled and thanked her, then put a hand to the small of Eva's back, like he had every right to be doing so. He was thankful she didn't even flinch. As it was, the back of her dress had dipped down in the back to the middle of her back, showing more skin than he remembered when she tried it on. To him this felt a little more intimate than it should. He had to hand it to her, she was taking her role in stride and going with it. He figured if Kris could be a fly on the wall, he would, and he would be bugging him all night, watching him hold Eva's hand.

"I see table 15 over there in the far corner," she said, as she looked up at him and smiled.

They made their way through the sea of people hobnobbing and found their seats. There were place cards with their names on them. Jake noticed that the group that had made Eva uncomfortable, would be sitting with them too.

Eva was looking all over the room, taking everything in. The Rooftop Garden was a beautiful covered open-air space, with views of the Downtown Cityscape and views of the track. The tables were covered with white linen table cloths, with stunning red rose centerpieces. The outer rim of the room had high top tables with similar, but smaller red rose centerpieces. It had a great view of the track, where the Derby would be taking place in a few days.

At the far end of the space was a large intricate bar, featuring floating shelves with rose filled vases hanging precariously within the shelves, along with giant overflowing vases on each end of the granite stone bar, filled with at least two dozen roses, in each one.

The opposite end of the room held long tables made of rustic wood and wrought iron legs that displayed the night's buffet. There were metal pans and chafing dishes filled with a delicious assortment of food, along with a whole table of lobster, crab and shrimp that they had made into the shape of a horseshoe.

"Can you imagine trying to build that horseshoe out of seafood?"

Eva was star struck by how fancy everything was.

"Can you imagine how it will look after all these people dig into it," Jake said.

Eva laughed. "Won't be pretty, that's for sure."

"Would you like a drink? I can go get us something, if you want to look around."

"A glass of red wine would be great, thank you."

Eva watched him walk toward the bar, which was pretty packed and she wondered what Kris would think, if he was here. She figured he'd be giving them the stink eye all night, that was for sure. But he also knew, without a doubt, that Jake was not her type and nothing would ever happen. She looked at Jake standing at the bar and she had to admit that yes he was a very good-looking man, but that wasn't what held her attention. Kris was not only good-looking, he was caring, sweet, funny, loving, hardworking, and he loved his family, and doing things with them. Jake had a dangerous job, and was pretty much married to it.

While she walked the perimeter of the room, she listened to conversations, trying to hear any remarks made about Phillipe, and his murder, but not many of them mentioned him at all. They were all so into themselves and being at this high falutin party, getting to dish with professional jockeys. They didn't care about the dead. She found that to be very sad.

She made her way over to where the high top tables were and stood looking out over the expanse of the track in front of her. It was coming on dusk and the sun was making the sky beautiful shades of pink and orange. She inhaled and exhaled at the stunning view in front of her. She didn't hear Jake come up behind her. He put a hand on her back and she'd almost jumped out of her skin.

"Sorry, I didn't mean to frighten you," he looked contrite.

"Oh gosh, you're fine. I was in my own little world, I guess. The view is to die for, here."

Jake's eyebrows rose, and she corrected her faux pas.

"Sorry, bad choice of words."

He laughed. "It's okay."

He handed her the glass of wine and they both took in the amazing sunset.

"It is beautiful, isn't it?"

She looked up at him, and nodded. "Very."

"I don't get to do this very often, it's kind of nice."

That made Eva's heart sink. She thought about how bad his job could be and all he sees is the ugly part of life, and not the beauty of it, that she takes for granted.

"Your job must be hard on your psyche."

"It has its moments."

He didn't elaborate on it anymore than that, and Eva took that as her cue to not ask for more.

"Want to get something to eat, it looks like people are at the buffet now?"

She decided a change of subject was safe and the food did look mouthwatering. She was starving. She hadn't realized it until she began drinking her wine and it was having an effect on her already. She needed food to counteract that.

"Sure. I've been eyeing that seafood ever since we walked in."

"You and Kris with your love of seafood. It's not my favorite, but I do like salmon and cod, but that's as far as I'd go."

"I love seafood. I eat it any chance I get. The shrimp and lobster look especially fresh. I'm heading for that. I'll meet you back at our table."

Eva went to the buffet table and walked the length of it, deciding what she would partake in. There was so much delicious food, it was hard for her to decide. As she was forking a piece of prime rib onto her plate, she overheard a gentleman speaking about Phillipe's untimely demise.

"Did you hear, they are looking into Juliette Sutherland for Phillipe's murder? I can't see her doing it.

"Really? I can see her having a motive. He was the only one who could probably have beaten her. You know they found him in her horse's stall? " "

Eva didn't listen to that conversation long. She had already determined it wasn't Juliette that committed the murder. Eva hadn't gotten any bad energy off of her, at all.

As Eva walked toward the table she was assigned to, she noticed most of the group she saw earlier, that made her jumpy, were sitting at their table. She stopped short, as the dark vibe hit her again.

Jake noticed Eva's resistance to continue to their table and walked to her side quickly, but subtly. He put a hand to her shoulder, and she didn't even jerk at his touch this time. He whispered in her ear, making it look like an endearing husband whispering sweet nothings.

"Are you okay," he whispered, gently smiling.

She smiled back at him, keeping up her appearance. "I'm fine. There is someone in that group though, that I don't trust. I believe one of them could be the one you're looking for."

This pulled him up short. "Seriously?"

"Yes, but don't be obvious, keep up your persona. I will be fine. I might be able to narrow it down as we sit with them."

"Okay Mrs. Long, I'll let you do your thing." He gave her a sweet smile, as he looked down at her.

Eva looked to Jake, giving him a look that nearly dropped him to his knees. Her smile was beautiful and genuine. He now knew how Kris felt. It took him off guard and he didn't like it. He didn't want to know what he was missing, not having a special person in his life. His life didn't accommodate for such things.

153

Eva noticed the change in him immediately. She put her hand to his chest and felt his heart pounding. She was worried.

"Are you okay?"

He recovered himself quickly. "I'm good," he said smiling.

Jake motioned her toward their table, pulling out the seat for her.

He knew most of their table mates, as he had questioned every one of them. He introduced Eva to them, as his wife. She nodded and kept her cool. She was polite and sincere, as some asked her how she liked Louisville, and asked if she'd ever been to the Kentucky Derby before.

Penelope asked, "did you bring a special hat to wear for the Derby?"

"Oh gosh, no. I totally forgot all about that. Is there a good place to find one or do you think they would all be picked over by now?"

"Oh, you must go to Forme' Millinery Hat shop on Main Street," Penelope told her.

Jake piped up, "I'll have to take her over there tomorrow. Can't have her being hatless at the infamous Derby, now can I?"

Eva laughed at his try at humor, as did everyone else at their table.

She started in on her dinner, enjoying all the deliciousness, without kids fighting. She looked over to Jake, and noticed he too, was enjoying the seafood he was eating.

They all settled into a comfortable silence, as they all dug into the food on their plates. Unfortunately she knew looks can be quite deceiving. Eva was doing her best to act normal, but she was feeling the sudden dark energy coming off of someone at their table.

She wondered if anyone else could feel it, or if it was just her. Eva looked around the table. No one seemed to be bothered by it, or at least they weren't showing it, but as she was about to continue to eat, she caught Kai looking at her, with what she thought was a baneful look on his face and just as quickly, it was gone, replaced with a friendly smile. As if on cue, Chloe did the same thing. Eva was feeling that creepy unsettling feeling and she didn't like it. She kept a smile on her face as she continued to eat.

Was the dark energy she was feeling coming off of those two? She wasn't getting much off of anyone else at their table. Juliette and Brett seemed to be in their own little bubble. New love, she thought. Penelope and Florant were discussing horses and their temperaments.

She couldn't shake the feeling, something was off. She unconsciously grabbed Jake's hand under the table and squeezed it gently. He looked at her, surprised, then he saw the fear in her eyes, she was clearly shaken by something. He couldn't exactly ask her what was wrong, right then and there. He gave her a knowing look and gently held her hand. He hoped that she felt some semblance of security knowing that he was with her and wouldn't let anything bad happen to her.

Kai and Chloe, along with Brett and Juliette, got up from the table and headed in opposite directions. Penelope and Florant had been answering some questions from a few of the reporters that had shown up at their table, so Jake thought this would be a good time to walk around the room. If nothing else, he could get Eva somewhere where he could talk to her and ask her what was wrong.

He got up from the table, held his hand out for Eva and asked her, "would you like to head out to the patio?"

She took his hand, but said nothing. They walked to the patio, where it was becoming twilight. The open air patio had white twinkle lights strung from the ceiling, making it look festive and fancy.

Eva looked up to the sky and closed her eyes for a second. Her spidey senses were off the charts in this place and she needed to calm herself. Jake couldn't help noticing how keyed up she was. He wanted to ask her twenty questions, but he also had to play the part of the ever doting husband.

He decided to do what any good husband might do and he put his arm around her pulling her in close to him. God bless her, he thought. She went with it.

He leaned in a little, "What's going on?"

She was surprised that he'd picked up on her feelings. Was she that obvious? Of course she was, she practically broke his hand a minute ago while he was trying to eat. She was going to have to work on her poker face better, if that was the case.

"Was I that obvious?"

"Not obvious, but when you grabbed my hand I knew something was wrong. And your eyes told an even better story. What is it?"

"I don't know if you want to talk about this now, it might blow our cover."

"Oh...do I need to sit for this?"

She couldn't help but laugh a little, but then turned serious. "I believe the murderer is here."

That, he was not expecting. "What?!" He had said it a little too loud and noticed people staring at them. He smiled and tried to recover himself. Jake turned her to face him and he pulled Eva into a hug, "sorry, you took me off guard."

"I shouldn't have blurted it out like that."

"Who do you think it is," he asked, still holding her close. If she was uncomfortable with him hugging her, she wasn't showing it.

"I've got a couple people giving off a dark type of energy. It's something I've felt before. I'll need to go into the barn and you'll have to take me to the stall where the murder took place. I will try one of my spells there, and see what we get, before we go any further. I don't want to tell you who, until I do the spell. I hope that's okay?"

"Okay. I think we should leave this party then, now. You can do the spell or whatever it is you do, before everyone gets back later. Will that work?"

"I'm game, if you are?"

They pulled away from the embrace, he took her hand and they made their way to the elevators.

The press conference was in full swing, as questions were flying. Eva and Jake stopped where they were as they heard one reporter ask about Phillipe's murder.

It was Terrence Rivers, Executive Board Member, who fielded that question.

"As horrible as the incident was, we really can't comment on it, until the authorities finish their job. We are trying to keep tonight light and fun and not weigh down the other jockeys. Next question."

Eva and Jake continued to the elevator. "That was the best answer he could give," she asked.

"The politics of business, I guess. He has to keep the money coming in, and if they focus too much on the murder, it will ruin buisness and people spending."

They exited the elevator and they made their way to where the valet parking attendant was. Jake handed him his ticket and they waited for their car.

"How long do you think we have until the others return?"

Jake shrugged his shoulders, having no idea, but he did have a few of his colleagues here, hiding in plain sight. The minute anyone from the ranch leaves the party, they'd let him know.

"Let's just get back to the ranch and get this over with, as quickly as we can," he said.

"Deal. I'll wait to call Kris later. But, I will give him a quick text, to let him know what's going on, if that's okay?"

"Yeah, that's fine. I'm sure he's anxious to hear how the party went anyway."

Eva sent her husband a quick text letting him know what the plan was. She told him that she'd call him later. Within thirty seconds, he'd texted exactly what Jake had said... *How was the party? Did Jake behave?* Eva let out a short laugh, "Wow, you really know Kris."

"Why, what did he say?"

"Pretty much exactly what you thought. *How was the party? Did Jake behave?*"

"Man, he thinks I'm a real player. Gotta tell ya, I'm far from it. I don't have that kind of time. You're the closest I've come to having a date, in two years."

"Okay, that's just pathetic."

"Yeah, tell me about it."

The rest of their drive went about the same, just small talk, with comfortable bouts of silence.

Chapter 28

Once they had both changed out of their dress clothes, Eva grabbed her book of spells, her bag of necessities, and they headed toward the horse stalls.

It was a relatively nice evening, with clear skies and an almost full moon.

They entered the barn and made their way to Juliette's old stall. Her horse had been relocated due to the police and FBI investigation, so it was virtually empty now. There were still traces of blood on the left over hay, but Eva ignored that.

She went about the stall, setting up her things. Jake stayed silent and just watched.

Eva looked his way and noticed him staring. "I'm setting a protection spell first. It's important."

"I'll just watch. If there is something you need me to do, let me know."

"I might need you. I'm going to do a spell that will take me to the past, preferably two days ago, in this very spot. I'll need you to hold a few things while I perform it, so I can get back to the present. It might look like I'm here, and physically I am, but technically I won't be. It's hard to explain. I've never tried this spell personally, but I've seen it done."

"It sounds like it could be dangerous. Is there a better one that won't possibly get you lost in the past?" He looked at her, truly anxious.

"This is the best one for this situation. I'll be fine."
She gave him one her radiant smiles that nearly knocked
his equilibrium off kilter.

"Okay. I believe you."

Eva wrapped herself in a white silk scarf, took the
container of salt and made a circle with it, as she stood in
the middle. She placed her white candles just outside the
circle, then poured pig's blood in a smaller circle, inside the
salted circle. She shook some baking powder over it. After
she lit the candles, she stood, closed her eyes and started
her chant.

*In the shadows evils hide, ready to draw me from
loves side, but with your help I shall be strong, banish all
that do me wrong. Send them away, send them astray,
never again to pass my way. So mote it be.*

Jake stood there in stunned silence. He had no idea
what to expect, but this wasn't it. He remained as quiet as
he could, not wanting to interrupt her.

Eva finished her protection spell and grabbed a black
candle that she had placed near her circle. She picked up a
couple of pieces of paper, a pen, and a vial filled with fast
action oil.

She began writing on one of the pieces of paper, the
date and time she wanted to go back to, and the other with
today's date and time. She would need Jakes help with the
second half of this spell, to get her back.

"Jake, I need you to come to the outside of the circle,
in front of me please. I can't do this spell without your

help. I'm sorry, I didn't want to tell you until right beforehand."

He walked slowly towards the circle, eyebrows knit together, concern etched in his face.

"I've never done anything like this, I don't know magic or spells, and all that hocus pocus stuff, Eva."

"Trust me, you don't need to be a witch to be able to help me with this. But, you are needed, or I can't do it. Please Jake, I promise, it'll be fine." She gave him a pleading look.

He stood in front of her, towering over her, worry clouded his big brown eyes.

"Okay, what do I need to do?"

She handed him the other piece of paper that she had written on, and he saw that it had today's date on it and time, but the time was for ten minutes from now. She then took the vial of oil and dabbed her finger into it. She made the sign of the cross over the paper in an oil stain. Eva also handed him another piece of paper, this one had *To Bring Me Back to the Present* written across the top, and what he assumed was a spell written out below.

"Okay, are you ready? I'm going to start my portion of the spell, to go back to two days ago, right before Phillipe supposedly was killed. Once your watch says the time on that paper, you start your portion of the spell, to get me back. Got it?"

"NO! What if something goes wrong? What do I do then?" He was panicking and having second thoughts about bringing her here.

Eva walked up to him, putting a hand on his chest, it was thumping hard. "Jake, I'll be fine. We have to do this. Trust me, please. Don't freak out if a wind starts to kick up and I'm still here. It will be as if my soul is traveling back in time, but my physical body will still be in this time. Don't do anything. When you see your watch say 10:15pm, then start the return spell."

His eyes grew large. He couldn't believe any of this would work, but he had no other choice.

"Fine. Let's get this over with. The sooner the better." Her hand was warm, through his shirt, and soothing.

"Okay. Step back a little."

He did as she said, then watched her get into the middle of the circle. She held the paper to her chest, and started the incantation.

I want to see the highest power, take me now, in the past, right now in this hour, take me back to the past!

Jake watched as Eva's hair started to blow around her face, the air was getting thick and murky, he could barely make out her form. He was growing more and more anxious. He promised her he wouldn't do anything. This was the hardest thing he ever had to do.

He looked at his watch every ten seconds.

Chapter 29

Eva opened her eyes and low and behold, a horse was in front of her. She jumped back, forgetting that the horse wasn't actually there. Well, it was, but she was in spirit form.

She looked around, but she didn't see Phillipe anywhere in the stall yet. She had arrived before the murder took place.

Eva walked around the stall, looking for anything that might stand out, when she heard the barn door open, and heard two voices in the distance.

Two killers, she thought...

The voices were growing closer and closer. One was definitely male, but she didn't immediately recognize it. It wasn't British, like she was thinking it would be. The other was female, for sure. A large shadow appeared to be coming into the stall, and it was carrying something, or rather someone.

He threw the body down on the ground inside the stall. "Damn, for someone so short, he is damn heavy."

"Or maybe you're just weak," the female stated, sarcastically.

The male figure whipped around, striking the female, knocking her down.

"You need to show me respect, or I'll make sure they find evidence that you killed Phillipe, instead of Julliette"

The small female whimpered, "sorry."

"That's better."

Eva couldn't see either one of them very well. She somewhat recognized the female voice as Chloe Rivers, which didn't surprise her, but the male was wearing a hooded sweatshirt.

They were arranging the body inside the stall, staging him to look like he'd been killed there.

"Crap on a cracker, turn around!" Eva was willing the male to turn in her direction. He'd turned every other way, but in her direction.

Just as the duo was ready to leave the scene, the hooded male looked directly at her. It was Kai Armstrong, with an evil glint in his eyes. She'd seen that look before. Probably the same look he was giving her at the party. But he was from England, like Juliette, where did his accent go?

She had so many unanswered questions.

****

Jake was still looking at his watch, noting the time was 10:13, only two more minutes.

He noticed Eva's body twitching, but seemed okay otherwise. There was still a slight fog formed around her. Jake couldn't believe what he was looking at. Thinking to himself, "would she really be able to find anything, or was he losing his mind even bringing her in on this?"

He held onto the paper with a tight grip. Looking at the time, he saw the numbers change to 10:15.

"Now. I have to get her back, now. God help me, let this work."

Jake took the other paper Eva gave him and started to recite the words before him.

Get this message now, as slowly and quickly as I bow, change the time and in the other place, in the future, I'll be found.

****

Eva continued to look around the stall after Kai and Chloe left, not finding much. She knew three things; one, Kai and Chloe were the murderers, two, the murder didn't take place in this stall, and three, Kai was not from England, but why he was speaking with an accent in front of everyone else? She stood and pondered all of this when she felt her body go slack.

"Oh... it must be time."

****

Jake waited and waited, but nothing was happening. Did he do something wrong, did he miss a word. He didn't think so. He looked over the words on the paper and he couldn't see any he missed. She was still standing there in suspended animation. He walked closer to where Eva was and went to reach out to her, but her body fell to the ground. A gust of wind whipped around her, and hay and leaves that were on the ground in the stall were swirling everywhere. He backed up a fraction, holding his hands in front of his face, not wanting the debris to get in his eyes. He watched as it all started to die down and he could see her form coming back into view, she was still on the ground, not moving. Worry seeped into his veins.

Everything came to a dead stop and he stood stock still for a second, before going to her.

"Eva! Eva!" He shook her limp body ferociously, on the brink of fear.

Eva began shaking uncontrollably. Jake crossed into the circle where she was lying and picked her up, carrying her to the middle of the barn. He held her on the damp ground, trying to control her shaking body. He had no idea what to do, or if this was a normal occurrence after performing this type of spell. This was totally out of his realm of understanding.

His voice came out rough and strained, "Eva, please wake up, it's Jake, I'm here. You're going to be fine."

A cough escaped from Eva's throat, as if she'd been drowning in a sea of water. She made short ugly gasps, trying to catch her breath. Jake sat her more upright in his lap, rubbing her back, "You're okay Eva, breathe."

Eva opened her big hazel eyes and saw Jake staring at her, worry and fear etched in his face. She didn't know what was going on, other than she couldn't stop coughing and gagging. He continued to hold her tight, rubbing her back, trying to ease her. She was shivering.

"Eva, can you hear me?"

She shook her head vehemently. She tried to talk, but nothing came out, her voice strained from coughing.

"It's okay, don't try to talk just yet. I'm going to ask you a few questions, and you nod yes or no. Can you do that?"

She nodded yes.

"Good. Are you okay?"

Again, she nodded yes.

"Good. Did you know that was going to happen when you did this specific spell?"

Eva shook her head no. He did remember that she told him that she had never performed that spell before and wasn't sure how it would play out.

"Okay. You did say you hadn't performed this spell before. I'm thinking you weren't aware of the after effects."

Eva croaked out a "yes. I'm…"

He stopped her from talking by holding his hand up. She closed her mouth and shrunk back into herself. She was a witch by birth, but she did not have as much experience as the rest of her family.

"Just sit for a minute or two and then we'll see how you feel, okay?"

She looked down at her hands and shook her head.

"Eva, I'm not mad, I was worried. Please know that. I hate to even ask, but did you find out anything?"

Her head shot up, eyes wide and she went to speak, but he stopped her. "Nod yes or no for now."

She nodded yes, quite enthusiastically.

Stunned, Jake turned her around in his lap, so she was facing him head on.

"Seriously? And before you try to talk, just nod."

Her coughing had stopped, but her throat felt raw, so she just nodded yes.

"Wow! I honestly didn't think you'd actually find anything. I guess you proved me wrong, huh?"

She smiled up at him, with a cocky little smile. She wanted to talk and figured she could by now. She held up a hand, to halt him from saying anything, so she could get out what she needed to tell him. He let out a sigh and agreed to hear her out.

Her voice came out pretty ragged, "I saw who it was. It was Chloe Rivers and Kai Armstrong. I saw them bring Phillipe into Juliette's stall. They didn't kill him here though. I'm not sure how, or where they killed him. And one more thing… I heard Kai speak and he did not have an accent, like he would if he was from England."

Jake sat stock still, mouth agape and floored by what she just said. He didn't know what he expected her to say, but that wasn't it.

"Are you absolutely positive it was both of them?"

"Yes, I swear!."

"Okay, okay. Now we just have to find out how and where they killed Phillipe. Got anything else up your magical sleeve? We need proof and some decent evidence. If it didn't happen here, then where?"

"I'll have to see if there is another spell I can perform to go back in time, but with a specific location in mind. Has anyone gone through Phillipe's room yet, at the Inn at St. James Court? I know Chloe saw him at the Bourbon

Inn, but I overheard him saying his room was at the St. James."

"I'm sure they have. The local authorities were processing everyone's location, as far as I know."

"Maybe they should process the rooms of each jockey, and all persons affiliated with Phillipe. That way no one in particular will think they are being targeted."

"That's actually a really good idea, Eva."

Jake shifted Eva around so he could get his cell phone out of his pocket and she realized for the first time, that she had been sitting in his lap, but for how long, she had no idea. She tried to angle her way out of his lap, but he held onto her. Eva looked at him, surprised, but he just held up his index finger, for her to wait.

She listened to his side of the call, which she figured was to the local cops who'd originally taken the homicide call. He took her advice and asked them to start processing the other locations, before anyone could clean up any more evidence than they already had. It may be a long shot, but it was all they had. Once he hung up, he picked Eva up and set her on the ground next to him, he stood and stretched his lithe body, then offered her his hand, to help her to her feet.

"I hope I didn't make you uncomfortable by holding you. I was really worried about you and what was happening when you came out of the spell. I've never felt that protective of any one person before. Kris would kill me if anything happened to you and frankly, I might have let him."

Jake was definitely growing on her. He had this highly protective big brother vibe going on. And she found herself liking that. Eva was never that close to her family, after her mother passed away.

"Thank you for helping me. I should have warned you that the after effects could be severe, but I didn't know how severe. And just so you know, I would never let Kris kill you," she said, smirking.

"Thanks."

"Now what?"

"Let's grab your stuff and get back to the lodge. I'm beat, mentally and physically. And, I need to get you some tea or something for your throat."

He looked at his watch and realized the whole thing, from arriving to the barn, to now, had only been forty minutes. It seemed like hours to him.

"I'm pretty tired. I could go for some tea, with a shot of Jack Daniels added."

That made Jake smile. "Girl after my own heart."

They gathered all of her supplies, including the candles that were no longer burning after all the wind,and placed everything back in her bag.

They walked the distance to the main house and noticed multiple headlights coming down the long stretch of drive towards them. They hurried up the stairs, taking two steps at a time to their floor, where their room was. They shut the door behind them and breathed a sigh of relief.

"That was a close call," Eva said, breathless.

"Yeah, I agree. Why don't you change your clothes and we'll head downstairs for some tea and maybe I'll find some JD lying around. We'll make it look like we needed to relax for the rest of the evening. How does that sound?"

"Works for me. I'll just be a minute."

Eva went to the bathroom, taking a change of clothes with her. She shut the door, locked it and sat on the edge of the tub, with her head in her hands and tears threatening to spill. She was terrified by the side effects from that spell. She wondered what might have happened if Jake hadn't been there. She quickly put that thought out of her mind, stood and went to the sink, splashing her face with some cold water. She quickly changed her clothes and emerged from the bathroom ready to go downstairs.

Jake was sitting on the couch when Eva came out of the bathroom and noticed her eyes looked glassy, as if she had been crying. That tore him up inside, but he said nothing.

Eva walked toward the door, "ready?"

Jake got up and opened their door, motioning her to go ahead of him. He shut and locked the door. She looked over her shoulder at him, smiled and asked, "do you think they do have any alcohol down there?"

He couldn't help laughing. "We'll take a look. If all else fails, I think Penelope and the rest are back, we can ask her if she has anything."

They heard conversations going on, on the main floor as they descended the stairs.

Everyone turned to look in their direction as they entered the great room. Brett was the first to say something.

"When did you two get back? Did you leave the party earlier?"

Eva piped up, "I had a bit of a headache, so we came back so I could take something. It was probably from the busy day of driving, then shopping, and the party."

Juliette smiled, "well, you didn't miss much, trust me."

Penelope was near the front door staring outside. "The police are here again. What do they want now?"

Jake cleared his throat and everyone looked in his direction. "They are here on my request. They will be processing everyone's rooms here, and at the St. James, as well as the Bourbon Inn. We believe that Phillipe was murdered elsewhere and dumped here, so we are looking into every jockey and person he was around the last forty eight hours of his life. I'm sorry for the inconvenience."

To their credit, everyone in the room seemed fine with it. And as Eva figured they would be, because she knew none of them had done anything wrong. She did, however, wonder what the chaos would be like at the St. James and the Bourbon Inn. She knew Kai was staying at the St. James Inn, but Chloe would be getting the same treatment, at her apartment, too. Eva kinda wished she could be a fly on the wall to see their faces.

Eva walked over to where Penelope was standing, "I'm sorry to bother you, but do you happen to have anything to drink?"

"Of course, I'm so sorry. I should have showed you earlier where everything was."

Eva followed Penelope into the kitchen, where she opened the refrigerator and the pantry, along with a closet that turned out to be a larger than it looked wine cellar of sorts.

Eva walked into the wine area and turned to Penelope, "now this is what I was looking for. Do you mind if I open a bottle, or is there one that is already opened that I could try?"

"You can open any of them, or I believe I have some chilled in the refrigerator, let me look."

"Thank you so much. I feel like having a small glass before bed, to relax me."

Penelope agreed with her. "I'll have one with you. Let me check and see if anyone else would care for one, while I'm at it."

Before she left the kitchen, she pulled a bottle of Merlot from a bottom shelf and set it on the counter, then went to take orders from the others.

Jake came into the kitchen where Eva was leaning against the counter, with her eyes closed. "Penny for your thoughts, Mrs. Long."

Eva smiled while keeping her eyes closed. She was already used to Jake just popping up wherever and it didn't even surprise her anymore. "Not much going on in here, at the moment. I think I'm running on empty, after earlier."

"I bet. It was hard to watch, I have to admit. I had never seen anything like it before."

Eva opened her eyes and stared at him for a second before responding. She could only imagine what he saw. It was near impossible for her to do a spell in front of Kris, let alone Jake. He must think she's a freak of nature or something.

"I'm sorry if I made you uncomfortable," she said quietly, with her head down.

Jake came closer, so only she could hear him. He put his hands on her shoulders, "don't. This is what I wanted you to do and you were a huge help. Yes, I had no idea what to expect and it was a surprise, I'm not going to lie, but it was also the most surreal thing I'd ever witnessed."

"Kris wasn't sure what to expect either. Sometimes I think he thinks it was all a dream."

"I have proof it wasn't a dream, Eva."

She looked up, "this is true."

Penelope came back into the kitchen, smiling at them, probably thinking they were sharing a moment. Jake slung an arm around his pseudo wife and smiled back at her. For her part, Eva wrapped her arm around his waist and smiled back.

"Penelope, do you need any help with passing out drinks," Eva asked.

"Sure, that would be great, thank you. It seems everyone could use a little relaxing drink tonight. The wine glasses are in the cabinet above you. We'll need six glasses. Agent Long, Officer Jackson took the crew from the crime scene unit upstairs, after I handed over the master key to him."

"Okay, great. Thanks for your cooperation."

"I don't have much of a choice, do I?" Penelope was mad, but understandably so. This was not only her home, it was also her business, her livelihood, and her only source of income. She knew her father-in-law was probably laughing about now. He would just love it if she went bankrupt.

Jake felt bad for her. He knew she was a widow and that this place was her life. "You could have refused, but that wouldn't have looked too good," he said, smiling.

"It's okay, I have nothing to hide. Now, how about we get the wine out there."

Chapter 30

When the crime scene team left and everyone headed for their respective rooms, Eva and Jake went to theirs as well.

Jake placed a call to his colleagues that had gone to the St. James, the Bourbon Inn, and Chloe's apartment.

While Jake spoke with his people, Eva decided to go to the bathroom and call Kris.

"Hey sweetheart, how's it going? Did you have fun at the swanky party?" He laughed.

"It was okay. These types of parties aren't my thing. The food was delicious though. Churchill Downs is a beautiful place…"

"But…"

"Okay, okay… I felt a really dark energy around some of the people there. It made me very uncomfortable and I've felt that same presence before."

"What do you mean, you've felt it before?"

"I can't put my finger on it yet."

"Okay. So, did anything else happen while you were there, that may help get this investigation finished?"

"Maybe. I did a back in time spell while we were in the barn tonight."

Kris made a strained sound on the other end of the phone, before commenting.

"And… what did you find?"

"I can't really say, just yet. Jake and the rest of the crew are still doing searches of rooms and apartments. He doesn't want me to divulge any information yet, not even to you. I wasn't thrilled when we said that, though."

"Ha, I bet. How's he handling all that spunk?"

"You're funny. He seems to be taking me in stride, thank you very much. He doesn't seem to be much of a people person though, kind of quiet and reserved. Was he that way in college?"

"No, he was pretty outgoing actually. He was Mr. Football and all the girls loved him. I'm guessing the hazards of his job are part of his problem, now. Why? Is he not behaving? Am I going to have to kick his ass? Is he not husband material?"

Eva stifled a laugh. "Kris, you don't need to kick his butt on my behalf. He's been perfectly fine and a gentleman. A little awkward sometimes, but like you said, his job may have something to do with that."

There was a knock on the door, "Eva, are you okay in there?"

"Oops, I forgot someone else may need the bathroom."

"I take it Jake needs in the bathroom? By the way, why are you locked in the bathroom talking to me, anyway?"

"He was on calls with his team and I wanted some privacy to talk to you. I miss you."

"Oh yeah? What were you going to talk about before I asked you twenty questions?"

"I guess you'll never know, will you? I gotta go, love you."

"Wait… crap, she hung up."

Eva opened the door to the bathroom, with an apologetic smile.

"I'm sorry, I didn't know you were on the phone in there," Jake said. "How's Kris doing?"

"No worries. He's fine, but probably bored. How did your calls go? Anyone find anything?"

"They used luminol and a dark light on everyone's rooms and Chloe's apartment to look for any trace of blood spatter. They found a little, and it was on the hall floor in Chloe's apartment. They swabbed it and are taking it to forensics for a DNA test, to see if it matches Phillipe's. Now we wait. We couldn't arrest her, because for all we know, it's her own blood. There wasn't enough to constitute a bludgeoning, so for now, I have one of my guys hanging around outside her apartment, in case she leaves."

"Can you get me into her apartment? I might be able to tell you for sure, before the DNA comes back."

"Are you going to do another spell? I don't know if my heart can handle seeing that again Eva."

"I'm sorry if I scared you earlier. This one would be an easy one and I wouldn't be going anywhere, exactly."

"I can probably get you into her apartment tomorrow, if that works?"

"Works for me. I'm too exhausted to do much else tonight, actually. I think I might go to bed, now. I'm going to make up the sofa, you get to bed. And don't try to change my mind. You know I'm much smaller and will fit on the couch. You, not so much."

Jake went to say something, but Eva held up her hand to stop him, then went to grab her pajamas and shut the bathroom door to him.

She finished dressing and walked out of the bathroom door, to find Jake laying in bed, dressed in pajama bottoms and a t-shirt, reading. He looked totally different from the suit, tie, dress shoes and gun, she was used to. He looked relaxed, younger even.

She made her way to the couch and noticed it had been made up already, a sheet, blanket and pillow had been neatly placed on it. She couldn't help but smile. Jake Long did have a different side to him, she was slowly finding out.

She pulled the sheet and blanket back, sat down, pulled her legs up, and she stretched out. She proceeded to fluff her pillow, and pulled the sheet and blanket over her, getting situated for a good night's sleep.

"Good night Jake."

"Sleep well Eva."

Chapter 31

Eva thought she was in a relatively deep sleep, until her eyes opened and she was standing in the dark of night, in the middle of the forest.

"Not again," she said.

Looking around, she found herself in familiar territory. She was back in Connecticut, where she grew up.

"No, no, no, this can't be happening."

Eva walked the length of the trail and smelled the familiar campfire scent. She followed the faint light glowing in the distance. She found herself in the same clearing she was at when she reconnected with her deceased mother, a month ago. This time she found a figure sitting on a long log, hunched over the fire. The figure, she assumed was her mother, was shroud in a gray organza dress, her tangled mess of hair falling forward, covering her face.

"Mom…"

"Eva," she croaked out

"Why am I back here, Mom?"

"You tell me dear. What brings you back to the mother you hate so much?"

"Really, we're going to start this off by going there, again?"

"Your hatred of me is palpable, I can feel it in your soul. But, I have a feeling I know why you're here. You're using your gift again, aren't you?"

Alma, Eva's mother turned to look at her daughter standing above her. Eva was stunned by what she was looking at. Every time she saw her mother in these crazy dreams, she seemed to be getting older each time. It was like she was aging ten years with every dream. How could that be, she wondered.

"What's with the worried look, dear?"

She hadn't realized she'd been staring at her mother in any particular way.

"Oh, um, nothing. Why am I here again, Mom?"

"Like I said, you're using your magic again. Want to tell me what you're using it for, this time?"

"I used a new spell to go back in time a few days, to see if I could help find another killer. It seems the FBI thinks I may be useful to them, in solving crimes. At least I can use my gifts for good."

She hadn't meant that to come out as sarcastic as it had, but it was out there now, and she waited for her mother's snarky response.

"Hmmm… I see. No need to get cocky with me, Eva. As usual, you jump into something that you think is for the good of mankind and you end up running with the devil."

"What's that supposed to mean?"

"It means, you have no idea who you're dealing with my darling. Not everyone is as they presume to be, remember that. You think you're so self righteous and on the side of good, but trust me, temptation is not that far away."

"If you think I'll go to the dark side of magic, like you did, think again. I have a soul mother, you let evil take over yours. Now, why do I always seem to return to this place, every time I practice magic?"

"Maybe your subconscious is in need of my help, my guidance, my approval…"

"I don't need anything from you. Last time the entity that took over you, nearly killed me and my friend. This is nothing like the last time," Eva said, and started walking away from her mother.

"Don't you walk away from me!"

Eva ignored her mother and continued to walk out of the clearing. A black mist rose around her, and wind whipped her hair straight up. She turned to see Alma standing with her arms above her head, her hair and dress swirling around her, and her eyes closed.

"Let me go!"

"He still wants you, he won't give up."

'Who?"

"You know who, Eva. I'm dead, he can't have me anymore, but you, you're still very much alive and he's seen what you are capable of. He wants you more than he ever wanted me. He's closer than you think."

"No! I won't give in to it. Where is it? How do I get rid of it, for good?"

"Oh darling, you think you won't give in to it, but he's very persuasive. I don't think you're strong enough to resist. I wasn't."

"I'm not you and I'll never be like you. Never!"

Alma laughed and laughed, all while tormenting Eva.

Eva took off in a sprint through the woods, narrowly missing low hanging branches. She was almost out of the forest when she tripped.

"Ow!" she cried.

She held her ankle in one hand and started rocking back and forth. Tears were streaming down her face. Eva rolled to her side lying there, sobbing on the wet ground.

"I want to go back. I want to go back, now," she cried.

She felt someone's hand on her shoulder, shaking her.

"Eva! Eva! Wake up. Wake up, Eva."

Eva jerked her eyes open, flailing her arms to remove the person touching her.

"Eva! It's me, Jake. Look at me. Please, look at me. You're dreaming. You were having a nightmare. Look at me."

Jake had a hold of her shoulders, willing her to look at him. He shook her, but not hard. He feared she might be having a night terror and didn't want to harm her.

Eva's vision was slowly clearing and she saw that Jake had a hold of her. She looked around and noticed she was sitting up on the leather sofa she had fallen asleep on earlier. She was back at the ranch. Safe.

She wrapped her arms around Jake hard, and wept uncontrollably.

At first he was taken by surprise. He knew she'd been dreaming and it was a bad one. Now here she was, crying into his chest, holding onto him for dear life. He was not used to this kind of display of emotion, at least not from someone he knew; victims' families, yes, but this was his friend's wife. What the hell was he supposed to do now.

Jake did the only thing he could, he wrapped his strong arms protectively around her and held her, until she was done.

She pulled back from his strong hold, sniffling and hiccuping. Her face was wet, her nose and eyes were red. She looked at him, embarrassed that he saw her like that. She was silent for a beat.

"I'm really sorry Jake. I don't know what came over me."

He sat up straighter, but his arms were still slightly wrapped around her. He looked down at the frightened, yet embarrassed look on her face.

"You had a bad dream, it happens to the best of us. No need to apologize."

"It was more than a bad dream. I've had these before." She wasn't sure how much to tell him. Um, how much has Kris told you about my past and my family?"

He looked a little perplexed by the question. He assumed she'd just had a nightmare and it was done.

"He didn't give me much of your background, why? Is there something else I should know?"

"Yes. You should know where I came from and what type of past I had. It may help you understand why I do what I do."

"Okay. Do you feel like talking about it now?"

"Yes."

"Do you want a glass of water or anything, first?"

"A glass of water would be great, thank you. And, it would probably be best if we get this whole *growing up as a witch* thing over with, now."

Jake let her go, and got up to retrieve a glass of water for her. He motioned for her to get on with the history lesson. He wasn't sure if he was ready to hear it, but he needed some background on her.

"Okay, here goes... I didn't have a typical childhood, as I am sure you've gathered, but I digress. I grew up in a small town in Connecticut. I have one sister, who is a year younger than me and she still lives there, as does my father. My mother is deceased."

He gave her a somber look, as if to say he was sorry for her loss. She continued before he could say anything.

"Neither of my parents had traditional 9-5 jobs, they were both witches, as is my sister and I, and my family before me. My father was a farmer though, for the most part. He and my grandmother, his mother, were Earth witches. They believed in thanking mother earth for the air, water, earth and fire. He would do spells to improve his crops and that sort of thing. My mother was a whole other ball of wax. She would conjure spells for just about anything; love, money, illness, revenge... you name it, she would have a spell for it, or she'd find one that would work. As long as you had the money to pay her to do it, she would do it. She was a sideshow freak. I hated practicing magic with her. I would purposely mess up a spell, just so I could get out of doing them, however, she would punish me for screwing up.

It wasn't until December 21, 1989 that I finally got to see just how bad my mother was getting. It was the "Return to Light" celebration. It was normally a night to rejoice in the white light of our magic and the Winter Solstice. My mother and her friends had other plans.

We would always gather at the same spot, to celebrate our heritage and the new Moons. It was a large clearing in the middle of the forest, just beyond our house, which sat on thirty acres.

This night was what changed my life forever. I didn't even want to go, but my father convinced me to do so. We got to the clearing and the bonfire was already burning bright. My mother and her friends were already there, dancing around it, chanting something I wasn't familiar with. She looked different and she didn't even acknowledge our presence, at first. As I watched the ceremony unfold, I noticed something forming inside the fire; a figure was taking shape. I had never seen anything like it. The wind started to pick up and the leaves swirled overhead. I stared into the flames as the silhouette started forming in the flames. A large head with horns and a long sleek torso was dancing in the flames. It wasn't of this world, I knew. My sister Amelia and I were sitting next to each other when our mother turned around; she stared at us, eyes black as pitch, not the beautiful hazel eyes we were used to. She smiled a maniacal smile and continued dancing around the fire, chanting in a different language.

Neither my sister or I was aware of what she was saying, but our father did. He ran over to her and screamed at her. He had seen the figure in the fire forming, too. He was doing his own incantation, to counteract the one my mother was doing, to try and rid the fire of the creature taking shape. My mother turned on him and put a spell in place that froze my father to the spot he was in. I had never seen my mother do anything to hurt my father before.

I ran to my father screaming, trying to move him, but I couldn't budge him. My sister was crying and hysterical. She had no idea what to do. I went and stood in front of my mother, looking her in the eyes, but it wasn't her, it was something else. I yelled at her to stop what she was doing, that I wanted my mother back, but the figure in the fire, and my mother were starting to become one. I continued screaming at her. I grabbed her by her shoulders, trying to shake some sense into her, but she picked me up and threw me across the clearing, into a tree. I'd hit my head pretty hard. Amelia had run over to me, to make sure I was okay. Nothing would ever be okay again and I knew that. I yelled at father for making us what we were, but all he could do was tear up. My mother's spell had rendered him paralyzed where he stood.

I made my way back over to where my mother was, looking at her long and hard. I realized that this was no longer my mother, it was the evil entity that had formed from the flames. They were one and the same. I didn't know what to do. I hated everything to do with magic and at that moment, more than ever, I knew I was going to have to use what magic I had, to rid my family of this evil. My grandmother had always told me, I was the light in the darkness and I had never quite understood what she meant by that, until that night. I made myself conjure all my magical strength and I pushed it through my hands, willing it to go away. Instead, a white light emanated from my fingers and when I pushed at mother, for her to stop, she flew into the fire. The flames screamed, turning from red, to blue, then to orange and back to red, all while the entity and my mother were still one, they separated into two, but they were dying together, or so I thought.

I killed my mother, or the shell of my mother. That person wasn't the mother I knew. After that night, I vowed never to use my magic again, for as long as I lived. I had put away the family book of spells into a wooden trunk and I hadn't gotten it out, until last month.

Before Kris and I got married, or even engaged, I had told him of my past, because I didn't want any secrets between us. He was fine with it, as long as I'd never use magic again. Of course, he revised that after I begged him to let me use it last month, but it was for good, not evil."

Eva watched Jake's face as he was processing the information she'd just divulged. She knew this might take a while, so she remained silent and waited for him to speak.

He flopped down on the leather couch next to her, blew out an excessive amount of air that he'd been holding in and looked at her. He just sat there and stared at her.

"Jake?" Eva felt anxious all of a sudden.

He remained silent for a beat.

"I'm sorry. I was just trying to picture this whole scene in my head. It sounds so much like something you'd see in a movie or read in a fictional book. This was your life Eva, really?"

She didn't blame him for being skeptical. It did sound far fetched to a normal human, but where she came from, it was anything but normal. She made it her mission, the day she and Kris had children, that they would have the most normal and carefree life. Up until a month ago they had succeeded in doing just that. Now look at her.

"Yes, that was my upbringing, until I met Kris, that is. I had not opened the trunk that housed my family's spell book, since I'd put it in there, December 21, 1989. I broke my promise that I made myself. I want my normal back, in the worst way Jake. I had not had dreams like I had tonight and the couple I had a month back, of visiting my mother, until I reopened my past.

She had opened a veil of evil the night she died, but from what I can gather, that veil hasn't closed back up with her death. It's just laid dormant, until recently. And because she is dead, it wants me."

"You're serious, aren't you?"

"Yes. You might not believe in such things, because you've never seen them with your own eyes, but true demonic evil exists. I know you've seen your share of this ugly world, but I'm not sure it's the same thing I'm dealing with. You never know though. It all could be one in the same. The devil himself, or those associated with him may inhabit people you see and they move on to the next one, causing this vicious cycle of crime and death."

Jake didn't know what the hell was going on. He wasn't sure if he was dreaming and he'd wake up and they would go on and continue with the investigation or what. Can it be real that there are such things as witches and demons? So many unanswered questions and he didn't like it. He knew one thing for certain, Eva was scared and tormented by what she had dreamt and he had to keep her from totally shutting down and leaving him to figure this all out on his own. She told him things that he had no way of getting evidence for, at least not without her.

"Listen Eva, I can't begin to understand what your life was like. I'm not going to pretend I'll ever get it, but you're here now and you're safe. Kris will do everything in his power to keep you and your family safe and I will too." He held his arms open for her. "Come here."

Eva was thanking her lucky stars that Jake wasn't calling the paddy wagon to come get her. She thought for sure she was going to be spending some time in a pink padded room after what she had told him of her past. And now, his arms were open to her. He wanted to show her that she was truly safe there. She inched closer to Jake on the couch and let him hold her tight. There was nothing inappropriate about his gesture, it was almost brotherly. She felt it. Eva always wanted this type of relationship with her own family, but alas, it would never happen and she had already accepted that truth, long ago.

Chapter 32

Eva woke up early, rubbing her still tired eyes.

"Morning sleepyhead."

"Morning Jake. What time is it," she asked.

"10:00."

Eva shot to her feet and started running around the room.

"Oh my gosh, ten? Why didn't you wake me up?"

"I thought you needed the extra sleep, especially after last night."

He looked at her wearily.

Eva stopped short, pressing a hand to her forehead, "so that whole thing wasn't a dream, I actually did tell you everything about my past?"

He nodded, "yes, and I'm glad you did. It helps me to understand this whole thing a little more, not that I completely understand how you can do what you do, but you know what I mean."

"I'm sorry I woke you last night and freaked you out. You're probably wishing Kris had stayed here with me, huh?"

"Don't apologize. I'm glad I was here and you weren't by yourself. You seemed genuinely upset by the dream you had."

"It's always disturbing when I dream of my mother. What she says to me in my dreams, has been known to happen."

Her statement made Jake's jaw tighten. He didn't think that was a good sign, at all. He decided to change the subject, instead of asking more questions."

"Well, why don't you go get ready and we'll go into town for a little bit, before I have to meet my team."

"Where are we going?"

"I'm taking you to find your Derby hat, of course. I figured we would check out that shop that Penelope mentioned, Frome' something. You can't go to the Kentucky Derby without a cool lid," he said, laughing.

"A lid? Funny. But, you don't have to take me shopping again. I can find the shop myself. You've already done so much with me..."

"Stop! Go get ready. That's an order... sort of."

Eva smiled back at him, grabbed her clothes and toiletries, then headed for the bathroom to get her shower.

While Eva was getting ready, Jake decided to give Kris a call. Kris picked up on the second ring, hesitation is voice.

"Jake, what's wrong? Did something happen to Eva?"

"Good morning to you, too."

"Sorry, I'm a little on edge."

"It's okay. Eva is fine. Nothing is wrong. You good now?"

"Yeah. What's up? I know you're not calling just to shoot the breeze."

"Well, I was curious actually. Eva had a pretty bad nightmare last night that had to do with her mother. I was wondering if this was normal? She was really freaked out."

Kris was silent for a beat, before answering. "She told you it was about her mother?"

"Yeah, then she proceeded to tell what happened to her mother, as well. That was heavy stuff."

"Hmm... she must really trust you. She wouldn't tell just anyone about her past. Is she okay? I knew I should have stayed at the ranch with you guys. I want to talk to her, make sure she's okay."

"Kris, she is fine, but she's getting ready at the moment. I can tell her to call you when she's done. Question... have you ever seen her do what she does?"

"Once. I wouldn't have believed it, if I hadn't seen it. She had been followed one night on her way home from work, I think I told you this story... Anyway, I was on the phone with her when it was happening. I immediately got in my car and made my way to where she was driving, to see if I could get a license plate or the make of the car. The car tried running me off the road when it determined I was with her. It wasn't successful and I ended up running the other car into an embankment."

"You may have told me about this. Did you guys go to the police?"

"I'm getting to that. We did go to the police, right after it happened and told them that the car was in the embankment, but of course, by the time they got there, the driver was gone and the VIN# on the car proved to be crap, so there wasn't much they could do. Well, my darling wife had other plans and would find out her own way. That was the first and last time I saw her do magic. She found a spell in her family book. After we purchased the supplies she needed, we went back to the embankment, that same night. Eva started to perform the spell and it was the strangest thing I'd ever seen. Jake, the person who had been driving the car appeared in the driver's seat. I took a picture and everything. I didn't know what to think."

"Dude… that's almost as crazy as the one she did last night."

"You were with her," he asked, more surprised, than questioning.

"Yes. I had a part to play in the spell. It was interesting, scary, terrifying, cool and intense, all at the same time."

Jake kept the fact that Eva had a little trouble coming out of it, to himself. He figured Kris had enough to worry about.

Kris was silent on the other end, then asked, "did she find anything useful?"

"Yes, but I can't say what it is, just yet. Sorry."

"I get it. She told me she couldn't tell me either, but I thought maybe you'd tell me anyway. I hope this all over soon. I'd like to have my wife back, man."

"Me, too. This is a weird one, that's for sure. I really do appreciate everything you both are doing, though. I am taking her shopping this morning, for a Derby hat. Apparently that's a thing."

Kris stifled a laugh. "You're taking Eva shopping? Good luck with that."

"What? I took her shopping for a dress yesterday. It went fine. She's pretty easy going, isn't she?"

"For the most part, yes, but you haven't been married to her for twenty years, and don't have kids to parent. You're getting the temporary Eva. The one away from kids and household duties, etc. I love her more than life itself Jake. Please keep her safe and behave yourself. She's easy to love."

Jake thought about that last statement for a second. She was easy to love, that was true, but she was also his friend's wife, whom he needed to protect.

"I gotta go, she should be ready soon and after I take her shopping, I have to meet with my guys on the next plan of attack. We're waiting on some blood results. I hope they come back today."

"Alright, good luck with the shopping and have her call me when she gets a chance, okay?"

"Will do. Talk to you later."

They both hung up simultaneously.

Jake sat on the couch for a minute, enjoying the silence when Eva emerged from the bathroom. She wore black skinny jeans with rips in the legs, a gray fuzzy sweater and black heeled boots. Her hair was up in a messy bun on top of her head, her make up was done and she wore a few tasteful pieces of jewelry. He thought she looked great, but not overdone. She didn't look like a mom to Jake.

Jake thought, this is probably what Kris meant when he said he had the temporary Eva. The Eva that got to take her time to get ready and do her makeup or whatever else she was doing in there. This was probably not the Eva that had to take care of two kids, get meals ready, keep the house cleaned, and help with homework.

Jake stood up and walked over to her, "Are you ready to go hat shopping," he said with a genuine smile.

"Can we get something to eat real quick first?"

"Absolutely. I think Penelope has some things in the kitchen, that she leaves out for guests. We can go see if there's anything good. If we don't see anything, we can pick something up on our way into town. How does that sound?"

"Works for me."

They headed for the kitchen, where Eva hoped to find at least some coffee. That was high on her priority list at the moment. When they didn't find any, Jake suggested they go get coffee and a quick breakfast sandwich from a fast food place.

Chapter 33

Breakfast ended up being on the go and that was fine with Eva. She desperately needed coffee, and a big one at that. After her mother showed up, yet again in her dream, and she had to relive her horrid past with Jake, she didn't sleep too well.

"So where to first," he asked, shaking her out of her thoughts.

"I thought we were just going to the hat store."

"Well, since I have a couple of hours until my meeting, I didn't know if there was anything else you wanted to see, or do, before I have to drop you back at the ranch."

"The hat store is good. Besides, I wanted to do some research on a few things this afternoon anyway."

"Penelope gave the name of another hat store downtown, besides Frome' Millinery; there's also Secret Beauty Hats, too. She said they do trunk shows downtown near the track this week. We can stop there first, then head to Frome', if you'd like."

"Sounds interesting, but you don't have to cart me around you know."

"I know I don't, but I'd like to get out a little, too and get some fresh air before I have to go back to work.

"Okay, that sounds good. Hats must be a big thing for this event. I love hats, but mostly straw hats or wool fedora's. You know, the gangster hats," she said, laughing.

The sound of her laugh was something that made Jake immediately smile. He liked to hear her laugh.

"You mentioned wanting to do some research, what kind of research are you wanting to do, if you don't mind me asking?"

"Oh, I was going to see what I could find on Kai Armstrong and Chloe. I'm sure you already have plenty, but I wanted to check their social media accounts, if they have any. I'm sure Chloe does, she seems like the type that would post every ten minutes."

"That's not a bad idea, but you don't need to do that. I can have one of our computer geeks look into them. I don't want anything traced back to you, okay?"

"It's something I feel compelled to do. Let's just say I'm going on a hunch from my mother and leave it at that."

Jake didn't dissuade her anymore and decided to let it go. He wasn't thrilled with her nosing around on her own, but kept his mouth shut. He found that in the short amount of time he'd spent with Eva, she would do what she wanted anyway.

They drove in comfortable silence for a couple of miles, until they saw what they assumed was the trunk show, set up under a large white tent across from Churchill Downs.

Jake pulled in and they both exited the car. They walked the distance to the tent, where there had to have been easily a thousand hats on display, for the picking. They had small ones, medium, large, extra large and, where is the person's face sized hats, and even intricate headbands.

Jake found himself in foreign territory here and let Eva lead the way. He watched her look over some of the more subdued looking hats, and he gave his opinion on a few that she had tried on. She walked to this one display that had a large black hat with a huge flower in the front. She picked it up and put it on her head, looking into a full length mirror near them. A sales lady came over to them, checking Eva out in the mirror.

"That one looks stunning on you. That one is called "The Winner". This one is designed in black lace with a spray of black dazzling sequins, with a ten inch silk lavender flower, to make it really pop. What do you think?"

Eva stood staring at the huge hat on her head and didn't know what to think of it.

"It's very pretty," she said, hoping she wouldn't offend the lady.

"What type of dress are you planning on wearing to the Derby, dear?"

"Oh, it's just a classic little black dress."

"Do you happen to have a picture of it? I can get a better idea of what would look good and we can go from there."

"I don't, sorry."

Jake piped up, "here, I have a one," he said, surprising Eva.

"Remember, that gentleman from the Press Party took one of us last night honey," he smiled.

She had totally forgotten. Last night had seemed more like a week ago, not less than 24 hours.

He showed the lady the picture on his phone. She took in the picture of the two of them, and looked up at Eva wearing the hat, then back at the picture.

"You two are a lovely looking couple. I'm not sure if that particular hat would do with that dress though. Let's see if there are any others you might like."

Eva looked in Jake's direction and stifled a laugh. *Lovely couple… if she only knew.*

After trying on twenty or so hats in all shapes, sizes and colors, Eva said she would think about it and come back later. She wanted to see what Frome' had as well, before making her decision. The hats were pricey and she didn't want to get just any old hat.

Once they were settled back in Jake's car, she asked, "I hope you don't mind taking me to the other shop. I just wanted to see what they have. Those hats aren't cheap. If I'm going to be spending over $200 on a hat, I want a unique one."

"I don't mind at all, I have some time yet. By the way, you are not paying for the hat, I am. It's the least I can do. I mean, you're getting paid through the bureau, too, but I want to do this. It's not like I have anyone else to buy stuff for, ya know."

"I can't let you do that Jake, I'd feel weird."

"Would it help if I got Kris' permission?"

He looked over at her and he was dead serious, he'd call Kris to get his permission.

Her chin hitched up and she looked indignant. "I don't need Kris' permission for anything, thank you."

He had to diffuse the situation quickly, she mistook what he was saying.

"I didn't mean that way. I just meant.."

She held up a hand, stopping him from going all flustered with his reasons. "I know, I'm sorry. I get a little nuts when people don't think I can take care of things myself. I know you meant it to be a kind gesture."

He breathed a sigh of relief, "then you'll let me buy you your hat? Please."

She looked at the desperation on his face and she couldn't exactly deny him. "Okay, but this is the last thing you buy me." She gave him a hint of a smile.

When they pulled in front of Frome' Millinery Hat Shop, there was a line out the door, just to enter.

"Oh, look at that line, maybe we should go back and get the other hat."

"No, we're going to check this place out. If there's that big of a line, there must be something good in there."

They went to the end of the line and stood waiting to get in. The line moved rather quickly, so it didn't take long for them to make it to the entrance. Once they were inside the store, it was hats here, there and everywhere. Jake thought the other place had a lot of hats. This place was like the Costco of hats.

They walked around the store for a while and after Eva had tried on a multitude of hats, she had narrowed it down to three. The first one was called the "Night Owl." This particular one, she learned, was a hand-blocked hat, with a black velour flip brimmed, with vintage white trim, circular horsehair and a black velvet bow, and it was a whopping $475. The second one she saved was called the "Black Speakeasy." It was beautiful. It was also hand-block made, in black and tan with a flipped brim, with feathers and the Frome' gold-plated logo emblem. The lady said it was a one of a kind piece. She also mentioned that it was made on a hand-block that was over 100 years old. Eva had no clue what that meant or the significance, but when she looked at the price, she nearly choked. The hat was priced at $550. Jake told her not to pay attention to the price tags.

She tried on the third hat she had set aside, again. This one was called, "The Red Ruby". It was a large red parasisal brim with curled feathers to add a fun flare. This particular hat priced out at $485. She looked into the big mirror and was turning from side to side, getting the different angles of how the hat looked. She spoke into the mirror at Jake. "So, which of the three do you think looks best?"

He made a face that looked like he was truly thinking about which hat looked best and he finally smiled and said, "I think the black one that had the tan feathers and had the flippy up brim, and the gold emblem. The Speak-Easy, I think it was called."

Of course he picked the most expensive one and the one that was a one of a kind.

"Really?" She grabbed the hat he was talking about and placed it back on her head again, for a second look. "You think this one looked the best," she asked.

"I do. Why, do you not like that one? You know I don't know much about these things, right? I'm kind of flying by the seat of pants with this whole wardrobe thing."

He had overheard a few ladies comment on the hat when Eva had tried it on the first time and they had been quite complementive about her in it, so he figured that was the one. He thought she was definitely a hat person, unlike some of the women he'd seen trying on some of the fancy hats.

Eva looked at herself again in the mirror, with the Black Speak-Easy hat on. She did the same turning from side to side, as she had done with the others. It was a stunning hat. She felt pretty and sophisticated wearing it. She just couldn't believe how expensive it was. That fact still gnawed at her.

Jake stepped up behind her and she saw him in the mirror looking like he was wanting to ask her something. "What?"

"Oh nothing. I was just wondering if you were going to wear your hair up or down for the Derby?"

He then took it upon himself to remove the hat and take the elastic she had holding her hair in it's messy bun out. Her hair fell around her. She messed with it a little while still looking into the mirror.

"I guess I'd probably wear it down, but I'll curl it or something. I just put it up real quick so we could leave, today."

"It's cute in the whole bun thing, too. I just wondered if you'd want to see the hat on with your hair down, as well. Sorry, I should have asked before I took your stretching thing out."

She smirked at him, "It's fine. I should see what it looks like with my hair down. It might not look right."

Jake still had the hat in his hand, so he stepped closer to her and she turned around to face him, thinking he would give her the hat, but instead, he placed the hat on her head and began moving some of her hair around before turning her back around to the mirror to see.

"What do you think," he asked. "This is still my personal favorite," he stated.

She stared at herself for a brief moment and her face had that giddy look.

"Yep, this is the one, definitely."

"Perfect."

Jake called the sales lady back over and told her they had made their choice. He asked if they had a box that they could put it in, so it wouldn't get ruined. She was ecstatic with their choice and had told Eva that she'd overheard other ladies commenting on how she looked in the hat.

"I'll take this in the back and wrap it and then box it for you. We have beautiful hat boxes that we put all of our hats in. The box is included in the price, too. Just remember to take the tissue paper out of the hat, before you put it on. I'll meet you both at the front desk."

"Thank you, Ma'am."

"Such a polite young man," she said to Eva. "You're a lucky lady."

Eva smiled and nodded at the lady in agreement.

Jake looked down at her, smiling his teasing smile, "You're a lucky lady, did ya hear that?"

"You can be a real goofball, you know that?" She was enjoying this side of him. They had far too much time to be serious and she found this side of him rather endearing.

They made their way to the front desk, but not without a couple of ladies commenting to Eva on how amazing the hat she picked out looked on her. It wasn't that she wasn't used to getting a compliment here and there, but it was a bit overwhelming to have a bunch at once. Her cheeks were turning a bright red, she was sure of it. She was polite and thanked them, then waited patiently with Jake at the front.

"See, I told you that was the perfect hat," he said all proud.

"I can't believe I'm actually doing this. We're going to the Kentucky Derby and getting all dolled up. This is nuts!"

"It's all part of the job," he whispered.

"Okay, but what if the job is over and done with before the Derby? Then what? You just spent a pretty penny on a hat for me, that I may not even get to wear."

"Oh, we're still going, no matter what."

"Hunnh…"

Chapter 34

After dropping Eva off at the ranch, Jake headed to the Louisville Field office to meet with his team, who had been keeping tabs on Chloe and Kai for the last 24 hours. He was anxious to hear if anything came of it.

Jake was a little nervous about leaving Eva to her own devices. He knew from past experience that she was quite resourceful and that worried him more than anything.

Once he pulled into the parking lot, Jake's phone rang. He picked it up, and it was the lab.

"What do you mean the blood sample wasn't human? Was it an animal's blood," Jake questioned the man on the other end.

Jake listened to the lab tech for a second, before he jumped in.

"Hold up. Before you go into the whole thing, are you close by, by chance? I'd like you to bring the results to the field office ASAP. I have my whole team here for a meeting. I think we all need to hear this and understand it a little better."

As the lab tech agreed to meet him and his team, Jake exited his car, shaking his head in confusion. *This has to be the weirdest case ever,* he thought.

Jake found his whole team sitting around a conference table, waiting for him.

"Hey everyone. Before we start the meeting, I have the lab tech from Forensics coming down to meet us. He will go over the blood analysis report from the blood taken at Chloe Rivers apartment."

One of his teammates piped up, "why, was there something wrong with the sample? Why couldn't he give you the information over the phone?"

"I'd rather you all hear what he has to say before I say anymore, if that's okay."

They all looked around the room, whispers of questions floating up to him. He felt their anxiety. This wasn't normal and he wasn't saying anything until the lab guy did his explanation.

He asked the two guys to his right, "anything of interest happen overnight, while you guys were watching Kai and Chloe?"

"Not much. Mr. Armstrong did show up at Miss Rivers apartment last night, but he just dropped her off. He proceeded to go back to his room at the Inn at St. James. It was maybe a half hour later that he came back out and headed back to Miss Rivers' apartment, but no other movement out of them after that. We still have a car on them though."

Jake smirked, "they probably noticed things were a little out of place at both of their residences. Too bad for them, that they both stay in publicly owned buildings and with warrants, we don't need their permission to enter, huh?"

A knock on the door to the conference room, stopped everyone's conversation and they all looked up to see an older gentleman wearing a lab coat, holding a large manilla envelope in hand. He held it up, hoping to get Jake's attention.

"Dr. Proctor, come in. Take a seat right over there." Jake pointed to the empty seat across from him. "If you wouldn't mind, please explain what your findings were, to all of us."

Jake introduced the gentleman as Dr. Davis Proctor, Head of Forensics, for The Jefferson Laboratory.

"Dr. Proctor, could you go over the report with us. I need a better understanding of what you mentioned to me on the phone."

"Of course." He opened his envelope and took out a thick pile of papers that looked like lab reports. "As I told Mr. Long earlier, the blood we tested ended up not being human blood."

There was a flurry of questions being thrown around the room.

Jake held up one hand, "hey, let him finish."

"Thank you. As I was saying, we found the blood to not be human. But, we also did a Raman Spectroscopy, which is a test that shows if the blood is animal. We use the PLSDA model, it stands for (partial least squares discriminant analysis) which differentiates the blood between human and animal. Now, you know human blood contains proteins called antigens and animals do not carry such proteins. What we have here is neither human nor animal and it is unknown to any lab analysis available to anyone. I've sent the rest of the sample via FedEx to the lab in Quantico to see if they can come up with anything."

"Okay, so this is the first time you've seen this? Is that what you're trying to say, Proctor," Jake asked.

Jake couldn't hide his frustration, even if he tried.

"Yes sir, that is what I'm saying. I've never seen anything like this in my thirty five years of experience."

"When did you mail out the sample that was left over to Quantico?"

"I sent it first thing this morning. They should receive it no later than tomorrow morning."

"I'll contact them as soon as we're done here, to have them put a rush on it. Thank you for your time Dr. Proctor."

The doctor stood to leave and walked over to Jake, they shook hands and he led the gentleman to the door. Jake re-entered the conference room to a barrage of questions from his colleagues, that he had no answers to.

"Everyone! I'm sorry, we have no definitive answers and I sure as hell got nothing, after that. I don't even know where to go from here. Has anyone gotten any useful information off the social media accounts of Chloe or Kai?"

One of the tech analysts spoke up, "there was a lot of activity on both Facebook accounts up until last week, then both accounts had gone dormant. Chloe especially; she had at least twenty posts a day before that. For it to go to nothing, is quite odd."

"That is really odd, for a college student. I wonder what that's about?" He thought that over briefly. "What about Kai's accounts?"

"He wasn't as active on social media, but there would be at least one post a day, again, until last week, then nothing since."

"Check in with the guys that are keeping a watch on them and let me know if anything comes up. I'm heading back to the ranch, to talk to Chloe's mother, Penelope. Call me the minute any of you get anything new."

They all nodded, stood, and left the conference room. Jake headed back out to his car, to go back to the ranch, beyond frustrated.

Chapter 35

Eva was sitting at her laptop in the main living area of the main house, when Juliette and Brett came in, holding hands. They looked happy with each other and that made her smile.

"Hi there you two," Eva said. "No training today, Juliette?"

"We were out on the track for three hours, earlier. We just came in to grab a sandwich. How's your day going?"

"So far so good. Jake took me into town earlier so I could find the perfect hat to wear to the Derby. I never knew it was such a big deal to dress to the hilt for the Kentucky Derby," she said, smiling.

Brett asked, "where did you go, I know of a few millineries downtown?"

"We went to the trunk show across from Churchill Downs, then went to Frome', which is where I found the perfect hat."

"Nice. Frome's has the best selection and some of the celebrities that come to town for the Derby always go there. You'll fit right in, I'm sure. Big hats and bigger mint juleps are a Derby staple," Brett pointed out, with a smile. "Have you ever had the signature Mint Julep yet?"

"No, I haven't had the pleasure. Where could I get one? Are they only at the Derby?"

"Oh no, they have them at all the restaurants in town, as well. Louisville is known for them. You should have your husband take you to Proof on Main for dinner while you're in town. They have an eclectic menu and a full array of bourbons, if you like that, but their Mint Juleps are legendary."

"Wow, sounds expensive."

"It's a little more upper crust, but well worth it. I should take you there, Juliette. How about we all go tonight? I can call and make a reservation for four, if you want."

Juliette got all giddy with excitement at the idea of going to a high end restaurant with Brett. The party last night was formal, but it was full of reporters and they didn't have time to truly enjoy the night together. She had been fielding question after question.

"Brett, do you think they'd still have open reservations for tonight, being it's such short notice and only a couple days from the Derby," Juliette asked.

"I'll make a few calls. It should be fine. Eva, do you think Jake would be fine with going to dinner tonight?"

"I'll ask him when he gets back. He's at the field office now."

"Okay, just let us know. I'll make the reservation for four, just be on the safe side."

"Sounds like fun, thanks."

They both waved goodbye to Eva and headed for the kitchen.

Eva went back to her search. She had been checking out all of Chloe and Kai's Social Media pages, looking for anything out of the ordinary. So far, all she found was that

Chloe had been the typical college student and displayed her whole life online, which in her opinion wasn't that smart. She had been pretty quiet that last week though, which she thought was odd. Kai on the other hand was not on as much. A few posts here and there, but nothing strange or unusual that would indicate a murderer. His posts had also stopped about a week ago.

She was just about to close down her laptop when she thought to check out Phillipe's Social Media accounts, too.

His Facebook showed a lot of pictures of him and his beautiful horse. Not many family pictures were posted, she noticed. Of course, there were the typical pictures of him and loads of pretty ladies from the races he had won, but not much else, to indicate anything unusual.

Jake came in through the front door and Eva noticed the grim line in his jaw. She knew something was wrong.

"Jake, you're back."

He hadn't even noticed Eva sitting at the table with her laptop. He walked over to her, wondering what she was up to and almost afraid to ask, after his earlier meeting.

"Hey. What are you doing all by yourself down here?"

She smiled that brilliant smile that always took him off guard, "oh nothing, just playing on my laptop. How was your meeting?"

"I'll tell you later. Right now, I'm a little hungry. Want to come in the kitchen with me to see if there's anything out?"

"Sure, but don't eat too much. Brett and Juliett asked us to go to a restaurant called Proof on Main for dinner, if you're able to, that is? I told them it would be up to you and your schedule."

He took her hand and pulled her away from her laptop, "We should be able to go to dinner with them. Would you like to do that," he asked, now smiling at her.

It was hard for him not to smile when he was around her. He didn't know what it was about her that made him turn to mush and emotions. Jake wasn't sure he liked it. She was taking away his edge.

"If you're able to go, I don't see any reason why we shouldn't. Maybe we can casually question them a little, too."

Jake let out a bark of laughter and slung an arm around her shoulder, walking them toward the kitchen. "You mean, I'll get to question them."

"Hey, it'll be less obvious if it was me that asked them questions, than you interrogating them, don't you think?"

Damn it, I wish she would not make so much sense, sometimes. Jake was thinking she might be onto something, but he'd have to think about it.

"I'll think about it. Can we eat first, I'm starving."

"You're as bad as my kids, when it comes to eating all the time," she laughed.

"Maybe I'm still a growing boy."

She looked him over and saw only hard muscle and a trim physique. She wondered where he put all his calories.

"Do you workout a lot, or do you have one of those naturally disgusting fast metabolisms?"

"I workout, but not everyday. I usually don't have time to do much, but a 5K run in the morning."

"Ugh, you're one those."

Jake stifled a laugh, "one of whom?"

"One who can eat whatever, do little exercise, and still be thin. It's not fair, ya know. I mean, I birthed two kids, I'm never going to have my pre-Mom body back, no matter what I do."

"Who says you look bad?"

"Me. I say I look bad."

"Well, don't say that."

"Ah, shut up."

He kept his smirk in place and kept his mouth shut, walking her to the kitchen. Penelope left sandwiches, a vegetable and fruit tray, along with a pitcher of lemonade on the Island.

They each grabbed half of a turkey and cheese sandwich, some fruit and veggies, and a drink. Eva retrieved her laptop and they took their food back to their room.

While they shared a quiet lunch, Jake wanted to touch base with Eva, to make sure she was hanging in there, but her phone started ringing. The way she answered the call, he knew it was Kris.

He felt bad being in the room, listening to their conversation, but it made him realize what a lucky couple they were. They truly loved each other. And that made

Jake want to re-evaluate his whole life. Will he ever find that kind of love, or was he really already married to the job?

After Eva hung up, she eyed Jake and the weary look on his face. Something was wrong, she thought.

"Penny for your thoughts."

He hadn't realized she'd hung up.

"Oh hey. I'm just off in a zone, sorry. How's Kris doing?"

She didn't buy it, but didn't press him either. "He's fine. A little bored, I think. I told him to go on the bourbon trail thing they have down here. He likes different kinds of bourbon and whiskey. That would give him something to do. And he's always asking me if you're behaving yourself, what's up with that," she asked.

"He's paranoid you're going to fall head over heels in love with me and I'll take you away."

He was joking, of course, but not by much, he'd bet money on it.

"That's ridiculous!"

Jake shrugged, then smiled a devilish grin, "can you blame the guy?"

Eva shook her head and laughed out loud.

"Alright, back to work. Did you find anything out when you went to the office?"

Jake gave her a grim look.

"You did find something out, what is it," she pressed.

"Sort of, but not really. Does that make sense?"

"Not even a little."

"Okay. Here's the thing... I had the head of The Jefferson Lab come down with the blood analysis results, so he could go over them with all of us, and what he told us, wasn't helpful at all, but it was also very strange."

"Strange, how?"

"The blood was neither human, nor animal."

He sat there and let her process that for a moment, before he continued. She had a little wrinkle in her nose that told him she was just as confused as the rest of them.

Yeah, so he sent the rest of the sample to Quantico, to see if they could make heads or tales of it."

"Hmm, that's not normal. Oooh, maybe it was an alien."

"Really?"

"Just a thought."

"Yeah well, we left those buggers in Roswell. Anyway, it's just annoying the crap out of me that we can't find anything definitive in this case. You saw what you saw, but I can't figure out how and where it took place, or what they used to do it. I know it was a blunt object, that's all I've got to go on. And until the coroner is finished with Phillipe, I got nothing."

Eva looked at him, still stuck on the Roswell comment. Was he serious or just messing with her? She put that remark on the back burner for another time.

"Okay, let's think about it for a second. Is there any way you can get me into Chloe's apartment?"

"Maybe, why?"

"If the murder occurred inside her apartment, I can perfom a spell there and we may get to see where they did it, and with what. If we can find out what they used, it would be a lot easier for me to locate it. In my own special way, that is."

Jake thought that scenario over in his head. He wasn't sure he could watch her do anymore spells. The first one was hard enough to watch.

Eva noticed that he was battling with himself, when she muttered, "it won't be like the last one, I promise."

He jerked his head up, "how'd you know what I was thinking?"

"It wasn't hard to tell, what with the pained look on your face and all."

"Am I always that easy to read?" That made him very nervous, considering his job was to consistently have his poker face on.

"No, I've just gotten used to your facial expressions. Normally I can't read people, but since we've gotten fairly close over the last couple of days, it's made it easier."

He wasn't too sure that made him feel any better. He was going to have to reign in his emotions better. Jake wasn't one to wear his heart on his sleeve, or give away any kind of emotion. This whole conversation was disconcerting to him and he needed a break from Eva St. Claire, and soon.

He stood up abruptly and headed for his suitcase, grabbing a pair of running pants, a t-shirt and his running shoes, and went to the bathroom to change.

Eva wasn't sure what was wrong, "Jake? Is everything okay?"

"I'm fine. I think I need to go for a run that's all."

He was dressed and out the door within five minutes, leaving Eva a little concerned and confused.

"What did I say?" She felt a lump in her throat. She wasn't going to cry. This wasn't anything she did, she knew that. *He just needed some fresh air, that's all.*

Chapter 36

Jake ran hard and fast, trying to gain his composure back. He felt he was losing his edge and all because of one small little woman. How could he let that happen. What was he thinking bringing her and Kris here, into this investigation?

His thoughts were muddled and not clear. That's why he was out here running like a madman. Running always cleared his mind, brought him back to the here and now, and he needed a clear head, or this would all fall apart, and fast.

He had his phone clipped to the inside of jacket, so when he stopped running, he pulled it out and dialed. His guy Jason answered on the second ring. "Hey, is there any way we can get Chloe out of her apartment, without her suspecting anything?"

"Probably. We still have the warrant for all of the locations we went to yesterday."

"It's still a viable warrant?"

"I believe so."

"Double check, just to be on the safe side, for me." A plan was starting to form in his head.

"You got it Jake."

"Perfect. I'm going to need that warrant later. I'll be out with Eva, Brett and Juliette for dinner tonight. I may do a little light questioning with them, but if you could drop off the warrant before 5pm, at the ranch, that would be great man."

After disconnecting from the call, Jake continued his run, feeling a little better. He had a plan and yes, he was taking Eva with him, so she could do her hocus-pocus. He might not like the idea, but he had her here for a job and he was going to use her for it. He was getting too emotionally involved with her and that wasn't good for him.

Jake vowed to continue with the charade, but he wouldn't show her emotion when they were alone. It was making him question things he wasn't ready to delve into.

He made it back to the ranch before four, to grab a shower, before they went to dinner.

He unlocked the door to their room, but Eva was nowhere inside. Jake thought he should've been relieved, but he felt uneasy instead. She was probably down in the main living area again, he thought.

Jake jumped in the shower and figured he'd look for her after that.

Chapter 37

Eva went off on her own, to get some fresh air and to put some distance between her and Jake. She saw him running down the main driveway, towards the ranch and she took off. She went out the back door before he got to the front door.

She made her way down to where the barn was, which housed all of the horses. She peeked in, and when she found no one was inside, she went in. She walked past all the horse stalls, taking in the beautiful creatures, petting a couple as she went. They were very docile and friendly.

Eva loved horses, but wasn't an avid rider. The last time she was on a horse, she thought, had to have been when they lived in Arizona briefly. She remembered taking the kids to the White Mountains for a MOMS Club outing and they all got to ride a horse along a short trail.

While Eva was reliving memories, she failed to hear the barn door open and footsteps walking toward her.

She turned around and was face to face with Kai Armstrong. She flinched at the close proximity, but didn't make a move to leave.

"I'm sorry. I didn't realize anyone was out here. I hope I didn't frighten you," he crooned, in his British accent, which she now knew was fake.

"No, not at all. Kai, is it? I was just taking a walk around the grounds and thought I would come visit the horses. They truly are something."

"That they are. Are you out here by yourself? Where is your husband?"

"He's right here," Jake said, a little loud, startling them both.

They both turned toward the barn door at the far end and Jake was standing there, fresh from a shower, dressed in jeans, a button down shirt, navy blazer, oxford shoes and his .9 mm clipped to his belt. He looked drop dead gorgeous and lethal. His game face was back in place and Eva was thrilled to see him.

She ran over to him, a little too eager, and put her arms around him. "There you are. I've missed you."

He played it out and held her in his arms.

She then whispered, "I'm so glad you came out here."

He placed a chaste kiss on her forehead, his eyes never leaving Kai's.

Kai took a step forward, stopped, then thought better of it. "Well, I'll see you two later, I'm sure."

They both just nodded and didn't say a word, until he left.

"Oh my God, I've never been so happy to see you," she blurted out.

"I'm glad I decided to come out here looking for you. When I didn't see you anywhere inside the main building, I decided to start walking the grounds; that's when I saw Kai head in here. Did he say or do anything to you, before I got here?"

"No, but he really creeps me out. You heard pretty much everything, I think. I can't put my finger on it yet, but there is something about him that isn't quite right."

"He's a killer, that's what."

"Besides that Jake. It's something in his mannerisms. I've seen it before, but…" And then it hit her. Eva turned white as a ghost, as it dawned on her where she'd seen it before.

"Eva? What is it? What were you going to say?"

She wasn't answering him. He grabbed her shoulders and shook, "Eva!"

"No, no, no, no, it can't be. It just can't be," she cried.

"What!?"

She looked up at him, her hazel eyes filled with pure fear, that's the only way he could describe it.

"It's him, he's back, but he was dead, I saw it with my own eyes. How can he…"

"Eva, who are you talking about, you're starting to freak me out, damn it."

She looked up at Jake, tears running down her cheeks, "The Dagon."

Jake looked at her even more confused than before. "Who?"

"Remember last month, the evil entity that inhabited Girard? I think he's inside Kai. He's found me, once again. He's the one that tried to take over my mother. She warned me, in my dream, that it would stop at nothing until it had me, but it didn't register, not until just now." Her whole body started to shake. Her words came out shaky, "he's come back for me."

Jake pulled her into his arms and held her tight. "Are you sure? Is that even possible? I thought Girard was dead."

She mumbled into his chest, "Girards' body was dead, not the entity that inhabited him. Which means, the other one is probably inside Chloe."

Jake had no words. They stood there, holding onto each other in the middle of the barn for a few minutes, before Eva pulled back.

"Now we know. I need to research what we're dealing with here. We need to see if there is any possible way to permanently get rid of them this time. I'm not sure what happens to them once their host body dies."

"Their *host body?*"

"Let me put it to you this way… Kai is not exactly Kai anymore."

This has got to be a joke, he thought.

You're kidding, right?"

"No, I'm not kidding. I need to get back to my laptop and see if I can find anything that we can do to get rid of the Dagon, for good."

"What exactly is a Dagon?"

"A Dagon is a type of demon, and I know they exist. I've seen him three times now. Please know that I am not crazy, Jake."

He didn't think she was crazy, he just wasn't ready to admit that such things existed. Though it shouldn't surprise him, since he has seen some of the most horrible people ever to walk this earth.   He has seen what kind evil they are capable of.

"Okay, let's get back to the main house. What time are we supposed to go to dinner with Brett and Juliette?"

"Oh gosh, I completely forgot about that. I believe Brett was going to try for a 7pm reservation tonight, if he was able to get it."

Eva looked at her watch, "it's just 4:15 now, I've got some time to look into this."

They headed outside and walked at a good clip towards the ranch.   Eva was on a mission now.

Chapter 38

Heading to the steps to the front door, it swung open, and Brett was heading out, as they were coming up.

"Hey Jake, Eva... I was just looking for both of you. I was able to get a 7:00pm reservation at Proof on Main. Are you both still available to go to dinner with Juliette and I?"

Jake nodded, "sure, that sounds good. If anything should change, I'll let you know."

"Perfect, we'll meet you both here at 6:30, if that works?"

"Sounds good, thanks," Eva said.

"Okay, I'll see you then. I've got to go check on the horse's food and water supply."

Jake and Eva headed inside to their room. Eva was running up the steps with one thing on her mind and that was her need to find what it was going to take to get rid of The Dagon, once and for all.

Once inside their room, Eva wasted no time pulling her laptop out and bringing it to life. Jake kept quiet. He could see the determination in the set of her shoulders. He pulled out his own laptop and typed in "Dagon", to see if there was truly such a creature. And for the life of him, he couldn't believe the amount of sites on that exact name. He couldn't fathom what he was reading... *Dagon- Prince of Hell, one of the oldest demons that needs a body to possess, to walk the Earth. What the hell*, he thought.

Eva noticed the look on Jake's face, "you looked it up, didn't you?"

He gave her a startled look. "Yeah, how'd you know?"

"Your face never lies."

"Of course. It seems I lose any type of edge I have, when I'm around you."

"It's not that. You were your normal poker face when you confronted Kai. You looked... intimidating actually."

"Did I scare you?"

"Not me, no, but Kai wasn't sure what to do when you spoke up and you took him by surprise. I was sure he was going to show his true colors a second before you said something. I was really nervous. I never should have left the main house by myself. To be honest, I left when I saw you running toward the front door. I figured you needed some time away from me. I could tell you weren't in a very good mood when you left to go running, and I wanted to give you some space."

Jake was speechless. She read him perfectly and he didn't even know she was doing it. The one good take away, was when she said Kai was nervous by the look on his face. At least he can still appear to look like a hardass in front of the enemy.

"I'm sorry if I upset you so much that you felt the need to leave. I'm not used to having such strange emotions during an investigation. You make me feel things that I don't usually feel. Don't worry, they're not romantic feelings or anything, they're more of a protective nature. I want to keep you safe and happy. How dumb is that? Maybe I'm getting too old for this job."

Eva let out a small laugh, "you're not too old, and I'm flattered that you want to protect me. Actually, I was feeling the same thing. I feel like you're the big brother I never had. And Kris will be very happy that you have no romantic feelings for me whatsoever. It might be a dis towards me, but I'm okay with it. I don't have any romantic feelings for you either."

They both laughed and resigned to the fact that they just needed to get through the next few days, or however long it would be, until this murder was solved.

Jake looked up from his laptop, "I didn't mean that as a dis. I think you're very attractive, I'm not going to lie. But..."

This got a huge grin from Eva. "But... I'm your friend's wife and that would be wrong?"

"Something like that."

"Gotcha."

Eva went back to her research. She was able to find very little on getting rid of a Dagon. She went to her bag and pulled out her family spell book. She opened it and started searching the pages for anything on how to get rid of demons. She wasn't sure where to even start. The family book didn't have a table of contents.

Jake sat back and rested his eyes for a minute, hoping that would produce an idea. When it ceased to be helpful, he stood and walked over to the leather sofa where Eva was reading.

"Is this the book you get all your spells from?"

"It is. This book has been in my family since the 1600's. And before you even ask, yes a couple of family members were persecuted during the Salem Witch Trials."

"No kidding?"

"I wouldn't kid about that. Another reason I never wanted to use my *gifts*. People would think I'm a freak."

"I don't think you're a freak, you're unique. Have you found anything in there yet, that might help us?"

"Not yet, and it's frustrating as heck."

Jake had to stifle a laugh. He thought it was cute that Eva tried really hard not to swear. He guessed that it was the whole having kids that gave her such control. He thought he would definitely fail that one on the first day. Though he found himself trying really hard when he was around Eva, not to swear and he hadn't even realized he was doing it, until now.

"Oh, I think I may have found what I was looking for."

She read the spell to herself, and started making a list of what she would need to pull it off.

"I'll need to go buy a few things to make this work, but I think this might fit the bill."

"What do you need?"

She read the list of supplies out loud to him, "I'm not sure what a triangle of arts is. I'll have to look that up,and see if I can even get it. I may have to make one, myself."

She pulled her laptop out and searched for The Triangle of Arts. She found it immediately and pulled up a picture.

"Okay, this is easy enough. I have heard of this. It's also known as the Solomonic Triangle. It's a triangle of evocation. You can see I've not done a lot with summoning spirits. This is all new to me."

"What is the triangle for," Jake asked, curious.

"From what I can tell here, it's an equal triangular symbol, that has words or symbols of power on the outside and has a circle drawn on the inside. It's a tool used for evoking entities. The names that would go on the outside, are typically the 3 names of God; Tetragrammaton, Primeumaton and Anaphexeton, and then, it is also to spell Michael, split into three parts, (Mi-Cha-El), the center parts, between the triangle, and the circle. See how the triangle is shown here?"

"That's interesting. Do you know what it is supposed to do once you have this triangle thing made?"

"According to this, the symbol is to be placed outside the circle of magic and it's the place where I can evoke the entity. This is a must, to be able to do this safely. It is a tool that is supposed to keep the entity in a confined place, while interacting with him and it protects everyone around it, too." Eva read verbatim, from her family book, while Jake listened intently.

I think we should still see if we can get into Chloe's apartment. I want to do a spell to find out if that's where Phillipe was killed and what they used to do it. You need to be able to arrest them for his murder, then I can do the *Demon trap*. And pray to God it works."

"I'll give Jason a call. He was going to check on the warrants they had for her apartment. I wanted to see if the warrants had a "suspect has to be present" clause in it. I'd rather be able to go in when she's not there, so you can do your thing."

"Have I met Jason?'

"You've probably seen him when he and my team were here yesterday, but you haven't formally met him." Jake retrieved his cell phone and sent a quick text to Jason, to get an update.

Eva had lost all track of time, while she was researching and wanted to call Kris before they left for dinner. She knew he had to be getting bored.

"I'm just going to call Kris real quick before we go." She walked into the bathroom, since that was the only real place for any privacy.

Kris answered after the first ring. "Hey beautiful, how are you? Make any busts yet?"

"Ha ha... not yet, but I think we're getting close. What have you been up to all day?"

"I actually went out to explore a little. I found the Stitzel Weller Distillery. It's not far from downtown Louisville. It was a neat place."

Kris sounded excited and anxious to tell Eva of his experience, so she waited for him to dive into how his field trip went.

"They make Bulliet Frontier Whiskey there. I tried a few different types that they had on their tasting menu and I was partial to their Blenders Select, it's more along the lines of a Black Label Whiskey; higher end and pretty smooth going down. I ended up buying a bottle."

"I bet you were in Whiskey Heaven," Eva said, smiling. She was thrilled that he'd gotten out of the hotel.

"It was a cool place. I'll have to take you there sometime, after this is all over. Which reminds me, when is this all going to be over?" Eva could hear the smile over the phone, but he was also serious.

"Hopefully soon. We have a few things up our sleeve and hopefully we'll be able to try them later tonight, after dinner. We are heading out to dinner soon. Brett and Juliette wanted us to accompany them to a restaurant called "Proof on Main.""

"Sounds swanky. Jake still being a good boy? How's he handling the whole being married thing?"

"I hope it's not too swanky, I'm not dressed up for that. And yes, Jake is fine. I think we are more like brother and sister. He's got that whole overprotective thing going on. I'm not really sure how he's dealing with the married thing. He more or less just goes with it."

"Brother/Sister, I'm fine with." Kris laughed.

"Alright, I better be going. We have to meet them downstairs at 6:30. I hope you have a good night, and I'll keep you updated if anything else comes up. I love you."

"I love you, too… Always and Forever."

"Ditto," and she hung up.

When Eva emerged from the bathroom, Jake was on the phone, looking as if something significant had happened. He held up a finger to her, letting her know he'd be a minute.

"Sorry about that. Are you ready to go?"

"No problem. Is everything okay? You looked like something happened and you weren't happy about it."

"It's nothing. We are able to get into Chloe's apartment, without her being there, so that's a step in the right direction. I figure we'll go after we're done having dinner, if that's okay? I would really like to know where this murder took place. The sooner the better."

"Yeah, that's fine. Are we going to come back here, before we go to Chloe's, or should I pack my stuff into a bag and take it with us?"

"We'll go right from the restaurant, so you might want to pack whatever you're going to need."

Eva grabbed her purse and the backpack she brought. She threw the items she would need to perform the spell, into the backpack and made sure her cell phone was one her, as well.

They headed downstairs to meet Brett and Juliette. The two of them were already waiting at the front door, but it looked like Brett had just gotten there, so they hadn't been waiting long.

"Hey there, you two," Eva greeted them with a genuine smile. "I hope we haven't kept you waiting long."

Juliette piped up, "not at all, I had just come down not even a minute ago."

Brett held a hand out to her, and she took it eagerly. "Are we all ready to go?"

Jake took that as a sign that he should do the same and held his hand out to Eva. Taking it, she gave his hand a gente squeeze, that only he would notice and he smiled down at her.

"Are we going in one car, or two," Brett asked.

Jake turned to Eva, but answered Brett's question, "is it alright if we take two cars? I was thinking of taking Eva around downtown Louisville after."

"Yeah, sure that's fine." And by the look Brett gave Juliette, they were good with their decision.

Brett gave Jake the address of the restaurant, so he could put it in his GPS and they got into their cars and headed out.

Chapter 39

The drive to Proof on Main was an easy one and without much conversation, but Eva was fine with that. She could tell Jake had a lot on his mind and she didn't want to pry.

Proof on Main was a farm to table restaurant in the heart of Louisville. The interior boasted a modern eclectic array of busts and pin up photography, as well as objects and artwork from the personal collections of some prominent residents. Brett was giving them the whole back story.

The seating was a variety of tables and chairs, nothing matched. They had booths that were done in taupe velvet and the table was made of natural wood, stained a dark color and had wrought iron legs. Most likely locally made.

Eva looked around the restaurant in awe, after they were seated. The walls were adorned with a variety of wallpaper styles. Not one area had the same feel or look to it. It was bigger inside than it looked. They were told they could take it upon themselves to walk around and check out the art that was on display, too. The hostess said that the artwork gets changed out every few months, so there is always something new to look at.

They were seated in a booth that was made partially table and two chairs and part booth style seating. Brett and Juliette took the two chairs, which left the booth seating for Jake and Eva. Jake was good with that, as he didn't like having his back facing an open area. Too much room for surprise. He liked seeing what was coming at him.

"Wow, this is quite a unique place," Eva said. "What do you suggest, besides the mint julep to drink? What food have you tried here, that's good?"

Brett had his menu open, "I've been here a few times. I'm friends with the chef. He's amazing, The Braised Beef Short Ribs are exquisite, but so is the Char Grilled Pork Chop. I personally feel like a Bison Burger. It's done perfectly, every time."

"Jake, what are you going to get?" Eva was having a hard time choosing what she wanted for dinner.

"The Bison burger sounded pretty good to me," he said.

Juliette had decided on the Grilled Pork Chop and Eva had narrowed down her choices to that, or the ribs.

They placed their drink orders while they were still reviewing the menu. A few minutes later their waiter came back with their drinks. Eva had ordered the mint julep, along with Juliette, and Jake and Brett were both drinking Manhattan's.

After deciding on her dinner choice, and the waiter leaving, Eva took a small sip of her drink and her eyes lit up, "this is so good. What is all in this? I may have to try to make them at home."

"There's bourbon, simple syrup, mint leaves, and then it's usually garnished with a mint leaf and angostura bitters. You would use a mortar and pestle to grind the mint leaves, then put them into a shaker along with the bourbon, simple syrup and ice. It's a pretty simple recipe, but you need to use good bourbon."

Eva was typing all of the ingredients into her phone. She was definitely going to be making these once she gets back home.

"Thanks. I like a sweeter type of drink. I'm not big on the hard tasting ones, like the Manhattan."

Jake was looking around the restaurant, taking in every face and looking for all the exits. Old habits die hard. Being safe in every situation was second nature to him.

Brett noticed Jake's eyes darting everywhere. "Is everything okay, Agent Long?"

Jake smiled, "yep, perfect. I just like to know what's in my environment. I don't like surprises."

Juliette was cautiously looking around to see what was around her. "Have you made any headway in the murder of Phillipe?"

Jake didn't want to give away too much information. "We have a little more than yesterday, yes, but I can't really discuss it. You understand."

She looked embarrassed for asking, but she recovered, "Oh, of course."

Brett put his arm around her chair, in a comforting gesture. "She didn't mean to pry, we're all a little on edge, being that the Derby is only a couple of days away."

"I understand. And I am hoping we can wrap this up as quickly as possible. If I may, can I ask you a couple questions about Kai Armstrong?"

She nodded.

"How long has he been in town?"

"As far as I know, he arrived the day that Phillipe was killed, but he could have been here before that, for all I know. The first time I saw him was when he came to the ranch after we'd gotten home from dinner. Why? Is he a suspect? I can't see him doing this. He didn't even know Phillipe."

"I'm not saying he is a suspect, I'm just trying to put a timeline together of everyone that had any contact with him. And, being that you were his ex, and he seemed to want to reconnect, do you think he would do anything to help your chances of winning the Derby?"

"Wait, what are you saying?" Brett was getting heated. "You think he killed Phillpe, so her competition would be taken out? No way. She can, and will win this on her own."

Jake gave Brett a look that told him to take his temper down a notch, because they were being watched now.

"Sorry. I just can't see someone doing that."

Juliette looked at Brett and put her hand on his chest, "Thank you. I just think he's got too many unanswered questions Brett."

"Well, can you see Kai doing this," he asked her.

"No, not really. But, he was acting a bit out of sorts the night he came over to see me. Claiming we were still together, and whatnot. I didn't like it. He made me feel uncomfortable."

Jake decided to change tactics. "What about Chloe? Do either of you know much about her and her relationship with Phillipe or Kai?"

Brett was afraid to say much about Chloe, since she'd been after him for a while now. Juliette however, had no problem talking about her. "She apparently met Kai at the Bourbon Inn bar the night he came in from London. At least that was his alibi. We had seen Chloe earlier that evening at Sarino's. She had been with her grandfather then. There was talk that she had met with Phillipe later that night, too, so I don't know which story is true, to be honest. She's also not my biggest fan. She's had the hots for this one, here," pointing at Brett.

Jake's eyebrows went up in question at Brett, and Brett just nodded in acknowledgement.

"Do either of you know much about Chloe? Other than she has taken a liking to Brett and Kai?"

"She's used to getting what she wants, from her grandfather. Ever since her father passed away, Chloe is the only one he'll give any time to. He doesn't speak to Penelope. I'm not sure why though," Brett said.

"And that would be Terrence Rivers, correct?"

"Yes."

Just as Jake was about to ask more questions, the food arrived and everyone decided to halt the questioning and dig into their dinners.

"Oh my gosh, these short ribs are amazing," Eva gushed. "How's the bison burger," she asked Jake.

"Probably the best burger I've ever had. Do you want to try it?"

Eva was very tempted to, but felt it might be a little awkward. Jake was posing as her husband, but really wasn't and shouldn't be sharing food, she thought. Or could she? It looked really yummy. "Oh hell, I'll just try a little bite. I've never had bison."

He handed her his burger. She took a tiny bite and closed her eyes, "wow, that's good."

"You barely got a bite," he said, laughing.

"I wanted to leave you some."

Brett and Juliette laughed.

Jake's phone buzzed with a new text. He glanced at the screen, *"Kai and Chloe left her apartment. When were you going to do your search? We'll continue to follow them."*

Eva looked at Jake, who was typing a response to whomever had just texted him. "Is everything alright?"

"Fine. We may have to cut our dinner a little short though. I'm sorry."

He looked anxious.

"That's okay, I'm almost finished anyway. Do you want to go now?"

"No. I really want to finish dinner," he gave her a side glance, revealing a small smirk.

"That's too bad. Does it have something to do with Phillipe's case," Brett asked.

"Maybe."

As they finished eating, Eva was feeling a little nervous and didn't have much of an appetite, now.

Jake looked at her and felt horrible for cutting their dinner short. He could tell she was on edge now, because she stopped eating and grew quiet.

He whispered to her, "I'm sorry, please eat the rest of your dinner. I didn't mean to ruin it. Everything will be fine."

She smiled back at him, "It's okay, I'm actually getting full. And, I know the job is why we're here."

Juliette was sort of eavesdropping on them, not on purpose, but she couldn't help it. She smiled at Eva in pity.

"It must be hard on your marriage for him to have this type of job, that takes him away all the time, huh?"

Both Jake and Eva looked at her, not sure how to respond. They both smiled and Jake was about to say something, but Eva beat him to it. "Sometimes it's harder than others, but I know how hard he works and what he's doing is making the country a safer place." And she knew that was the truth.

Jake was speechless, he sat there silent, but gave her a full on smile.

"Cheers to you. That's the best way to look at it, Eva," Juliette said, raising her glass to her.

Jake had finished his dinner and was calling their waiter over to ask for the check, when Brett spoke up, "Just put it all on one check, this is on me. It's the least I can do."

"No, you don't have to do that." "No, I insist. If you all need to head out, go ahead. We'll take care of this."

Jake shook the other man's hand and thanked him profusely, as did Eva.

He pulled Eva to her feet and continued to hold onto her hand as they walked to the car. Once in the car, they drove in the direction of Chloe's apartment.

Chapter 40

They arrived at Chloe's apartment a little after 8pm, itt was full on dark outside and there wasn't much traffic around the area.

After Jake parked their car, Eva retrieved her bag out of the trunk that had her supplies in it. Neither of them spoke as they headed toward the entrance. The doorman opened the door for them.

"Hello folks, who are you here to see tonight?"

Jake took his badge and the warrant out for him to see, then told him which apartment they were going to.

"We need access to Chloe Rivers apartment. Is there a manager here that can give us the access we need?"

"Of course, let me ring Mr. Gregory. He's usually in his office until late evening."

"Thank you."

He pushed a couple buttons on the console inside the entry and was immediately talking to someone, Jake assumed it was Mr. Gregory.

"He'll be right out, to escort you up."

"Much appreciated."

They all stood silent, until Mr. Gregory walked up to them.

"Hello. I'm James Gregory, the manager here. Robert said you're with the FBI and need to get into Miss Rivers apartment? I assume you have a warrant?"

Jake handed the warrant over to the man, who looked to be in his late 50's, to early 60"s. He had salt and pepper hair, a slim, but lean build, his face was pretty ordinary, nothing stood out about him, not even his clothes. He wore a middle of the road priced navy suit, white dress shirt, with a red tie, and wore plain black dress shoes.

The man read over the warrant briefly and returned it to Jake. "If you'll both follow me, I'll let you into her apartment."

The elevator ride was quiet. Eva stayed close to Jake, not saying or doing anything. The doors dinged open and they followed Mr. Gregory down the hall to Chloe's front door. He pulled out a large set of keys and inserted one into the lock. He proceeded to escort them inside. They took a few steps into the foyer, looking around and taking note of everything, and how it was displayed, so they could put everything back where they'd found it.

Jake turned to face the older gentleman, "okay, I think we'll take it from here, thank you. A few of my colleagues from my team will be here shortly, I would appreciate it if you'd tell the doorman to let them up."

"Of course. I'll see to it that they are allowed entrance."

Jake shut the door and started walking through all the rooms, doing a cursory look while Eva gathered her gear.

"Did they ever tell you where they picked up the trace of blood that they found," she asked. "I'll do the spell in that spot."

"Yes, it was on the living room wall, close to that far end table. Do you have everything you need?"

"I think so. I'll start the protection spell first, just to be on the safe side. You may want to stand over there, near the kitchen. You'll still be able to see everything from there."

Jake walked into the kitchen and leaned against the counter, watching her methodically place candles and salt in a circle around her, as well as wrapping herself in the white silk scarf she had used the other night. He wasn't sure if it was a good or bad thing that he was getting used to seeing her this way.

She finished the protection spell and placed two white candles outside the circle of protection she'd created and drew another circle of salt and baking soda around the candles; she then proceeded to put four rocks around the candles. She lit each of the candles and filled a bowl with water, then placed it in the middle of her candle circle. Placing a drop of pigs blood into the bowl, Jake noticed it turning the water a pinkish hue.

Eva held her hands out in front of her, closed her eyes and began chanting,

"Hermes, keeper of what disappears, Hear me now, open your devine ears,

What is lost, I now wish to find, help me stop being blind,

Direct me to what I seek. Show me where this blood came from, how it did appear

By Fire, Air, Earth and Sea, show me what I seek."

She continued to chant the spell eight more times, while Jake noticed the water in the bowl started swirling.

He leaned over a little to get a better look. He could see something in the water that hadn't been there before.

Eva opened her eyes and looked into the water. The swirling had slowed and an image was forming. She had to squint to see what it was trying to show her. The images were getting clearer, and she could see faces coming into view, one of which was Kai's. He was holding a large metal object. Chloe and Phillipe were standing closer together, but they looked to be arguing.

Jake had made his way over to stand next to Eva, by the sheer pull of curiosity.

"What are we looking at here," he asked.

"This is where Phillipe was murdered. Keep watching."

The images continued to get clearer and they could now see the three were arguing, when Kai, who was holding a large iron horseshoe, swung it right at Phillipe's head. He didn't go to the ground with the first hit, and not before he took a good swipe at Kai's face. Chloe took the horseshoe from Kai and took her own swing at him and he crumpled to the ground, not moving. Kai took the horseshoe from Chloe and ran his finger along the iron and licked it clean.

Eva's eyes went wide and her stomach was queasy. Jake looked on in horror.

"That is the most disgusting thing I think I've ever seen," he said.

"I've seen worse," she stated, matter of factly.

"We need to find that horseshoe. We have the murder weapon and the location. Do you have anything special you can do to find where they dumped the shoe?"

"You're getting a little too used to me doing this and it's a little disconcerting," she grinned.

"Yeah, how do you think I feel."

"Let me clean this up and see what I can do to find a location spell. We have more information now, so it should help me some."

They both cleaned up the salt and baking powder off the floor, then dumped the water into the sink.

She had her book open, looking for another spell she could do and Jake was on his phone.

"Kai and Chloe are at some club, so we still have time, if you can find something to do."

"I'm looking."

Eva paged through several more spells, until she finally found one she thought would do the trick. "I think I found one."

"Do you have what you need to do it?"

"Yes."

She began frantically moving around the living room, setting up another circle of protection, and digging into her bag, searching for what she needed. She had picked this particular spell because it didn't need any crazy items to perform it.

Jake walked over to her, grabbed her hand, "hey, you don't have to rush, we have time. You look panicked. Just calm down, okay?"

"Easy for you to say."

She grabbed a gray and a purple candle from her bag, set them on a small tray that she had brought from home. She lit both candles, staring at them intently. Eva knew what she was looking for, now she just had to picture it in her mind's eye.

Jake brought her out of her concentration, "what is this spell you're doing now?"

She looked at him with annoyance all over her face. "Shhh… you'll see, but I need complete silence so I can concentrate on the horseshoe."

"Oh, sorry." He made the zipping of lips, with his fingers across his mouth.

"Thank you," she smiled.

Eva began to stare at the candles once again, picturing what she was looking for. She started speaking out loud, reciting the spell.

Object I see, come to me, wherever ye hide, I shall see and as my work so mote it be. What I lost, help me find, so I may restore my peace of mind, bring it to my sight. Bring it this very night. As I will it, so mote it be.

She chanted the incantation three more times. Jake saw her eyes reflecting the flames from the candles and felt mesmerized. The flames began to dance and grow taller as the flames weaved in between each other. Eva stared directly into the fire, with the changing shapes of the flames, it started to show her the horseshoe and it's location.

"I see it," she blurted out.

"See what?" Jake couldn't see anything, but the flames. He looked closer, but saw nothing except the candles burning brightly and the flames dancing.

"The horseshoe, I can see it. She's carrying it with her." Eva could see Chloe open her purse and where there was only lining, she split it open and it was inside. Eva thought it could be a hidden lining, but she wasn't sure. She noticed the color and brand of the purse. It was a black Prada handbag.

"Where does she have it stashed?" Jake looked curiously at Eva. "She is keeping it in a secret lining of the Three thousand dollar black Prada handbag that she carries. I could see the normal inside zippered pocket, but once she opened that, she pulled at another hidden area within that, she had to have made it herself. The horseshoe is inside that."

"Are you sure? I didn't see anything form in the candles. How did you see that?"

"You're just going to have to trust me on this one, okay?"

Eva started cleaning up, by blowing the candles out and running her fingers over cold water and squeezing them over the hot wicks, to cool them off faster. She put everything away that she had taken out of her bag.

Jake wasn't sure he could take her word for it, or not. He didn't think he'd have probable cause to search Chloe's purse.

Jake was brought back to the here and now when his phone rang. "Yeah?"

Eva looked over to him, and he looked angry.

"How did you lose them? When? Do they know we're here? Damn it! We're leaving now." He hung up and Eva had only gotten the question side of the conversation and she started worrying.

"What happened," she asked.

"They figured out they were being followed and ditched my guys. From what my guy gathered, Chloe received a phone call from someone and whoever it was, told her that her apartment was being searched by feds, so they took off."

"Oh dear God, not what?"

"Now, we get out of here, drive around the block and come back, hoping they return."

She grabbed her bag and headed out the door with Jake on her heels. They were in his car and rounding the block, when Chloe's car flew into the parking lot, but she spotted them and continued out the other end, barreling down the street.

"Hold on," Jake said.

Eva was no stranger to fast driving, what with her husband Kris and her having to outrun some nut who was tailing her a month ago, on her way home from work. She had been terrified.

"Maybe we should have taken my car. They probably recognized yours right away."

"A little late to think of that now, don't ya think?"

He was being funny, while flying in and out of traffic on the hunt for crazy people. She couldn't help the nervous laugh that escaped out of her mouth.

Jake looked at her sideways, "did I miss something funny?"

"Sorry, nervous habit."

They continued their fast paced driving and weaving in and out of traffic for twenty minutes, when they'd lost them. "Damn it! Where'd they go?"

Jake had been on a conference type call with his guys, telling him where they were heading the whole time, hoping they could all converge on the duo, but somehow they were able to lose them.

"Sorry Jake, we never did catch up with you guys, due to an accident on 60, going West."

"It's okay."

Jake slammed his hand against the steering wheel, completely feeling defeated. He didn't know what to do next.

"Hey guys, meet me back at the ranch in twenty minutes, okay?"

They all came back with, "Roger that."

The drive back to the ranch was quiet, by choice. Neither Eva, nor Jake had anything to say. Eva's heart was slamming into her chest, doing 100 mph., and flashbacks were on the periphery of her mind. Remaining quiet was her only solace. She tried her best to keep her breathing as steady as she could, without alarming Jake. Eva could feel the frustration rolling off his shoulders in waves.

When they pulled into the ranch parking area, Eva got out of the car, grabbed her bag and walked head down all the way to the entrance. Still not speaking a word, she fished out her key to their room and headed up that way. Jake moved to catch up with her. "Eva, wait."

"What?"

"What's wrong? Are you racing away from me, for a reason?" He caught up to her, put his hand on her elbow, to turn her around so she was facing him. "Talk to me, please."

"What do you want to talk about Jake?"

He took the key she had in her hand, unlocked their door and motioned her in. After he shut and locked the door, he spun around to face her. "There's something wrong. What is it?"

Eva's head hung low. "Flashbacks."

Jake knew most of what happened a month ago, but not everything. Eva had to deal with some seriously evil stuff then, but he wasn't sure if that's what she was talking about.

"Flashbacks of last month, or something else?"

"Last month and twenty years ago. I've seen my fair share of messed up stuff. I've seen things no one has ever seen before and probably never will. But, you know that already. I'm sorry, I just need to rest. I'll be fine. I think I'll get a hot shower and call Kris. I miss him. And, you have your guys coming soon, so you'll have to leave anyway."

Without thinking, Jake pulled her into him, holding her in a tight embrace. He had nothing to add to what she said, so he just held her.

Chapter 41

It was after midnight, and Eva was laying on the couch that she was using as her bed. She had gotten a hot shower, which had lasted a good half an hour, until the hot water turned cold and she couldn't stand it anymore. She talked to Kris and told him about their eventful evening, and as she expected, he was worried for her and wanted to call Jake and tell him she was done, and he'd take her back home. It took her a good fifteen minutes to get him to calm down and let her finish this out. She had a job to do and she was going to see it through until the end.

Eva drifted off to sleep and no sooner had she done that, she woke with a start. Only she wasn't on the couch, she was outside in the all too familiar wooded area in Connecticut again.

"Not again..."

She wondered why it was always the same place she'd return to. Eva set off down the trail, as she had many times before. She knew exactly where it would lead her, and the fact that she just went with it, she thought, should worry her more than it did.

Once in the clearing, there was no bonfire like she was used to seeing, but there on the knotty pine log, was her mother, hunched over, looking ragged.

"Mother? Why do you keep bringing me here in my dreams?"

Her mother didn't even look up. "Eva, it isn't me who needs something, from you, I'm dead. It's you, who needs something from me."

"Okay. What do I need, that always brings me back here?"

"I see you haven't lost your stubbornness."

"Get to the point, Mother."

"He's bound to have you, dear. He will not give up easily."

"Who? What are you talking about?" Then it dawned on her. "The Dagon. You're talking about the Devil's Dagon. He's the one who tried to take over you, isn't he? He didn't die when Gerard was killed, did he?"

"No, he didn't. He and his mistress are not easy to kill my dear, but you already know that, don't you? You found a way to trap them though, didn't you?"

"How do you know that? Wait, the one that was inside Gemma...it took over Chloe, didn't it? I knew it."

"Yes."

"What's with the one word answers? I need help here. We need to get rid of them, for good this time. Why do they want me so badly?"

There was a long moment of silence, then Alma stood up; she turned toward her daughter, her eyes closed. As she opened them, they weren't the hazel color she was used to, they weren't even human. Eva stepped back a few steps. "Mom?"

"Your mother was stupid to bring you back here. I'm growing tired of her trying to block me from having you all to myself."

Eva jumped back, "what did you do with my mother?!"

"She's momentarily gone. I wanted to speak to you, myself. You are a smart woman, Eva, but I will do whatever I have to do, to have you as mine. Your husband and even your fake husband won't be able to help you."

Eva felt the power welling up in her hands, going up her arms, just as it had the night she killed her mother.

"You will NEVER have me!" She yelled at the top of her lungs. "You will be going back to hell, where you came from and you will never be able to hurt anyone else again, once I'm done with you." She knew this was a bunch of bravado on her part, but it was all she had.

The entity grew angry, "how dare you talk to me that way." It started vibrating and wielding wind all around them.

Eva raised her arms to the air, where a brilliant white light emerged from her hands, "I want my mother back, now!"

The Dagon yelled in an ugly tone at her, "you'll never see her again!"

Eva lowered her hands, pointing them in its direction and the white light penetrated the shell of her mother, making the white light turn to red. The Dagon shrieked and swore up and down, until her mother's form crumpled to the ground.

The body of her mother lay motionless on the dirt covered ground. Eva didn't so much as move. She waited a beat to see if she would start to move, or breathe. Nothing happened. Eva started to walk in the direction of her mother's body when it went into convulsions.

Eva yelled, "mother!"

The convulsions stopped after a few seconds, and Alma layed there limp and unmoving, again. Eva ran to her and knelt on the ground pulling her onto her lap.

"Mother, wake up! I know you're still in there. Please wake up!"

Tears streamed down Eva's face, as she rocked her mother's limp body in her lap.

Eva whispered in strangled tears, "you can't keep doing this to me. I can't take much more."

Alma opened her eyes, which were the beautiful hazel they once had been, and looked at her daughter, "I'm sorry Eva, I truly am. You're so much stronger than I ever was. I couldn't resist him, but you can. It's one of the reasons he wants you so badly. You are stronger in more ways than you realize."

Eva sat there on the ground continuing to hold her fragile mother, crying uncontrollably. She rocked back and forth holding the older woman. "I love you mom. I always have and always will."

Something or someone was shaking her shoulders and talking, but the words were muffled. Eva felt like she was under water.

"Eva, wake up. You're dreaming again."

Jake was shaking her so hard, trying to bring her out of her dream state. He didn't want to hurt her, but nothing seemed to be working.

"Eva! Please wake up!" He brushed the hair out of her face and was stroking her cheek gently. Eva's eyes slowly opened and they looked frightened. Jake stayed quiet, because he didn't want to scare her anymore than she already seemed to be.

"Jake?" She felt groggy and weary, definitely not rested.

"I'm right here Eva."

Eva tried to sit herself upright, and started yammering nonsense. "He's back Jake, he's come for me again. It's the same one as last time. He didn't die. I knew it. I knew he hadn't died. He's going to do to me what he wanted to do with my mother."

"Who Eva?"

"The Dagon"

Jake sat back on his heels, not sure what to do, or what to think. She thought this Dagon was a real thing, or person.

Jake sat on the floor next to the couch where Eva was sitting. "What is this Dagon, Eva? You mentioned it earlier, but you didn't give me a lot of details. Is it a person or thing? I'm not sure how or what to make of this."

"You think I'm crazy, don't you?"

"No, I don't think you're crazy, I just want to understand better what I am dealing with."

"The Dagon is considered one of the devil's right hand men, and is high ranking. He or it can inhabit a human and take him or her over, fully. That is what we are seeing now, in Kai and Chloe. They aren't dead, but they also don't have any idea the things they are doing. We have to track them down and you have to arrest them, or get them into custody somehow. I know how I can get rid of the evil entities, remember I was explaining a little bit about it to you yesterday?"

Jake was quiet, he still didn't fully believe in this good vs evil inhabiting another body thing, but he wasn't entirely dismissing it either. It would definitely explain a lot about some people's behavior.

While Jake was still silent, Eva continued, "I'm going to need a few things to trap the demons. I'll be going out first thing in the morning."

"Oh? What do you need to buy for this demon trap?"

"I need to make a Triangle of the Arts, which I showed you, so I'll need some craft supplies, as well as a few more candles, and something I can use as a charm or vessel to contain the spirits."

"Where does one go to find these things," he asked, ruefully.

"A craft store. But, I really need to try and get some sleep, I'm drained, as I'm sure you are, too. I apologize again, for waking you up."

"You didn't wake me up, I had just come in from meeting with my team and talking to Penelope. I need her to see if she can get in touch with her daughter. She tried calling her when we were downstairs, but it went straight to voicemail. I really hated to tell her what was going on with Chloe. That lady has had enough heartache, with losing her husband, her father-in-law not being very nice to her since his son passed away, and now her daughter being suspected of murder."

"That had to be hard on you. I don't envy your job, but you are good at it. Anyway, we should get some sleep Jake."

"Are you going to be okay now?"

"I think so. Thank you."

Chapter 42

Eva woke up earlier than she had planned, but not as early as Jake, since he was nowhere in the room. When she checked the bathroom, she noticed his running pants and shoes were missing, so she assumed he was out jogging off some of the stress.

Once she finished getting a shower and getting ready, she headed down to the kitchen in search of something small for breakfast and a much needed large cup of coffee.

There was a nice spread of muffins, croissants and fruit, along with yogurt and assorted juices in carafes on the island and a large stainless steel coffee urn, with togo cups and lids, with sugar and creamer in all varieties. *Ahhh, nirvana,* she thought.

She immediately grabbed a plate and took a giant blueberry muffin, a few pieces of fruit and a yogurt cup, then poured herself coffee and made it the way she liked; two splenda and two creamers.

She went into the dining area where there was a long wooden table with benches on both sides and spindle back chairs at each end. She sat down to the empty table and devoured her breakfast.

Eva was taking the last few bites of her muffin when the back door opened and Jake came through, sweating profusely.

"Wow, how many miles did you run this morning," she asked.

"I only did five. I didn't want to be out too long, I've got too much to get done and I don't know where to even begin." The defeated look on his face made Eva's heart, break.

"Don't you kiss your wife good morning dude?"

They both turned around, startled out of their conversation, to see Brett standing in the kitchen doorway, with a plateful of food.

"Huh? How long have you been standing there," Jake questioned, annoyed he hadn't heard him nearby.

"I walked in just as you came in the back door. And I think your wife deserves at least a good morning kiss," he said, teasing.

Eva looked horrified and Jake looked to her for some help. This was out of his comfort zone, and guessed it was way out of her comfort zone, as well.

She recovered quicker than Jake had and smiled serenely at Jake, "well, what are you waiting for, an invitation?"

Jake's eyebrows rose a good two inches off his head, a little confused. "Umm, I should probably get a shower before getting so close, don't you think?"

Brett let out a bark of laughter. "Man, how long have you two been married? A week?"

"It sometimes feels that way," Eva said, smirking at Jake.

Jake didn't like being goaded, so he gathered himself up and went over to where Eva sat, bent down, and laid a big old kiss, square on her lips. It lasted longer than he intended. When he pulled back, her face had turned a pinkish hue, and the look on her face made him smile bigger than she had ever seen him smile before. She was taken aback, and temporarily speechless. He had thrown her off kilter. Jake wasn't sure why he was proud of that, but he was.

Brett smacked Jake on the back, "that's what I'm talking about. Kiss her until she's speechless." Jake just smiled at Brett as if some sort of male bonding ritual had just occurred, and Eva was not privy to the insider information on that one.

Brett took his food and left out the front door.

Eva was still rooted to her seat, not sure what to say next. Jake turned to her, a sheepish smile forming on his face, "sorry, I didn't know what else to do."

She just shook her head, "Kris is gonna kick your butt for that one," she stated, jokingly.

"I know. I promise, it won't happen again. I have to run upstairs and grab a shower. We put a BOLO (Be On the Lookout) for Kai and Chloe with local and state law enforcement agencies. I'm hoping to get something soon."

"You know, if they get picked up, you need to do something to get them to release them into your custody, so I can do my thing, right?"

"Yes, I know. I'm still figuring out where I can take them, so you can do it. What are your plans for the day? Do you have your cell phone with you?"

"I'm heading out soon to go to the local craft store, to pick up what I need. I'll have my cell phone, of course."

"I also want you to wear the earrings I gave you that have the audio recording device in it and I want to put the locator in your arm, as well. It will last a few days at the very least. It's just a precaution, since you'll be out of my sight today."

He also had a bad feeling in the pit of his stomach that something was about to happen, and he never took chances with those feelings. Jake went with his instincts 90% of the time, and 89% of the time they were right.

Eva could see the worry in his face. She agreed to wear the earrings, and to have him inject the locator into her arm. She planned on calling Kris anyway, to tell him everything that was going on and she'd also let him know that she would now be wired, so he should get his software ready.

Chapter 43

Eva was on the road, heading into town where she found they had a big box craft store. She called Kris on her way, to let him know she was all wired up.

"Hey beautiful, how's everything going?"

"It's going."

"Uh oh, what's going on?"

"I'm on my way to a craft store, to get some supplies I need. But, I wanted you to know that Jake has me wearing the earrings and he also injected the locator into my arm, too. He says it's just a precaution, but I think it's more. You need to get your computer stuff ready, in case something happens to go down today, okay?"

There was a moment of silence on Kris' end, and Eva knew he was doing some deep breathing exercises, trying to calm himself, before he said something stupid.

"Alright, I'll get everything set up. What do you need from the craft store?"

She explained to him everything that she had found out about on how to trap a demon, and she told him about her dream with her mother last night, too. He never once interrupted her. He just listened, more than likely taking notes along the way, too. She knew him so well.

"Oh, and one more thing, there was an incident this morning."

"What kind of incident?"

Eva wasn't sure how to tell him that Jake kissed her, but it was necessary to keep up their pretense of being married, so she just blurted it out. "Jake kissed me."

She waited for the barrage of questions to follow that statement, but they didn't come.

"Kris? Did you faint?"

"No, I'm here."

"Well, say something."

"Was it necessary for him to do that?"

"What? I guess. It was a matter of keeping up the pretense of us being married. The stable manager said something about us basically not showing any affection towards each other and Jake didn't know what else to do, so he planted a kiss right on my lips."

"And?"

"And what? There was nothing there. No sparks, no fireworks, not even an electric jolt, at least on my end," she said with a laugh.

"Good to know, but I already heard about it," he said, with slight humor to his voice.

"Jake was that worried that you'd kick his butt? I told him you would."

"Apparently he believed you."

"Jeeze, some tough guy he is. Anyway, I have to go, I just parked at the store. I'll talk to you soon. Love you."

"Always and Forever," he said, before hanging up.

Eva smiled at that.

As she made her way through the large store, where she found most of what she needed, except she still needed some sort of charm or vessel as a containment for the evil spirits. She had seen a home decor store in the same plaza that she was in, and would go there after.

Eva took a little extra time to let herself look around the craft store and decompress. This was one of her favorite stores.

After a good half hour of browsing the various aisles and picking up a few extra things she figured she couldn't live without, she checked out. Eva dropped her bags into her trunk and went to the home decor store to look for something that looked like it could hold a couple of evil spirits.

She entered the home store, grabbed a cart and felt the urge to window shop. She'd been so stressed the last few days, she was feeling somewhat normal walking up and down the aisles of paintings, shelves, furniture, and vases.

Eva was in an aisle that had chests in a variety of sizes, and figured this is what she needed. She looked at a couple larger chests made of wood, but decided on a small one, that she could easily carry with her anywhere. It was made out of some sort of stone, possibly granite, or marble. The chest she picked was solid and had a very secure lock in the front that was made of some sort of metal.

She took her items to the counter, and the cashier had complimented her on the choice she made in the chest. She had even asked Eva where in the store she had found such a beautiful piece. The cashier said she was going to try to find another one on her break, for herself.

Once Eva was back in her car, she felt the need to text her mother-in-law and check on the kids. She was missing them terribly, and was looking forward to being home with them, even if they did constantly fight.

Kris' mom replied almost immediately, with a picture of the kids making goofy faces, and saying they were being angels. "Of course they were angels, Grandma and Grandpa were probably spoiling them silly and I'll have to deprogram them once they are back home."

Still, she smiled at the picture, and sent them an equally goofy faced selfie of her back, which garnered her a laughing emoji back.

The whole way back to the ranch she had her stereo up and sang to her playlist. Her stress level was a lot lower by the time she reached the ranch.

Chapter 44

Jake and his team were out scouring the city for Kai and Chloe. They had gone to Terrence Rivers office to see him and question him on whether or not he had any ideas of where Chloe could be. He had him try to call her cell phone, just as they had Penelope the night before. But, to no avail, he also got her voicemail.

Terrence Rivers had his granddaughters back, and didn't believe one word Jake had said to him about Chloe. When one of Jake's teammates confronted him about his relationship with his daughter-in-law, they found out the reason he disliked her so much, was because she didn't want him as a partner at the ranch and stable business and that had subsequently rubbed him the wrong way.

After Jake had done a thorough background check on Mr. Rivers, he didn't blame Penelope for not wanting him as a business partner. He was in pretty deep with gambling debt and other shady business deals.

When Jake returned to the ranch, to grab something to eat, he went up the room first to get Eva.

"How was your shopping trip," he asked.

He was looking at the bags she had piled on the coffee table.

"Productive, thanks. How was your day?"

"Not so productive. But, I was getting hungry, so I came back here for a bite. Do you want to join me?"

"Sure, I'm getting a little hungry myself."

They headed down the stairs, when Brett came running up the front steps, and swung the front door open, letting it bang off the wall. He was panting and trying to catch his breath, looking at Jake wide eyed and crazed.

"Jake, you have to help me. I'm worried about Juliette. She left me a voicemail saying that she got a call from Kai, and that he asked her to meet him at the Bourbon Inn to talk. I tried calling her, but she's not answering her cell phone."

"Okay, calm down. What time did she leave the voicemail?"

"Two this afternoon. I even went to the Bourbon Inn to look for her, but she wasn't there, and her car is gone, too. I looked all over the parking lot there, and nothing. It's been two hours and I still can't get a hold of her."

Jake saw the desperation in Brett's eyes and heard it in his voice. He too, was worried about what might have happened to Juliette, especially if Kai was what Eva said he was.

Eva had a horrified look on her face, and immediately ran up the stairs to Juliette's room. She started pounding on her door, yelling for her. "Juliette!? Are you in there?" No answer.

Jake had followed her up the steps, "what are you doing?"

Looking deflated, Eva dropped her head down, "I was just hoping she might be in there."

Jake pulled Eva to him, "she's going to be okay, we'll find her." At least he hoped they would.

He took his phone out and called his team. He was explaining the situation when it dawned on him, "Brett! You said you couldn't find her car anywhere?"

"Yeah, it's not here and it wasn't at the Bourbon Inn."

"What kind of car does she drive and do you happen to know the license plate number?"

"She drives a newer model Mercedes GLS SUV, the bigger one, and her license plate is a vanity plate of sorts, it's HRSRCR, as in Horse Racer."

Jake relayed the information Brett gave him to his teammate and had him put another BOLO out for Juliette's car, in hopes that they would find them all in her car.

Jake asked Brett for Juliette's cell phone number and gave that to his tech guy, to see if they could get her location by tracking her cell phone.

"I'm heading over to the Bourbon Inn to meet some of my team, and question some of the employees. I also want to see if they have any video surveillance on their property. Are you going to be okay here for a little while," he turned to Eva, in question.

Remembering to act like she was his wife, she gave him an endearing look, "I'll be fine, don't worry about me, just find Juliette, okay."

"That's my plan." He gave her a quick kiss on her forehead and headed back downstairs, with Brett on his heels. Jake whirled around, "you stay here, in case she calls or shows up."

"I thought I'd go with you," Brett said.

"No. I would rather you stay here."

"But..." Jake cut him off before he could argue anymore, and bolted out the door.

Chapter 45

Eva called Kris, "Hey K, how's it going?"

"Hey sweetheart. It's been pretty uneventful here, how about you?"

She waited a beat, then went into the full blow by blow of everything that had developed over the last hour.

"Crap! Eva, this is how it all started last time. I don't like this at all. I think I should be over there. I can keep an eye on things there, while Jake is out doing his thing."

"No, you can't. Just stay where you are. If anything develops, I'll let you know."

"Ughhh… I hate this. Fine."

Eva's phone beeped, meaning she had another call coming in, "hold on Kris, I have another call coming in."

"Okay."

"Hello?"

"Eva?"

"Yes, this is Eva, who's this?"

"Oh, come now Eva, I know you know who this is. Don't play coy."

Eva sank to the floor, stunned silent.

"Eva?"

Jerk out of her shock, "Yes, I'm here."

"Good. Now, listen very carefully. If you want to see Juliette again, you'll do as I say. Are we clear?"

"Yes. But, I want to talk to her, to make sure she hasn't been harmed, first."

"Always so demanding, aren't you?"

There was a loud screeching, then a low grunting noise, "hello?"

"Juliette? It's Eva, are you okay? Have they hurt you at all?"

"Eva, help me! This guy looks like Kai, but it isn't Kai."

The phone went dead briefly, and sounded like it had fallen and hit something.

"Juliette!"

"You've heard her, she's alive, for now. Now, I'll tell you where to go, and be here by six, or she will suffer the same fate poor Phillipe did."

"Don't hurt her. I'll go wherever it is you want me to go."

"Good girl. I want you to go to the EP Tom Sawyer Park, then head to the Sauerkraut Cave. Where these people come up with the names of these things, I'll never know. Anyway, be here by six, or else. And Eva, I'll know if you let on to anyone where you're going."

And, he was gone.

Eva took a second to regain control of herself, before she went back to Kris.

"Kris?" Her voice was strained, but she felt she pulled it off.

"Yeah. Who called you? You had me on hold for a while."

Think Eva...

"Umm, it was Chrissy. She wanted to know when I thought I'd be back to work."

"Oh. They can't make it without you, huh?"

"Not on their best day," she replied, jokingly.

"Wow, modest aren't you?"

"I need to do some research, so I'll call you later, okay."

"Okay. Love you."

"I love you, too. Always and forever."

Before he could say anything else, Eva ended the call, grabbed for her bag and dumped the contents of her shopping bags onto the floor.

She took the construction paper out, and markers, along with the picture she found in her family's book, of the Triangle of Arts. She drew the triangular symbol with a thick black marker. The paper she bought was a heavyweight construction paper, almost the texture of cardstock. After drawing the triangle, she wrote the names of three Gods in each corner, Tetragrammaton, Primeumaton and Anaphexeton. She then wrote out Michael, split into the center spots between the triangle, so it looked like MI-CHA-EL and then drew a circle in the middle. The circle is the symbol designated as the confines of the magical practitioners circle.

Once she was happy with the end product, Eva gathered the rest of the items she had purchased to do what she planned to do with The Dagon, and put everything in her backpack, and headed for her car. She glanced at her watch, it was already 5:30. She didn't have much time. She caught a glimpse of her left hand and noticed she hadn't grabbed the sapphire ring that she had brought with her. Eva turned on her heel and ran up the stairs to her room to retrieve it, and ran into Penelope.

"Easy Eva, where's the fire?"

"Oh my gosh, I'm so sorry. Did I hurt you?"

"No, I'm good. Where are you going in such a hurry?"

"Umm, Jake asked me to drop off some stuff to him, at the field office."

Penelope's face went from a smile to a grim line. "Oh. Has he been able to find Chloe yet? She looked as though she didn't want to know the answer, but felt the need to ask.

"Not that I know of. You heard Juliette is sort of missing in action, right?"

Penelope looked stunned. "What? When?"

"Brett got a message from her earlier, that she was meeting Kai at the Bourbon Inn to talk and she hasn't been heard from since. I'm sorry to dump that on you and run, but I really need to go grab something out of our room and get moving."

"No, that's fine. Please keep me informed about Juliette."

Eva just shook her head in acknowledgement and proceeded to her room.

She opened the door to her room, grabbed her duffle bag and pulled out the blue velvet box. She opened it and grabbed the ring. She placed it on her right ring finger and took off.

Eva put the address of the park into her GPS, and thought she should probably text Kris, too, before she left.

You might want to turn on all the tracking and audio stuff. I'm headed out. Love you, always and forever, please never forget that.

Thirty seconds later, her cell phone began to ring and it was Kris. She was expecting that, but refused to answer. Eva didn't want to lose whatever bravado she had been running on, and Kris would want to know where she was going and she couldn't tell him that. She didn't want to risk Juliette's life.

Chapter 46

Jake was sitting in the bar at the Bourbon Inn, questioning the manager and waiting to see the video surveillance, when his phone rang.

"Jake Long."

"Jake, it's Kris. Eva sent me a cryptic text and now she's not answering her cell."

"Whoa wait, what did her text say?"

"She told me I may want to turn on all the tracking and audio stuff. I think she's up to something. Can you try calling her? I have the tracking software going and I can see she's driving, I just don't know where she's heading. And she's keeping quiet while driving, because I can't hear her saying anything either."

"Damn! Okay, I'll try to call her and you keep track of her location. I'll call you back soon."

"Thanks!"

Jake hung up, and immediately called Eva. Her phone continued to ring and ring, until it went to voicemail. "Eva, call me! Don't do anything stupid, please. Kris is tracking you."

The manager's assistant had the video set up and ready to run for Jake. They all sat back and watched the timeline that they assumed was when Juliette might have shown up. The first few minutes was business as usual, then Jake noticed Chloe approach the bar and order a drink.

"Okay, that's Miss Rivers. Let's see where this takes us," Jake said.

Chloe received her drink order and sat at the bar talking nonchalantly to the bartender for what seemed like only a few minutes, until Kai approached her. He stood next to her, but never ordered anything. They were talking, but the conversation took on a sharper tone from what the video feed was showing. Chloe was getting annoyed and Kai's finger poked her in the center of her chest as he was speaking.

"Don't these videos have any audio on them?" Jake was feeling anxious. He wanted to know what they were arguing about.

"Sorry, we don't have audio on this system. It's quite expensive," the manager stated.

They all continued watching the two talk. The conversation seemed to take on a calmer tone, and then Juliette appeared behind them. She wasn't smiling, but she didn't have a look of fear on her face either.

"She looks fairly comfortable with them," the assistant manager added.

"Maybe... Wait, what is she saying? Damn it, can't anyone read lips?"

Kai took Juliette by the elbow and Chloe got up from the stool she had been sitting on, drinking her drink, and they all headed in the direction of the exit.

"Do you have any cameras outside, too?"

"We have one, let me grab the footage, hold on."

While Jake waited for the next video, he called Kris.

"Did you get a hold of her," Kris asked, without saying hello or anything .

"No, she's ignoring my calls, as well. Are you tracking her? What direction is she going in?"

"She's on 264, heading Northeast."

"Okay, as soon as I look at this last tape, I'm going to head in that direction, If you hear her say anything, or if she stops somewhere, let me know,"

"I will. And Jake, please get to her soon. She's my life man."

"I know."

"Agent Long, we have the video set up. I rewound it to the time we were just looking at, on the other one."

"Perfect, thanks."

The video was of the parking lot and luckily it was daylight. The duo had Juliette by her elbows and led her to her own car. Kai took the key from her, and moved her to the backseat. Chloe went to the backseat with her, while Kai took the driver's seat. Jake could see the terror in her eyes. He dug his phone out of his pocket and dialed.

"They are definitely in her Mercedes, I just saw the video surveillance from the Bourbon Inn."

He waited a beat, listening to the person on the other end, "We have the BOLO out on her car. I am heading out, I'll be in touch. Call me on my cell if you get any hits off her license plate. Thanks."

Jake thanked the Bourbon Inn manager, and took off at a sprint to his car. He called Kris again to see if anything had changed in Eva's direction.

"Anything new? Is she still heading in the same direction?"

"Yeah, she's still on 264. I can hear her breathing erratically every now and then through the audio, but she still isn't speaking. She knows I'm listening."

"She's not talking on purpose. Something must have happened after I left."

"Dude, she just got off Exit ramp 21 and she turned right onto Westport Road."

"Okay, I'm about 15 minutes from that exit."

"Can't you call in the local cops with this information?"

"I don't want to spook Kai and Chloe and have them turn around and do something stupid."

"Fine."

"Kris, I know how frustrated you are. Trust me."

"She's making another right onto Freys Hill Road. Where is she going?"

"Can you shrink the map grid and look at what's around there?"

"Yeah, hold on. There's a EP Tom Sawyer park coming up."

"Okay, let's see if she heads in that direction."

A minute went by and neither of them spoke a word.

"Eva stopped. She's at the park."

"I'm on my way. If you notice anything else, call me. If she starts talking, call me. Do you understand?"

"Yes."

Jake sped his way through a few traffic lights to get onto 264. His stomach was in knots. He couldn't let anything happen to Eva. He had to get to her soon.

Chapter 47

Eva parked her car in the public parking lot at EP Tom Sawyer park. She was a little early. She made sure not to say anything while she was driving, she knew Kris had no doubt started tracking her, already. She was banking on it.

"Well, I guess you know where I am. I'm sorry I couldn't say anything, they're watching me, I can feel it. I don't know how, or where, but I couldn't run the risk of Jake getting here the same time I did."

Eva grabbed her backpack and glanced down at her hand, the sapphire was sparkling in the early evening sun. "You saved me last time, I hope I don't need you this time, too, but just in case."

******

"Yes, I know where you are Eva, and Jake is on his way."

He knew she couldn't hear him, but he talked to her anyway. It made him feel better.

"What is she talking about, who saved her last time?"

******

You know how one of your favorite things is Sauerkraut? Well, I really hate it, especially today.

I'm getting out of the car, and I won't be saying anything else for a bit."

"Sauerkraut? What the hell does that mean?" Kris was confused.

******

Eva looked up, and the sky was getting darker. The night would settle in, in the next half hour. This didn't help her nerves at all.

She walked by families that were gathering their stuff up, and heading to their cars, to go home.

Eva kept walking, looking for the small trail. Before she left the ranch, she had looked up the EP Tom Sawyer park and found that it had been the location of Lakeland Asylum back in the day. This did little to comfort her.

She made her way to the archery range and found a small dirt trail that was barely noticeable, with all the ancient trees covering most of it. Eva found herself on a dark foggy trail, because of the darkness and moisture in the trees.

The amount of cobwebs stretching across the path, from tree to tree, should have been a warning of the threat that was about to come. Eva hated spiders, with a passion.

She could hear the flow of water from a small creek that must be nearby. As the trail rounded a corner, a large opening on the side of the hill appeared, and from what she could see, it dipped into total darkness, but she continued on, noting the amount of graffiti that was displayed over every inch of the brick and pillars.

The evil that lurks inside, from the past and what currently resides in there, was palpable. A sudden wave of nausea hit her in the stomach.

Once she reached the deepest part of the cave, that once was used as a storage facility for the asylum and also an escape for it's many patients, who never made it out alive, due to the cave being so dark and frequently flooded, she started hearing low voices. Eva wasn't positive of whose voices they belonged to, whether it was Juliette or Chloe, or if it was the spirits that had been here for decades?

A flicker of light showed ahead, and Eva headed in that direction. The voices started to become more clearer, the sound of someone sobbing caught her attention. *Juliette...*

******

Kris was listening to the background noise of where Eva had been walking at the park. The sounds of people milling around and the crunching of her foot falls on leaves was all he could hear. He wanted her to say something, anything. All he could hear from her was her uneven breathing.

"Say something Eva, give me a hint as to where you're walking to. This is driving me nuts."

He monitored the tracking device and she was still in the park that he could see. Kris' cell started to ring, and saw that it was Jake. "Hey, what's up?"

"Is she still at the park? I'm about five minutes out."

"Yeah, she's still there. All I hear is her walking and the people she's walking by. It's driving me crazy that she's not talking. She knows I'm listening."

"Maybe that's why she's not saying anything. She's afraid someone else might be listening, too. Remember when she was told to meet that Gerard at the airplane hanger?"

"Of course, but I try to block it out of my mind on a daily basis, why?"

"I think Kai called her and asked her to meet him and he might have threatened her or threatened to hurt Juliette, if she told anyone. She's waiting."

"Wait! What the hell?"

"What?"

"Her tracking is off. It's not showing up anywhere. It's like she fell off the face of the earth. She was there, then she wasn't. What happened? Where is she Jake?!"

"Calm down Kris. Where in the park was she when you last saw her blip on the map?"

Kris was marking different locations on the map as Eva was walking. He looked at the map to see where the last one was. His breath hitched, "the last mark I made was close to a place called Sauerkraut Cave. Jesus Jake, she's in that cave, I'd bet my life on it. She even hinted at it earlier. How much farther do you have to go until you're there?"

"I just parked. I'm hanging up now. If she starts talking, call me."

"Hurry!"

******

Eva held onto her bag tighter and found herself rubbing the sapphire with her fingers, nervously. She let go of her bag and placed it against the cave wall, before she got to where the voices were coming from.

She walked into what looked like a deep recess in the cave. It was damp and cold, and smelled of death and decay. Her stomach recoiled, but she held the bile down that was bubbling in her throat.

"Hello Eva, your timing is impeccable as always. I've missed you," Kai said, in a sardonic tone. "Come closer, I won't bite."

Eva was pretty sure that was a lie.

She looked around the cave, once her eyes adjusted and located Juliette, sitting on a rock, her hands and feet tied and a gag over her mouth. Eva's breath caught in her throat.

"Juliette, are you okay," Eva asked, worried.

The slight woman just nodded, tears streaming down her dirt crusted face.

"Okay Kai, I'm here, it's time you let Juliette go. I know she has nothing to do with this, it's me you're after right, Dagon."

Kai looked at Eva, unable to hide the surprised look on his face.

"Yes, she has nothing to do with us, does she? It's you Eva, that I want. You won our last encounter, but I'm done being nice. Your mother was supposed to be mine and I would have lived forever in her, but you had to ruin that, as well, didn't you?"

******

"Jesus Eva, what the…" Kris picked up the slight echoing as Eva spoke and figured she was inside the cave somewhere. He called Jake again, to relay the info to him, and to see where in the park he was.

"Hello?"

"Jake, they're all in that cave, how far away from the cave are you?"

"I'm almost there. How do you know she's in the cave, did she say it outloud?"

"When she started talking, the voices were echoing. Kai and Juliette are definitely in there with her, I heard her mention their names. I'm really not liking what I'm hearing though. Kai is apparently not who he says he is and he knows my wife."

"I know. Did she say anything about who he is, by chance?"

"She mentioned Dagon and he said something about her mother. I'm getting a really bad feeling about this. I'm coming down that way."

"No! I need you to stay where you are and keep recording whatever conversation they have. And she mentioned Dagon?"

Jake was internally cursing himself. *Damn it, she was right.*

"Yeah. She was right about Kai being taken over by that demonic entity, wasn't she? It's the same one that tried getting to her in Delaware and the same one that tried to take her mother, too, isn't it?"

"Jake sighed, "I believe so. Listen, I'm getting closer to the cave, I can see the opening up ahead. I have to go, I can't let them hear me coming."

"Fine, just get my wife out of there."

Kris knew he was acting unreasonable, but he didn't care, he wanted his wife back in one piece. He was wondering why he ever agreed to help his friend in the first place.

******

Eva was trying to figure out how she was going to perform the demon trap and get them to let Juliette go. She was beginning to think she hadn't fully thought this through. Juliette was too far away for the Sapphire to protect both of them. She needed them to let Juliette go first, then she'd deal with Chloe and Kai.

Chloe was standing guard over Juliette, petting her like a dog. It was unsettling, considering Chloe really didn't like her much to begin with, being that Brett had declared his interest in Juliette, and not her.

Eva inched her way closer to where the two women were.

"That's far enough Eva," Kai, T*he Dagon* screeched at her.

"Let her go then."

Eva needed them to let her go. She didn't need to explain to anyone else what she was.

Chloe looked to Kai for what she was supposed to do next. Kai seemed to be contemplating his next move.

"I'll let her go, if you agree to become mine, forever"

This statement made Eva want to throw up. The last thing she wanted was to be taken over by this evil son of gun. She'd destroy herself before she'd let that happen.

******

"Oh for the love of God, don't you dare Eva." Kris was sitting at the desk listening to the conversation, rubbing the back of his neck. Anxiety rolled through him like waves hitting the shore. It smacked him in the face over and over.

******

Jake was making his way through the dark cave, using the light from his cell phone. He heard where the voices were coming from and headed in that direction. He turned his light off, so they wouldn't see his approach.

He was walking, when he kicked something with his foot. It wasn't something that was supposed to be there. He turned his light on quickly to see what he kicked. It was Eva's backpack. Jake opened the bag to find the picture of the triangle she had told him about, along with five rocks and a small sized chest. He looked at it, confused as to why it was here, and not with her. Then it dawned on him, *she didn't want them to take her bag and find the items she was holding. They'd know what it was for.*

Jake picked up Eva's bag and took it with him.

The closer he got to where they were, the more wound up Jake was feeling. It smelled horrible, and it had a not so good energy flowing through the cave, that made it all the more important for him to get to where she was and fast.

******

Eva heard a faint rustling in the distance and was hoping to God it was someone she wanted to see, but for all she knew, it was just a rat scampering through the cave.

Kai was pacing back and forth, while Chloe continued to stand guard over Juliette, who kept her gaze focused on Eva.

Kai stopped in his tracks and looked over to the two women. "Chloe dear, will you stand her up please. I'm growing tired, and I need to complete the transfer into Eva here, and as she stated, this Juliette is of no use to us, anymore."

Eva jerked her head in their direction and noticed she had now been standing only a few feet from Kai. *When did that happen?*

Chloe grabbed hold of Juliette, knocking her off balance, making her fall to her knees. "Get up," Chloe scolded her.

"Untie the binding at her feet and she can," Eva said, sarcastically.

Chloe shot Eva a glaring look.

"Now girls, no cat fights," Kai said, practically laughing.

Chloe untied Juliette's ankles and hauled her to her feet. Juliette glowered back at her, furious. She let out a bark of laughter. "Your wrists are still tied up and your mouth is still gagged sweetheart, your look of anger doesn't scare me," Chloe chided.

Eva felt that it had to be the evil entity inhabiting Chloe, that was making her act the way she was, but she had no idea. She hadn't met Chloe before she was taken over, to know for sure.

"Let her leave, now. I'll stay, I promise," Eva begged.

"I don't usually bargain Eva, it's not my style, but I never wanted anything more than to possess you, and to feel the immense magical power you have inside you."

"Chloe, walk the young lady out of the cave and let her go," he said, with a wink.

Chloe did as she was told and took Juliette by the arm. She walked past Eva, smiling a cheshire grin.

Eva had a bad feeling in the pit of her stomach. "Wait! What is she going to do to her?"

"Always so suspicious, Eva?"

"When it comes to you and the evil you represent, yes."

Chloe turned back, looking at Kai. He merely nodded at her and she continued to walk away from them.

Eva absently felt for her grandmother's ring. It protected her before, she prayed it would do it again.

******

Jake heard the whole conversation and was listening to the footfalls of the women heading in his direction. He kept still, backed against the left side of the pitch black cave. Luckily his eyes had adjusted fairly well to the dark. He saw the outline of the two figures approaching him. He knew neither one could see him. He held his breath as they came closer.

The women were about to pass by him, when Jake grabbed for Chloe, putting his hand to her mouth, to stifle any noise that may come out of her. He immediately told Juliette to remain quiet, and that she was safe.

"Juliette, it's Agent Long," he whispered. "I need you to be very quiet, okay."

He saw her nod her head fast in acknowledgement.

"Good girl."

Jake held tight to Chloe's body with one hand, and her mouth with the other one.

"Listen to me Juliette, follow this path with your hands on the cave walls and get out of here. My car is in the parking lot. Go to my car and wait there. I'll take care of Chloe here. Now go."

Jake continued to hold onto Chloe for a minute, while she was trying to jerk and flail her body around, to free herself from his hold. Thankfully, he was much stronger than she was.

He decided to incapacitate her with a move he learned at Quantico, by putting his thumb and forefinger to a specific nerve around the neck and shoulder; it had her down for the time being.

******

"Are you ready Eva, to be the most powerful witch known to man?"

No she wasn't ready, nor will she ever be ready for that. *Think Eva, think.* She was tired of thinking and at her whits end.

Kai approached her like a lion approaching their prey. He was graceful, calculated, and determined.

She backed up a few feet, as he moved toward her.

"There's no use trying to back away, Eva. Your destiny is coming."

Eva, don't let him come any closer.

Eva looked around her, searching for whoever was talking to her. The voice was familiar, but she didn't see anyone, but Kai.

Kai was only a couple feet away from her, now.

Fight him, Eva!

"Mother," she asked.

Kai looked at her with a peculiar look on his face.

"No dear, you're mother is no longer here."

She knew that voice, but apparently Kai couldn't hear it, only she could. Was she losing her mind?

Kai raised a hand to touch her face; he had made it that much closer to her and she batted it away. She didn't want him touching her. The thought of him touching her repulsed her.

He backhanded her across the face, knocking her to the ground.

"Do you have any idea what you're dealing with? I've come back a few times now, you know it's futile to resist me. You can't get rid of me, Eva," he said through his teeth.

Eva felt the side of her face, checking for any bleeding, before looking up at the face of the devil.

******

"Shit!" Kris heard the blow that Eva just took. It nearly knocked him off his chair. He stood and started pacing the length of his hotel room. His nerves were shot. He was ready to leave, head to the park, and say to hell with the audio. His wife was in serious trouble, when he received a text from Jake.

Don't you dare leave that room. I've got eyes on her, now. She's okay, and Juliette is safe.

"Damn it, how does he get into my head so quickly?"

******

Jake was only fifty feet from where Kai stood, when he saw him backhand Eva. She sat up quickly, touching her hand to her face. She looked in the direction where Jake stood in the dark shadows and gave an imperceptible nod. She knew he was there.

He was having a difficult time not going to her, to make sure she really was okay.

Jake had Eva's bag that had everything she needed to do her thing, but he didn't know how to get them to her.

He had his 9 mm at his side, ready to aim if, and when necessary.

Eva must have made out the gun, and shook her head telling him not to shoot, or at least that was the impression he was getting from her.

******

Kai yelled down at her, "Get up!"

She got herself to her knees, breathing heavily. The blow had not only knocked her down, it had knocked the wind out of her, too. She looked up from where she was and saw Jake in the distance. He was about fifty feet from them, keeping himself in the dark shadows of the cave. Her heart did a little flip-flop of relief. He had found her.

Eva stood, looking Kai in the eyes. He was glaring down at her. "Are you done making me mad, or am I going to have to resort to other tactics?"

Eva smiled up at him, "I have no intention of letting you out of this cave."

He let out another bark of laughter, like he did before, at her bravado. He had to have had almost 70lbs. on her and at least ten inches in height, not to mention a lot more muscle.

"I don't know where you get your attitude from Eva, it definitely wasn't from your mother and your father was a weak man, but you, you entertain me."

Eva felt the smile almost fade from her face, it was pure bravado, she wasn't strong or brave, he was right. She was just entertainment for him, but she was also cunning, and had an ace up her sleeve, so to speak.

She decided in one quick move, to throw herself to the right of where she was standing and she yelled in Jake's direction, "shoot him in the leg, now!"

Everything seemed to happen all at once, but in slow motion. Eva was flying to the right, Kai was confused and turned to look in the direction she had been talking to and saw Jake come at him, gun in position, aimed at him. Kai hadn't been able to react fast enough, and the bullet hit him in the knee, taking him to the ground, instantly. Jake was on him in a second, flipping him over on his stomach, cuffs in hand, and shackling him. Kai lay there, in the dirt, cursing in five languages.

Jake went over to where Eva had dove and picked her up. "Are you okay?"

"I'm fine, now. Thanks."

He smiled with relief rushing through him. "Anytime."

Kai yelled in their direction, "you think this is going to stop me? You didn't even kill this body. You guys are a joke."

Jake looked down at Eva. "Is this where you do your thing? I found your bag out there in the cave, it's over there."

Eva smirked, "yep, it's time. Where is Chloe though? I need her here, too."

"I'll see if she is conscious yet?"

"What did you do to her?"

"Eh, just a little subduing trick I learned," he said, smiling.

Eva just shook her head and watched him walk away.

She looked over at Kai, who was hopping mad now, and bleeding from the knee cap.

"Do you really think these cuffs will hold me, Eva?" He looked at her, smiling, and that's when she noticed the color of his eyes change from green to black, and the color of his skin had turned an ashy pigment.

Even in the dim lighting from the lantern, the change was less than subtle. She was on borrowed time.

"Jake, if you can hear me, hurry up," she squealed.

Laughing resonated inside the cave, and it was Kai, looking more, and more inhuman by the minute.

Jake stepped back into the part of the cave where Eva was and she blew out a huge sigh of relief, "thank God, I thought you went back to your car to retrieve her or something."

Chloe was handcuffed as well and Jake had a steel grip on her, trying to control her spasming body. She was not a happy camper, at all. "Sorry, this one has quite the attitude."

"Put her next to Kai, on the ground."

Eva pulled her Triangle of Arts out of her bag, along with the five rocks, and the chest.

Kai yelled, "what are you doing, Eva?"

He saw the Triangle of Arts first, then the chest, and he flinched. That was the first time she had seen him show any kind of fear, or anxiety in front of her.

Jake dropped Chloe on the ground in front Kai. He stood with his 9 mm trained on both of them. "Now what?"

Eva placed the drawing approximately four feet from the two of them and placed the rocks evenly around it, with the chest, now open, in the middle of the drawing.

Kai's eyes went wide and his face contorted. "Don't you even think about it, Eva!"

Eva looked over her shoulder in his direction, and gave him a sly smirk, and went back to setting her stuff up. She opened her book to the page she had marked.

Eva went to stand in front of the Triangle, her arms out in front of her, bent at the elbows, and palms up. She began the incantation immediately.

"Powers of the witches rise, course unseen across the skies. Hear me beckon, hear my plea. Dagon and Lillith, I summon thee"

A scream escaped from Chloe and her body contorted on the ground in front of them.

Jake pushed her back down, and continued to hold them at gunpoint.

"What's happening to her?"

"Ignore it Jake, let me continue," Eva said.

"By the power of the elements I bind thee here and now! Never again to be set free, by any means or anyhow."

A low, deep throaty growl came out of Kai, and his body started convulsing. There was a string of curse words that followed, but Eva continued.

"Guardians of the ancient towers grant me now, the sacred powers. Let these spirits never be set free. Contain these spirits in the chest at my feet. For such as my will, and so mote it be.

A swirling force of air encircled the recess in the cave, and the ground below them started to shake. The tremors almost knocked Eva to the ground, but she was able to bend down to one knee, before she lost her balance.

Jake was balancing himself, so he stayed on his feet, his gun never losing sight of the two on the ground.

Eva gathered herself and got to her feet, watching a smoky gray mist emanate from Kai and Chloe's body's. They continued to seize, and contort. Jake watched in awe.

She walked closer to where Jake was standing, looping her arm in his, and with her other hand, she touched the sapphire ring, gently stroking it with her thumb. She immediately felt the invisible shield wrap around them. A normal person wouldn't feel anything different, but she knew it was there. She kept them in her protective cocoon for a few minutes, until the bodies of Kai and Chloe stopped twitching.

Eva heard the lid of the chest slam shut and looked to the two forms now lying limp on the ground. "I think it's done," she said.

Jake looked from her to the bodies on the ground, who were no longer moving. "I'm not sure what to do now. Got any ideas?" He gave her a long questioning look.

"Haven't I had enough ideas? I'm not even sure what to do with that chest yet?"

"So, the evil spirits that were inside Kai and Chloe are actually in there?"

"I believe so. I'll know after we check on them."

Eva knelt down and put her hand to Chloe's neck, checking for a pulse. She let herself breathe a little easier, after she felt one. Jake did the same, with Kai.

"We need to get them out of here, somehow. And how are the FBI going to deal with this? Both of them were possessed by evil entities; they didn't consciously commit the crimes."

Eva was worried about how this might go down, or how Jake was planning to explain this.

"Leave that to me, we have the audio that Kris has been recording. I've gotten through weirder stuff than this, trust me."

The mention of Kris, threw Eva into a panic. "Oh God, Kris. He's probably just freaking out and madder than a hornet at me, because I didn't pick up his call earlier. I was too scared that they were possibly l even here."

"He knows Eva, I've been in touch with him a few times, since you texted him."

"Oh, good. Was he hopping mad at me?"

"More worried, than mad. Let's see if we can get these two to come around, huh?"

After a few minutes, Kai and Chloe were conscious and talking, but very confused.

Jake was going to take them with him, and Eva was taking the chest, and stowing it in her bag, along with her drawing. She left the rocks where they were.

When she emerged from the cave, Juliette was sitting on the ground waiting for them. When she saw Kai and Chloe come out with Jake, they weren't handcuffed. Her face twisted with a mix of anger and fear.

"Why aren't they handcuffed or something," she questioned.

"I'll let Eva explain that to you," Jake said, matter of factly.

She gave him a disgusted look back.

"Juliette, you'll ride with me and I can fill in the blanks as best as I can. I'm going to call the ranch, and let them know you're okay, then we'll have someone come get your car."

Eva opened the passenger side door for her to get in and placed the bag carrying the chest, in the trunk.

Before she dialed the ranch, she sent a quick text to Kris.

We're all okay, which I'm sure you heard. I'm going back to the Ranch, to get Juliette settled. I'm sorry I didn't pick up your call earlier, I couldn't risk it. Forgive me, please. Love you, always and forever.

Kris responded within seconds, *"You're forgiven. Love you, always and forever.*

Eva felt her heart constrict and tears sting her eyes. The fear she'd been keeping at bay was threatening to take over, but she tapped it back down and called the ranch.

Chapter 48

Brett was on the stairs of the main building when Eva pulled up to the roundabout drive, with Juliette. He ran down to open her door, squatting down, checking her over, making sure she was okay. She was no worse for the wear, a little dirty, but nothing a hot shower wouldn't take care of.

The whole way back, Eva went into as much detail as she could, about what happened, and why Kai and Chloe hadn't been handcuffed when she saw them. Eva was pretty sure she might have to perform a forgetful spell on Juliette, just to be safe. The less people who know about what she is, the better. And, she didn't think Juliette would want to remember those horrific few hours.

Once Brett got her into the main building, Eva texted Jake.

I have an idea of where I can put the chest. How's everything going there?

She left the backpack in the trunk and made her way inside. Penelope wasn't anywhere to be seen, so Eva headed upstairs to her room, locked the door, and locked herself in the bathroom, to get a shower. She felt filthy after trekking though that nasty cave. She felt things inside that cave that weren't normal and she wanted to wash it all away. Eva stood under the hot spray until it ran cold. Her muscles and nerves had mellowed, but it would take a while for her to unsee what she was truly capable of.

Jake had left her massage while she was in the shower, saying that Kai and Chloe were being interviewed, and it looked like they would be let go.

Apparently he had Kris meet him at the field office with the audio, and they were all going over it now. That made Eva cringe a little. She was glad she didn't have to be there listening to it.

There was a knock on Eva's door. "Hold on," she said.

She finished getting dressed and went to the door. Juliette was standing there, with Brett at her side. She was clean and dressed in jeans, and a sweater, looking better. Her hair was in a messy bun on top of her head, just like her own.

"May we come in for a second," Juliette asked.

Eva opened her door wider, so they could enter. "How are you feeling," Eva asked, genuinely concerned.

"Better, thank you. You... you saved my life." Juliette pulled Eva into a tight hug. "How can I ever repay you?"

"I was happy to do it. I'm just glad it's all over. And, I'm pretty excited that I get to go to the Derby, and see you race tomorrow."

That made Juliette smile. "I'm not sure how well I'll do, I haven't been able to train much in the last few days."

"You'll do great. Um, have you thought about what I mentioned to you earlier? Do you want me to take care of those memories?"

Juliette looked at Brett, then back to Eva.

Eva figured she had told Brett everything. "I'm sorry, I figured you told him everything already, was I wrong?"

"No, I did tell him. I'm worried that it will take away all my memories, like him," she whispered.

"No, no. It will only take away the bad ones from the last day, no more. Only the bad memories."

"Okay. I want you to do it then."

Brett looked apprehensive.

"She won't lose any memories of you, I promise," Eva said, trying to ease his mind.

He just nodded, and Eva went to retrieve a few things from her backpack.

She came back with a bowl, salt, and baking soda, along with a white candle. She lit the candle and placed it on the coffee table in front of the couch, where Juliette was sitting.

She filled the bowl with water, and added the baking soda, then stirred the mixture. She then took the salt and made a circle with it, around the bowl, which she then placed on the table next to the candle.

Eva sat next to Juliette and had her turn towards her. Eva took Juliette's hands in hers. Brett sat in the club chair on the opposite side of the room and watched.

Eva began the incantation, "Purge Juliette's mind of recents sights and sins, of memories dark and grimm. No longer dwell in her heart and head. Be gone, cruel memory after all is said, so mote it be."

She let her hands go from Juliette's, and waited to see what would come next.

Juliette looked at Eva, as if she had just gotten there. "Eva, how was your day, today? Did you do anything fun or exciting?"

Eva looked to Brett and smiled. It worked.

Brett stood, and walked over to Juliette, putting his arm around her, testing her. She looked up at him, and gave him an endearing smile. "We had a lot of fun with you and Jake last night at dinner. Where is he?"

Brett exhaled a breath he'd been holding, and relaxed instantly.

"Jake is at the field office. He should be back later."

"Oh great! Well, we better be going, we have dinner reservations."

They left Eva's room, holding hands and smiling. That alone changed Eva's whole mood. "Too bad I can't perform that on myself. There's a few things I'd like to forget," she said to herself.

She was watching TV, when she heard the key in the door. It opened, and to her surprise, it wasn't just Jake, but Kris was with him.

Eva jumped out of her seat and ran over to him, flinging her arms around his neck and jumped into his awaiting arms.

"You're here!" She had him in a death grip.

"I'm here," he said in a strangled voice, but was laughing, too.

After Eva detached herself from her husband, she went over to Jake and hugged him. "Thank you for bringing Kris with you. And, thank you for keeping it together in the cave. If you hadn't, I would have lost it."

"Hey, it's all in a day's work, for this guy."

"Yeah yeah, hotshot FBI guy. So, what happened to Kai and Chloe?"

"After all the big wigs went over the audio, and then listened to everything I witnessed, they figured they really couldn't hold them. They were pretty confused. They listened to the audio, as well. They were dumbfounded. It took a lot of explaining, but they know everything that happened, and they have been told never to mention it to anyone, ever, or there will be hell to pay. You should've seen their faces."

"I bet. Do they know it was me? Do they remember my face, or recall me in any way?"

"I'm not sure, why?"

"I gave Juliette the option to have the bad memories from the last 24 hours, taken away, and she let me. She doesn't remember any of it. I'm just wondering if I should try it on them."

Kris gave Eva a look of disbelief. "You can do that?"

"Yes. It's the first time I've tried it, but it seemed to work."

"So, you've never erased my memories," he asked, nervously.

"NO! Like I said, this was the first time I'd tried that spell.

Jake laughed, "Don't even think about doing that to me, I want to remember everything I saw you do. It was crazy, but pretty cool."

Kris gave Jake a scowl.

"What? You've seen what she can do, you can't think it's not cool."

Eva spoke up, "Anyway, if you want to mention it to them, by all means do, and let me know."

"I will broach the idea to them."

A big smile formed on Eva's face. "Now... do we get to go home," she asked, hopeful.

"No," Jake said.

"Why not?"

"I spent over $600 on a hat, dress, shoes and jewelry, and you're going to wear them, to the Kentucky Derby, tomorrow."

He looked to Kris, "sorry dude, she's my date to the Derby."

Kris rolled his eyes at him. "Fine. But if you kiss her again, I'll drop you like a rag doll."

Chapter 49
The Morning of the Kentucky Derby

Today's the big day, the Kentucky Derby. Eva was getting herself ready, in her new dress and hat that Jake bought her, a couple of days ago.

She looked out the bathroom door when she heard the sheets rustling, Kris had still been asleep, but was beginning to stir. Jake had been nice and took Kris' hotel room last night and let him stay at the ranch with her. He'd had to do a lot of explaining to Penelope, of course, otherwise this would have looked awkward.

Eva smiled down at the sweet sleepy face.

Kris opened his eyes and Eva was still smiling at him. "Good morning sunshine," he said, sleepily. "You're up early. Did you sleep okay?"

"It's not that early, it's almost 11am, and I slept better last night, than I have all week."

"Me too. It was a pretty rough week for me, too, not having you next to me. It was especially hard knowing you were shacking up with my friend."

Eva laughed, "You had nothing to worry about. Jake was generally a perfect gentleman. Speaking of which, are you sure you're okay with me going to the Derby with him, today?"

"Yeah, it's fine. I hope you guys have fun. I may try to hit another distillery. They may not be too busy today, what with the race and all."

"Call us if you need a ride," she said, and went back to getting ready.

While Eva was doing her hair, she was thinking of where she could secure the chest that contained the evil spirits. She had thought about taking it to Connecticut, and burying it in the location it had all started, but didn't think Kris would be too keen on that idea. Another idea came to her, and that was to put the chest inside a fire safe, but not until after she wrapped the chest in chains and put a heavy duty lock on it. She wasn't taking any chances of having that thing open by accident.

Grabbing her new hat, she heard a knock at the door, and after Kris opened the door, she knew it was Jake, by the sound of his voice. They were chatting away, so she finished putting herself together. She had on her little black dress, with her new Black and Tan Speakeasy hand-blocked hat, with feathers and the Forme' gold-plated logo on it. She placed it perfectly on her loosely curled blonde highlighted head. She paired the dress and hat with the black pointed toe, ankle strap four inch stilettos, and silver jewelry she had worn to the press party.

Eva opened the door to the bathroom and emerged, to two men staring at her, open mouthed, and suddenly speechless.

"I'm not sure whether to be flattered that I have you both speechless, or insulted," she said, grinning.

Kris was the first to speak, "you look stunning. I'm not sure I want you going anywhere with this guy," he said, giving Jake a look.

Jake rolled his eyes at Kris, "really dude, we're doing this again? She has no interest in me whatsoever. But, you do look very pretty Eva. I'd be happy to have you by my side today, at the Derby."

She shook her head, smiling at both men, "Thank you, both of you, and he's right, I have no interest in him, whatsoever. Besides, he has a really crappy job," she said sarcastically.

"Are you ready to go?"

"Yes, I'm ready, if you are. I have a question to pose to both of you, real quick."

The two men looked at each other, confused, but let her continue.

"I've got a couple of ideas on what to do with the chest containing you know, the two heathens. The first place I was thinking of was to bury it up in Connecticut, in the woods beyond my childhood home, where all this mess started, or we buy some heavy duty chains, and a really good padlock. I'd wrap the chest up in the chains and lock it, and store it in a fire safe. Do any of those sound like they would work?"

Kris spoke up immediately, "I really don't want you going back to the place it all started, so I vote for the fire safe, if you think that'll be secure enough."

Jake looked like he didn't know one way or another, so he agreed with Kris, that they should get a fire safe. "If you're going to put that chest into a fire safe, I suggest you not keep it on your property, though. I can find a storage facility for you."

"Okay, that should work," Eva said. "I'd rather it not be in our house anyway."

"Alright, now that that is settled, are you ready to go bet on some ponies, and drink a couple of mint juleps?"

"Absolutely."

Eva gave Kris a kiss and hug goodbye, and she headed downstairs with Jake.

When they got to the entryway, Penelope and Chloe were standing there, all dressed up and obviously heading to the same place Eva and Jake were.

Penelope smiled at them, "are you going to the Derby?"

"We are," Jake stated. "I'm guessing you two are heading in that direction as well."

"Yep, we're waiting for Kai to pick us up. I wanted to thank you both again for what you did," Penelope smiled at them, knowing that that was all she could say. They were ordered not to mention the incident in any detail.

Jake nodded, and smiled at the women. "You're welcome. I hope you can both enjoy today."

He put his hand to the small of Eva's back, and guided her out the front door.

When they reached the bottom step, Kai was pulling up to the roundabout drive. He quickly exited his car, and met Jake with a handshake. "Agent Long, Eva, thank you for everything. I don't know where I'd be if you two hadn't, well, you know."

Eva held his hand, "just go enjoy today and know that it's over, now."

Kai nodded in acknowledgement, and went up to the front door, and headed inside.

"Maybe we should gather everyone in your room later, and you can perform that memory spell on everyone that was involved in this investigation this week."

Eva thought he said that, jokingly, but she wasn't 100% sure.

Chapter 50
Kentucky Derby

Eva and Jake got to Churchill Downs and it was a much different scenario as it was the other night during the press party. Today was the big race. Women were dressed to the hilt, men looked dapper in their suits, and the energy was infectious.

When they got inside, there were lines at every betting cage, and Eva noticed a few celebrities milling around; one was one of the Kardashians, she was positive, but she also saw one of her favorite chefs, Guy Fieri, with his wife.

"Jake look, it's Guy Fieri," she said, giddy as a school girl. "His one show on the food channel is my favorite. You know the one where he goes to all these different restaurants around the country?"

"Oh yeah, I know which one you're talking about."

"Should we get in line to place our wager on the one horse I know is going to win," she asked, giving him a sly smile.

"We're betting on Juliette, and her Tennessee Whiskey, aren't we?"

"Of course."

After they placed their bets, they found where their seats were and Jake left Eva there, while he went in search of the infamous mint julep for her.

Eva was taking in her surroundings. Churchill Downs is a beautiful race track and they were blessed with a warm sunny May day. She sat there people watching for a few minutes, noticing the ladies hats, and some were full on large hats, and a few she noticed were headbands with adornments on them. The dresses ranged from super frilly, to understated elegance and Eva found that she fit right in the middle. She had gotten quite a few compliments on her hat, and people asked where she bought it. She was truly enjoying herself.

Jake returned with their drinks and took his seat next to her. They cheered to a happy ending of a crazy week, and sat in comfortable silence for a few minutes.

Terrence Rivers was walking in their direction, a man of many moods was Eva's thoughts on the older man. He stopped when he got their row of seats, and held his hand out to Jake.

"Thank you, Agent Long." He smiled at Jake, and proceeded on his way.

"You are the man of the hour," Eva said, teasing.

"I guess, but you did a lot of the work. I wish I could tell people that."

"No. I'm glad only a few know what I am. I'd like to keep it that way."

The jockey's were taking their spots and everyone was turned facing in their direction, waiting for the gun shot to go off, to signal the beginning of the race. It was only a one and a quarter mile race, but to be the first to the finish line was the goal of every jockey out there. The rose garland, made up of four hundred red roses, and the gold trophy, was the prize. Every single jockey had their eye on that prize.

Eva saw Florent Prat was at one end and Juliette and her horse were positioned toward the middle.

The gun sounded, and off they went. The horses seemed so close together, like they would run into each other, but as they rounded the first curve, Eva could see the distance between them was actually more than she thought. Juliette was holding her own, and Florent wasn't far behind. He was gaining on her, but she was currently trailing behind two other horses.

Eva was thoroughly getting into the race, yelling and cheering Juliette on. Jake stood and watched, quietly.

The announcer was rattling off the racer's positions, and when he announced that Tennessee Whiskey was gaining, and coming around into first position, Jake started cheering.

It seemed like an eternity, that one and a quarter mile, but once the announcer yelled, "It's Tennessee Whiskey by a yard! Yes, Tennessee Whiskey, ridden by Juliette Sutherland has won the Kentucky Derby!"

Eva jumped up and down, screaming, "We won!"

Jake smiled and gave her a high five. "How much do you think we won?"

"I think we won about six grand," she said, continuing to jump up and down.

"Really?"

"Yes. We would've probably won more, had we played the trifecta, but I don't understand all that."

"I'll take six grand," he said.

"I kind of feel bad for Florent, but at least he came in 2nd place."

After Eva and Jake collected their winnings, they went to the winners circle where they watched them place the rose garland over Juliette's horse, and hand her the gold trophy. She was beaming. Brett wasn't too far away, watching with pride in his eyes.

Eva had a good feeling about those two and was relieved that everything turned out the way it did. It could have gone South quickly.

Jake dropped Eva back at the ranch, after they'd said their goodbye's to everyone. They stood by his car, neither one not knowing what to say to the other.

Eva stepped up to him and gave him a gentle hug, "you be careful, okay."

"I will. I guess this is goodbye, until the next time, huh?"

"You really think there's going to be a next time," she asked hesitantly.

"There's always a next time, Eva," he winked at her.

"I was afraid you'd say that."

The End

Thank you for taking the time to read, Die at the Races, an Eva St. Claire mystery.

You can follow M.K. Stabley on Instagram @m.k.stableyauthor, or on Facebook @authormkstabley.

If you would be so kind, I would greatly appreciate it if you'd leave a short review on amazon and/or goodreads.

Acknowledgements

I'd like to take this opportunity to thank **Tricia Russell, Alan Riehl and Tami Fry** for proofreading the very rough draft of this book. They have been huge supporters of mine and their opinion meant a lot to me, as I fanagled my way through the second installment.

It looks like I'll be able to take this group of crazy characters and make it into a series. I honestly wasn't sure if more than a sequel would happen, but it looks like Eva, Kris, and Jake are not quite finished working together.

Made in the USA
Middletown, DE
08 January 2023